THE MOMENT

Vito raised his head to look at her in the dim bedroom light.

"What's the matter?" he whispered.

"Nothing, darling."

"But you're crying," he said. "Did I do OK? I tried to do what you told me."

Iris laughed despite her tears and tightened her arms around his neck. "You don't know how OK you were . . ."

And from that moment everything began to change, as a boy became a man, and a woman's idle erotic fancy turned into an all-consuming obsession of desire and possession. . . .

A Cold Wind

by Burton Wohl

in August

AN AUTHORS GUILD BACKINPRING.COM EDITION

A Cold Wind in August

All Rights Reserved © 1960, 2008 by Burton Wohl

No part of this book may be reproduced or transmitted in any form
or by any means, graphic, electronic, or mechanical, including photocopying,
recording, taping, or by any information storage or retrieval system,
without the written permission of the publisher.

AN AUTHORS GUILD BACKINPRINT.COM EDITION
Published by iUniverse, Inc.

For information address:
iUniverse
1663 Liberty Drive
Bloomington, IN 47403
www.iuniverse.com
1-800-Authors (1-800-288-4677)

Originally published by DELL Publishing, Co., Inc.

Because of the dynamic nature of the Internet, any Web addresses
or links contained in this book may have changed
since publication and may no longer be valid.

The views expressed in this work are solely those of the author and do not
necessarily reflect the views of the publisher, and the publisher
hereby disclaims any responsibility for them.

ISBN: 978-0-595-53038-0

Printed in the United States of America

A Cold Wind in August

1

Early summer in New York. The skirling and fluting, the calliope of spring is done. Forgotten, almost all of it, except for an occasional tiny rattle, like that of a mechanical snare drum which has turned itself on in the middle of the night. That, and a lacy wisp of steam. June is here. Summer is here. Spring is done.

At Rector Street the noonday spill of typists, stenographers, be-girdled, be-gauded, be-Katherine Gibbsd, clots the streets. They carry with them, like three hundred thousand gum-chewing graces, into the bowers of Bickford's an odor of Noxema strong enough to turn pot roast to stone.

Uptown, plump mamas thrust snake plants into the sun bidding them fiercely: grow a little. In the '40's men walk a chafed crotch walk stinted by last year's Sanforized suit. At Penn Station a man struggles with his train window and falls back dead of a broken heart. Only the first, more to come.

And in the East '60's the day rises out of the river, humid, tasting of the tide. Up and down the rows of apartment houses there is a soughing of air conditioners, ruminating gritty air.

In one of these apartments is silence, petulance, distress. The air conditioner is still.

Iris Hartford, drifting lazily between sleep and waking, pressed the pale-blue sheet against her naked breasts. Slowly, because it was most important, she began to make her first inventory of the day. Starting first with the interior of her head, she opened her wide gray eyes to their widest, not seeing, just letting the light in. There was, thank God, no trace of hangover. No fiery eyelids, no ache in the corners of the eye sockets.

Gratefully, but with a little shrug of regret and reminiscence, she closed her eyes again. She always liked making love when she had a hangover, it was really the best time. There was that musician, she remembered, Eddie? Frank? Freddie?—no, Chuck. That was it.

Alto sax. The Chimera Club. What was it he used to drink? Pernod. Jeezus! she thought to herself. But it wasn't so bad when you got used to it. And in the mornings when they woke up, maybe eleven, twelve o'clock, they would make love.

Iris liked that because she would be half asleep at the start. And then, little by little, she would awaken, feeling her body come awake through a padding of headache and fatigue. It was a good feeling, an almost total detachment.

She would lie there, she remembered, with her eyes open, watching—watching—Chuck, that was it—watching him move and feeling him move as if it were happening to someone else. Then deliberately, because it *was* kind of unfair, and he *was* a nice guy, really a *sweet* guy, she would abandon her detachment and she would begin to move in response. And if she moved long enough and hard enough she would feel the stabs of headache pain and this—funny, really weird—made it even better.

Then after a while he got tired of the affair. So did she. She shrugged again. They always started the same way, ended the same way. Nowhere.

Thinking about it made her lonely. She went on with her inventory. Hair? Not until tomorrow. She might wash it herself. That would give her something to do over the weekend, instead of going up to Connecticut with Juley Franz.

The thought of Franz threatened to invest her but she stubbornly excluded it. Moving her hands under the sheet she ran her fingers up and over her breasts and experimentally pressed the nipples. They began to harden and she smiled.

What a pair of tits, she said to herself, actually whispering it aloud. "Great. The greatest." Then she moved her hands down over her flat stomach, and over her narrow hips.

Tightening her leg muscles, she lifted her legs and pointed her toes, feeling the powerful thigh muscles. Hard as rock. Good for another ten years, she thought. No worry there. The breasts would be the first to go. Well, she reflected, there was always surgery. But she didn't want to think about that now. Anyway, it would be years before that would be necessary and she might be out of the business. She might be married to Juley Franz, to anyone, she thought quickly.

Impulsively, she got out of bed and walked to a fulllength mirror. Standing face to the mirror she placed both hands flat against her diaphragm and twitched her breasts. First the right one, then the left, then alternating, then both together. They snapped and jerked in response to her muscles and nerves, like trained animals. Flip, flip. Then she spread her knees and did a slow rotating movement of her stomach and pelvis and ended it with a sharp upward jerk of her breasts.

The greatest, she told herself.

Before leaving the mirror, she turned sideways and examined herself again. Not the slightest bit of drop. No crease on the underside where the downward slope of the breast met her rib cage. She twitched them again, very quickly.

"Boing!" she said, and tweaked her nipple as if it were a puppy's nose. She grinned.

Then she stopped still and froze. What the hell was wrong? Something was wrong. What in the goddam hell was it! She could feel the sweat starting to form on her palms. What was it! Was there someone in the apartment? Panic rose. What—

Oh, for christsake, she told herself.

The air conditioner was silent. Goddam thing. She reached for her robe and walked to the window. The machine emitted no air, no sound. She twisted the switch on and off, turned the dials. On the blink. Damn thing never was any good.

That's what she got for letting Juley Franz give it to her. If I'd have bought it myself, she thought, I'd have gone down to Saks, no, not Saks, but Macy's or Gimbel's or somebody and bought a good air conditioner and that's that. But Juley has to buy everything wholesale. He's always got a friend in the business who can get it for half the price and then— She stopped. The guy who installed it was a big strong black boy.

He thought she was going to let him make her. She laughed. No more niggers. No THANKS! It always gave her such a shock to see their hands on her.

How old had she been? She tried to remember. Nineteen, twenty? Was she married at the time? She frowned, biting her knuckle. That was—that was after Johnny wrecked his car, *her* car, really, and she was visiting him in the hospital with a couple of the boys from the band and . . . Now it came back to her.

They went up to her apartment and then they all got high and she wound up in bed with the both of them. That was the last time. "Whew!" she said aloud. She wanted a bath. But first the telephone.

The voice at the other end of the wire was thin but resonant. Mr. Pellegrino. She liked him. He wasn't one of those soft, white wops. Too bad he was so old, fifty, maybe.

"I'm terribly sorry to disturb you at this hour, Mr. Pellegrino—" and then, having fed him the line, she waited. The Great Lady bit. Smiling impudently, she doodled at the stiff bristles between her thighs.

"No, I don't think it's serious," she went on, "because I had the whole thing gone over just a month ago. Probably just a switch or a fuse or something. But it's Saturday and I thought maybe if it isn't very difficult maybe you—"

She laughed, a genuine laugh. Mr. Pellegrino said he was scared of air conditioners. He was convinced that they only blew out an evil wind like the *sirocco*. Did she know what the *sirocco* was? No, but that was all right. She liked talking to Mr. Pellegrino. He would send his son up.

"All right, but tell him to wait till I've had my bath. I can't hear the doorbell. . . .

"Thank you *ter*ribly much, Mr. Pellegrino, it's really *very* sweet of you. . . ." More Great Lady.

Then she went in to take her bath.

Pear's Soap, Iris thought, holding the brown, translucent cake in her hand, is the only thing to use. It was English soap and—naturally—the English knew what kind of soap was best for English skin.

Iris's skin was English. She was proud of that, grateful for it. Thick, astonishingly white and fine-grained, a wonderfully smooth substance and so opaque that no vein showed beneath it. Other girls had blue veins on their breasts but not she, not even a shadow, not a trace. And nothing on her legs either. Anxiously she examined the inside of her legs at the knee. No veins showing through.

Iris liked being English, having an English skin, an English body. Not a *cheap* English body. Not like the broad who taught her about Pear's Soap. Actually, she wouldn't have admitted to the girl that she "got the idea" from her because the girl was just a tramp. And her teeth were so bad. That was always a giveaway. Iris remembered having read it somewhere: the cheap English, the poor slobs, all had bad teeth.

She must remember some time to ask her mother about her father's teeth. Funny, in all the pictures of him, she couldn't tell whether he had good teeth or not.

Poor bastard never smiled, she reflected. He had left her mother when Iris was ten. Bingo! Goom-by.

But—she sighed—probably her mother had it coming to her. She tried to imagine her mother in bed with her father but she gave it up. Her mother, she thought, must have been a lousy lay. God knows, I'm bad enough, but at least I know how to fake it. And sometimes I get a hell of a kick out of it. But her mother—

"Men are all for themselves. Every blessed one of them." Iris remembered her mother saying it. She said it often. If she could have brought herself to use a stronger expression she would have used it. But Iris knew well enough what she meant: that men were selfish, demanding, lustful, *improper*. Iris was very fond of her mother, she felt sympathy for her mother's hard and lonely life. And, in a way, even though she had longed for affection as a girl, she couldn't blame her mother for her flinty, undemonstrative nature.

It was part of her breeding, Iris told herself; it was because she was English. When she herself was a grown woman she began to take pride in the fact that the older woman never allowed the two of them to become intimate. "Improper," Iris said to herself when she thought about it, smiling. Hard-nosed old bitch, but you had to hand it to her. She didn't ask for any favors.

From the time she was ten, when her father disappeared, Iris was alone. Thinking about it made her angry. She felt tears starting to form in her eyes and she constricted her face muscles to keep the glands from functioning. For a moment she stared fixedly at the hot water tap, holding her face rigid, keeping her brain rigid until the impulse to cry was contained. Tears, even the slightest amount, made her eyes look rotten.

Thirty years old and still a loner, she said to herself. She had liked her father. She had been proud of him too. She could remember herself telling the other kids at school, "My daddy is a brew-master over at Busch's." This was when they were living in St. Louis before her father went away.

He was a big man, she remembered that; and he had a waxed mustache. Sometimes he would let her put the wax on. It smelled lovely like candied violets. She smiled to herself in remembrance. To this day she couldn't *stand* the smell of candied violets. What would a head-shrinker say about that?

Should she go to a head-shrinker? Sometimes she thought it might be a good idea. . . . But hell, she knew what was wrong.

If her father hadn't gone away and if she hadn't had asthma as a child and if she hadn't started out being so ugly . . . funny, the asthma went away when she was fourteen. First time she got laid. So who needs a head-shrinker?

She wasn't mad at her father. In fact, she had looked him up once when she was in Detroit. He was living across the border in Canada. Still big but he'd put on some weight. Was in the insurance business. Had a young wife, not much older than Iris. He was a little embarrassed at first but he got over it.

"Ah see yuh've koom on," he had said in his broad Yorkshire way of speaking. Iris was wearing a mink coat and had borrowed someone else's car, a dark-green Cadillac. She had come on, all right, she remembered, and strong.

They had talked easily for an hour or so. He had asked about her mother. But he wasn't making any apologies. He wasn't sorry about anything, didn't seem to need anything. Hadn't even missed her, not really. There wasn't any reason for her to stay longer. At the door, she remembered, she had paused and asked him, "I see you've still got your mustache—does she"—gesturing at his wife in the other room—"put it on for you—the wax?"

He had played it just right, she recalled.

He smiled. "No," he said, "you're the only girl Ah've ever had in to help me shave."

Just the right touch, she thought, gratefully. Not too sloppy, not phony. It made it much easier for her to go away. She didn't tell her mother about that when she went to see her. She told her mother about the visit but not about the mustache business. Her mother would have been embarrassed.

She was glad her mother drank tea and always wore a hat. She always wore a hat too, and gloves. She was glad her parents were English even though she was born in St. Louis and had gone to school there and had, at the age of fourteen, opened her legs for the first time to a young seminarist from the Lutheran College not three blocks from her home. He was from Wisconsin. Bad Axe. She never forgot that. And she never forgot either her sense of surprise, her feeling of having been invaded —without, as it turned out, being in the least part overwhelmed. Later, she also recalled, he cried. She could still see that young mouth, soft and anguished, in that white, bony face, like the pictures of Christ that the Puerto Rican musicians carry around in their wallets.

It wasn't until she was eighteen and had already been married and divorced and had been with so many men that she no longer could remember their names, even though she tried to keep a list—it wasn't until then that she realized why the seminarist had cried. She realized it one night when she had allowed a leathery young soldier from Texas—he looked part Indian—to take her home.

"What I got to do?" he had shouted at her in a final burst of exasperation. "What I got to do, beat yo' brains out? Don' it mean nothin' to yuh, nothin' at all?"

"Keep your voice down, slob, I don't want the neighbors complaining. All you think of is yourself. Yourself, nothing but that."

"But that ain't the truth. Hones' t'God, if you'd only let go—"

"Why the hell should I? I'm doing what you wanted to do, aren't I? You got what you came for, didn't you? What the hell do you want me to do, light up like a Christmas tree because you've got that great big rod on you? What makes you think you're so different? You're all alike. All alike." And suddenly she remembered the seminarist and understood then, only then, why he had cried. She was half-drunk and she began to laugh.

The soldier clouted her for that. She was out of the theater two days with a swollen face.

After that she learned caution. She never got hit again. At times she had come close to it and there was one man who used to put his fingers at her throat but he hadn't the courage to stiffen his thumbs. She knew it.

"Go ahead," she had said, totally unafraid. "You're bigger than I am. You can hurt me. Go ahead and hurt me."

That was one weapon she had acquired: contempt.

And the other was class.

That was why she was glad she was English. It was the raw stuff, she felt, of class. Not quite sixteen when she joined the chorus line of a St. Louis night club, Iris soon found a vocation which became, in fact, her career. Awkward, still pudgy with traces of teen-age fat, she became a strip teaser. She took her clothes off, more or less to the accompaniment of music, and underwent artificial but childishly fierce orgasms on a tiny night-club floor.

What distinguished this performance, however—apart from her growing beauty, which was even then apparent—was a kind of gentility, a trace of bourgeois constraint. It was far more real than the pretended coyness of the other girls who shared the stage. It was, for the middle-class gentlemen in the audience, a re-evocation of their own wedding night, idealized, of course, a fantasy come true.

And for the working men, those who aspired but who had not yet attained middle-class status and who yearned for women beyond their reach, it was at once a promise, a vindication, and the confirmation of a dream.

Almost from the outset, Iris was a smashing success. She went through many changes of billing before she reached the top of her profession as "Beryl Cobalt—

The Daddio-Active Girl." And she moved from the burlesque theater circuit to the expensive night clubs—the "class rooms"—of Las Vegas, Chicago, Miami. But she never lost that quality of the beautiful, reserved—even aristocratic—gentlewoman turned avid by demonic lust. She preserved, perfected this quality, made it the motif of her act. The act became a morality play—in reverse. And men paid handsomely for the privilege of imagining themselves as "Beryl's" demon—enough so that she now earned about $40,000 a year.

Still, Iris's class was more than a theatrical device, a bit of business. It also became a part of her off-stage life. Over the years she had fleshed-out the image of bourgeois respectability. She lived, whenever possible, in the "better" hotels. She dressed with taste and even considerable style. She became a snob but not simply a Mrs. Babbitt. The Babbitts in her audience, and their wives, were, she felt, irretrievably vulgar, "squares, dirt."

What she sought was good taste, sensitivity, discernment. If she found it or thought she found it in a Negro trumpet player, a bartender, an industrial tycoon, she went, generally, to bed with him. And if, as it almost always turned out, she found coarseness, boorishness, insensitivity, she quit the bed or, in some cases, turned the man out.

You either had class, Iris thought, or you didn't. If you didn't have it, it made no difference who you were or what you did, you were a bum.

For forty weeks a year Iris Hartford was "Beryl Cobalt," a strip teaser, an "exotic" dancer. But she was not a bum. And for twelve weeks of the year, the hot summer months, she left the stage and lived anonymously as Iris Hartford in a small, handsomely ornamented apartment in New York. It was a kind of retreat, a re-examination and a reaffirmation of her credo.

During those three months Iris devoted herself to the cultivation of her body, her darling, her child. This was, of course, a constant ritual, but never so lavish as when she retired to New York. In addition, and more important, she practiced the ritual of gentility, of class. She visited the smartest shops, she bought expensive, patrician-looking clothes. She read books, modish and often difficult books, and sifted the offerings of the great city, shunning all that she considered common or square.

She brought these things, her purchases—clothes, books, a china teapot—into her apartment only after the most intense deliberation. They had to be worthy before they could be consecrated, before they could be installed in what was, in fact, a shrine.

This was her quiet, purposeful time. She did not limit herself to celibacy, though her affairs during this period generally took on a subdued, decorous quality, consistent with her role. But she did observe an unfailing rule: no suitor was allowed into the apartment, not even for a cup of coffee, not while she was making a last-minute change of gloves or purse. She kept him, if necessary, waiting outside the door.

Nobody, she was determined, is coming in here but me. There's not going to be any screwing on *that* bed. Nobody's going to walk out that door but me.

She kept her temple inviolate, just as she kept the gates of her body open. And she would have preferred to have intercourse on the seat of a car or in a shaded doorway, if need be, as casually and spontaneously as a mongrel bitch, than to bring a man to her chastely ruffled bed. The sanctity of the place was a source of pride.

Even now, in her bath, she savored the pleasure of uninterrupted devotions. She held her small, smooth right hand up for inspection. The fingers glistened with soap sheen and the crimson nails were as perfect as halves of almonds.

She would give herself a long, lazy manicure, she decided. That would carry her through the early afternoon. Then she stopped—

Impulsively, she reached for the phone and dialed a number.

"Mr. Franz, please." She waited. A rich male voice

came over the telephone. It was strong, aggressive. It conjured up the scents of expensive shaving lotion, expensive cigars. It suggested power, luxury, motion.

"Baby. I been waiting on pins and I don't want to say needles on account maybe this phone is tapped and the narcotics boys are listening. So what's with you, doll?"

"Clown," Iris said. Then her voice became small, girlish. "I'm taking my bath."

"How do you like that? At eleven o'clock in the morning!"

"Don't you wish you were here?"

"Now, bab—"

"All warm and squichy and slippery, mmmm. Juju, wouldn't you like to come take a bath with me?"

"Listen, what are you trying to do to me? I mean, this is a business office and my secretary is here, I mean—you know." He laughed. Then, still laughing, but forcing it a little, he asked, "So what about this afternoon? Can you get away?"

"No. That's what I wanted to call you about. You go along without me, Juju. I want to stay home."

"But that's silly. What fun will it be—all right, I'll stay here with you."

"You're crazy. Don't stay here for me. Go. Play golf. Get some sun. You need it."

He paused. "You got a date?"

"Yeah." She laughed shortly. "I got a date with a kid to come up and fix that lousy air conditioner you bought me. It's out of action again."

"Look, I'll send a man right over—"

"No, no. Never mind. I've taken care of it. Look, Juju, have a good time. Call me when you get back, all right?"

"All right, kid, but you'll be missing a swell party. Country gentry and all that stuffery."

"Stuffery puffery. 'By."

"You sure you don't want—"

"Sure I'm sure. I want to stay right here in my apartment all week long, I mean all weekend long, and cook for myself."

"I think you're out of your lovely mind."

"Sure, but that's why you love me."

"I do, baby, you know that, don't you?"

"Balls! But you're sweet. 'By. Call me."

She hung up the phone and sighed. Jee-ee-ee-zus! Then she smiled. He was a good guy, Juley. Fun. She felt much better now. And hungry. It would be pleasant, she thought, to make breakfast and then eat it in bed. But then she remembered Pellegrino's kid was due to come up and fix the machine. She had better put some lipstick on.

The residence of Alessandro Gaspare Pellegrino, Esq., late of Florence (Italy), the East Bronx, Queens Plaza, and currently of East 64th St., had less in common with the dwellings one and two stories above his head than it did with the residence of any *concierge, portinaio,* or *hausmeister* a good three thousand miles from his right elbow.

It had what all such places have, a window critically poised between the light of day and the gloom of the interior so that the two were never distinct. It also had, as all such human kennels have, an unobstructed view of the port of jeopardy—in this case, a narrow, walled alley used by cats, delivery boys and the man who read the gas meter. And finally, it had Alessandro Gaspare Pellegrino himself, who, because he had a respect for pageantry as well as for the absurd, sat almost constantly at this window in the hope that some day, someone—a cat, a delivery boy, the gas meter man, it made no difference—would recognize in his pose an outrageous parody of the scholarship of St. Jerome. To Pellegrino it had seemed only fair to provide a key to this charade, so he had placed—not quite a lion, but a shiny, black ceramic panther on the window ledge.

On a large table within arm's reach was an assortment of objects to which Pellegrino would address himself during the course of the day. There were books, a work on colonial bacteria, another work on utopistic societies and the entire Municipal Code of the City of New York, which he was considering—half-seriously—committing to memory. There was also a knife and two apples on a plate, a bundle of gnarled black *sigari toscane,* the malodorous Italian cigars, a partially knitted gray sock and, finally, his son who was bent over a plate and stuffing himself as delicately and purposefully as a young black fox.

"Ah, *figlio mio, figlio mio,*" Pellegrino mumbled in a tone of absent-minded lament.

"What's the matter?" the boy asked, reassured by the familiarity of his father's musing style. There was no need, he felt, to look up or to halt his intake of food.

"What's the matter?" Pellegrino repeated. "Nothing. *Un bel' niente.* And the less there is, the less I want. And the less I want, the more I have. This is a paradox, Vito *mio.* And paradoxes are not for young people, they are for old people, like knitting. They are a way of passing the time."

"Did you call up the oil company?" Vito asked.

"No. What for? It's summer. Who needs oil in summer? Ah, oil, the olive oil from Liguria, the first pressing." He smacked his lips. "I swear to you, Vito, it is like—you could drink it better than Coca-Cola."

"Papa," the boy, Vito, looked up and gazed at his father through long black lashes, the whole upper part of his face alert, knowing, secretive, like a fox's mask. "Papa," he said, smiling, with milk still on his lips, "you're crazy."

"And you're fortunate," Pellegrino said tartly. "God help you if I were sane."

"You gonna get sore at me?"

Pellegrino held up his hand in a gesture that signified peace. He was not angry. "I'll call the oil," he said, "you'd better get off your behind and go fix that machine. She probably don't know to turn the button up or down. Mmmph! what a woman. A *madonna. Che coscie!* That's what the Romans say. What thighs!" he said. "Vito, look at me."

"Leave me eat."

"Look at me." He laughed again. "Pick up your face. *Arrossolato,* blushing like a girl. Ah, Vito, Vitellone." He got out of his chair and grasped the boy at his slim neck.

"Some day you are going to have a woman like that. Not now. Now you are still a little too young. Now the girls are better for you, nervous, impatient. But later, when you get to be a man—"

"All right, so I'm not a man. Is that my fault?"

"Oh, Vito, I just tease you." He grabbed his son's black hair and turned the young face up so that he could look into his eyes. "Vito, tell me something," he said, looking deeply into his son's black eyes. "It hasn't happened yet, no? You are still a virgin, no?"

The boy winced and his dark cheeks colored. He tried to take his father's hand away from his hair.

"Goddamit—"

"Don't swear," Pellegrino said, holding up a finger in warning. "I don't tell you what to do, I just ask you a question: are you still a virgin?"

"Jesus Christ!"

"All right," Pellegrino said. He smiled and slapped Vito's face affectionately. "All right. Don't worry about it. Soon, it's going to happen. You're going to be a man, Vito. You're going to be such a man—you'll have so many women. Believe me. I'm happy for you."

"Ahhh—" The boy pushed his chair away and threw his father a look of pride and embarrassment. Then he went to the mirror over the sink and carefully combed his hair. His father watched him, deeply touched by the boy's beauty.

At moments like this he was grateful for the presence of his son, not merely because of the blood they shared, not priding himself for having sired this quick and graceful creature, but simply because Vito was something beautiful, something luminous and gleaming in the self-imposed austerity of his life.

Hope had died in Alessandro Gaspare Pellegrino, slowly, branch by branch, joy by joy, like a failing tree. It had never been a flourishing tree. It was twisted, spare, born in the narrow back streets of Florence as was Alessandro himself, and as he was also, twisted—crippled from birth—it was rooted in layers of stone. And these layers of stone had once been flowers, the sweetest, most brilliant flowerings of the human heart and mind. All crumbled, all pressed, one on top the other and turned to cold stone. The justice of God, a flower. The sweetness of Christ, the divinity of man, the eternality of art, the sovereignty of reason, all flowers turned to stone.

And so, nourished only by his anarchistic dreams—a dream of poetry, politics and paradox—and by the slender vitality of his own youth, his hope grew cautiously. Enough so, at least, that he could marry, contrive passage to America and settle in New York. Once there, a young man with a stunted leg, a passionate face, and a pale and gravid wife, a young man who, moreover, found few companions to share his luxurious dream of uprooting all of these misshapen stones, overturning all the benches of the courts, toppling the bishops' mitres from their heads, erasing all the torment of mankind with one last exquisite burst of dynamite—once there, his withering began.

What was it, how had it happened? Ugliness. He would have answered: ugliness, first. But then, of course, no one had asked the question. So that was the second thing, loneliness. And one thing more—cynicism, that colorless, icy Florentine poison which he had drawn into himself from his native stone. Ugliness, loneliness, self-doubt, quite enough to stunt a man.

Even so, Alessandro's hope, though it put forth no new shoots, did not quite end until one day when he stood black-suited, holding his small, four-year-old son wrapped in oil cloth against the November rain in "Brook-a-leen-a" waiting to throw a handful of wet earth into his wife's grave. Then it was done. *Basta.* No more.

Unable to work at his trade as a furniture maker he took a job as a "super" so that he could look after the boy. From one dark, furnace-reeking hole to another he moved, carrying with him his Dante, his chisels and awls, a curiously whimsical engraving of Bakunin which made him appear an early 19th century fop—a macaroni—and his son.

Vito alone was his treasure, his bronze. His figurine. And it was an awesome thing to see, more real than fanciful, how the boy re-evoked his heritage, almost as if the genius of Florence were inherent in his limbs. From a Della Robbia figure he developed into a boy of Verocchio; then a Sansovino; a Donatello, lithe, tentative, hermaphroditic; and finally, into the slim, muscular youth of Cellini with his full, curving mouth, his saracenic nose and his eyes like blackberries in the sun.

Vito, now sixteen, preparing to mount four floors to repair Miss Iris Hartford's sullen air conditioner, had become the young Perseus, holding not the head of Medusa but a screwdriver and a bit of rag. He was, his father thought not without envy, going to the apartment of that beautiful blond madonna and it struck him suddenly that Vito's errand was more than fitting, it was classically apt.

"Vito," he said, "good luck."

"Huh?"

"Good luck. *Buona fortuna.*"

"What are you talking about? What's good luck? To fix a lousy air conditioner?"

"Ah, the machine—" Pellegrino made a gesture. "No, the woman. Who knows, eh? Eh?"

"Cut it out, will you? I never even talked to her before."

"Sure, I know. But you've seen her. She's been here for three weeks now. For a boy your age all you have to do is see her. Then, pom! The mind begins to race and—"

"Look, will you cut it out? Leave me alone." He jammed the screwdriver in his back pocket and closed the door. His father smiled at him through the glass and he made an obscene gesture with his arm. Vito made a throwing motion, then opened the door long enough to say, "Cut out the crap. And call the oil." Then he was gone.

2

Waiting for the elevator to come down from the fifth floor of the converted brownstone, Vito whistled soundlessly between his teeth and boomed his knuckles on the metal door. Stuffing the rag in his back pocket, he balled his left fist and let go a fast jab at his metallic reflection. Cut him up, he thought, confuse him, dazzle him, then—fast! In with the right hand. To the midsection. Not to the jaw. That was for suckers. A guy could break his hand if he wasn't set for it. Like this. Jab, jab, feint with the right, jab again. Then—wham!

The door gave out a satisfying boom. He dropped his hands, pleased. Hardly breathing. He placed his hand against his tee shirt to feel his heart beat. Like a drum beat, steady. He was in good condition. He thought a lot about his condition and worked on it. Every morning, fifty push ups, fifty deep knee bends and twenty pull ups on the bar he had rigged in the alley. He felt his forearm. Getting hard. In another six months it would be a lot harder. He wished he had a tennis ball. If he could remember to carry a tennis ball around with him he could squeeze it whenever he had a couple of moments and that would give him a forearm like stone.

Maybe he could find a ball game when he got finished upstairs. He was feeling hot today, ready for anything. He wrapped his hands around an imaginary stick and took a powerful swing.

Just then the elevator door opened and a woman started to emerge and then halted, startled by his contorted pose. It was Mrs. Rosensohn in 4-A.

Once, only a couple of months ago, he had delivered a package to Mrs. Rosensohn and when she opened the door she was wearing just a housecoat. He didn't think she had anything under it. One of the seams of the housecoat was broken and he could see the flesh of her stomach pressing through. He couldn't take his eyes off it. She smiled at him and then went to get her purse to give him a tip. When she came back she left the bedroom door open and he could hear a radio playing music.

She had given him a dollar. Then she looked at him in a teasing way. "Do you like to dance, Vito?" she had asked. "Would you like to dance with me?" She had held out her arms, her head tilted to one side and at that moment he hadn't thought of her as a woman who was past forty and who was fat and who had curlers in her hair, one of which was threatening to escape and fall. He had only felt terror and the urge to flee.

Afterward, when he got to bed and thought about it, he decided that he had no way of knowing what she had meant. Did she want to make him? Impossible! Yet, the way she looked, and with nothing on underneath, not even any pants. . . . Once he had seen a girl without pants, a girl in the neighborhood, but all he'd been able to see was a little hair. It didn't look much different. . . . But a grown woman! It must be different. He had promised himself that if there was another opportunity, if he could get Mrs. Rosensohn alone again—well, he wasn't sure what he would do, but he would go along.

He rattled his fist against the metal paneling of the elevator so that it sounded like thunder. Slowly, far too slowly for Vito's taste, the elevator rose, bringing the sound of rising thunder gradually, like a stately tempest to the morning quiet of the fourth floor.

Moving soundlessly on his sneakers over the springy carpet, Vito approached Iris Hartford's door. He wiped his palms on his trouser legs and then grasped the knob of the little Georgian knocker. A soft musical bong sounded behind the door. He waited. There was no other sound. He was about to raise his hand again when the door opened softly. Iris, wearing a white, frothy dressing gown, her blond hair piled high, looked at Vito with a steady, smiling gaze and said, "Good morning. Who are you?"

"I—uh. I'm Vito Pellegrino. I live downstairs. Uh, my father said there was the air conditioner—uh—"

"Ah. You're Mr. Pellegrino's boy. The super."

"Yeah."

"Oh, wonderful. It was terribly nice of your father to send you up. I was just perishing—well, not that it's so hot yet, but it will be and that terrible machine makes all the difference—but come in."

She stepped aside so that Vito could enter and his nostrils flared at her scent. He felt he wanted to take a deep breath, fill his lungs with it. He had never smelled a woman like this before. It reminded him of an expensive department store.

Iris preceded him, walking through the foyer into the white-carpeted living room. It was airy, sunlit, gold and white and it seemed scented with the woman herself. Vito had never been in such a beautiful room. And when she stopped in front of the window and turned to face him, he knew he had never seen such a beautiful woman before. He held his breath. He was afraid to speak for fear that his breath might reach and offend her. He put his hands behind him and could feel drops of water rolling down the side of his body and stopping at his belted waist.

"Here it is," she said, "this horrible beast. You see?" She flicked a switch. "Nothing. By the way, have you had your breakfast?"

"Oh, no," Vito said quickly. "I mean yeah. I ate downstairs before I came up."

"You sure? Not even any coffee?"

"Oh, sure."

"Well," she smiled at him. "I'm going to go in and

finish dressing. If you need anything, just call me. You'll probably need some newspapers or something, won't you, to spread over the rug?"

"Yeah, I better. I'm such a slob." Vito laughed.

"You couldn't be. But I'll get you some newspapers anyway." Iris moved quickly, her filmy white skirts trailing prettily behind her and Vito heard her high heels tapping crisply across the kitchen floor. Then she was back in the room again, holding out a folded newspaper. He felt enormously awkward, moving forward to take it from her hand. This time her scent came to him mingled with the warmth of her body and he felt it almost physically, as if he had been struck.

Closing her bedroom door behind her, Iris moved quickly to her dressing table and sat down briskly. Smiling into her mirror, she looked at her face and watched her features widen into a grin. Her own look, her feeling of gay expectancy surprised her. What a divinely handsome boy, she said to herself. Then she turned and put down her comb. She opened the bedroom door and called into the living room.

"What did you say your name was?"

Vito cleared his throat and looked up. He was removing the plastic grille of the air conditioner. "Vito," he said, looking at her. It was easier to look at her when he was doing something.

"All right, Vito. You call me if you need anything. By the way, I'm Iris."

"Oh." He nodded his head and smiled.

She closed the bedroom door and went back to her dressing table.

Cute, she said to herself. Darling. And what a gorgeous build. Those long eyelashes. God! He almost looked like a fag. Maybe he *was* a fag. You couldn't tell about all of them. Anyway he was too young. Well, come to think of it, she had been young too and that boy, the one who cried, he probably hadn't been any older than this one. And of course, all Latins matured early. He was probably hung like a young horse, more like a young hound. How lovely it would be to—

"Oh, wow!" she said aloud to the mirror. "Wow, wow, wow! Cut it out. Cut it the hell out. What's with you, girl?"

She started to put on her stockings and then changed her mind. Tossing them back into a drawer, she stepped to her closet and drew out a pair of raw silk trousers which fitted her like an outer membrane. Then she slipped off her dressing gown and examined herself in the full-length mirror. It was a pose she particularly liked, naked above the waist, her pointed, chalk-white breasts suspended over the slim, natural silhouette of her lower body. The narrow hips encased in trousers, and the trousers themselves, gave her a biform look, female above, male below.

Should she wear a brassière? No, she decided, smiling to herself. Give him a thrill. A cheap thrill. She reached for a thin silk blouse and started to button it when she realized that she had not completed her face. The eyebrow pencil that she needed was in a purse she had left in the hall. For a moment she thought of asking the boy to bring her the purse and she would stand there, blouse open, breast bare and take it from him. That would give him a thrill, all right. Knock his goddam eyes out.

Putting her dressing gown on again, but not fastening it, merely holding it closed at her breast so that her white trousered legs showed through, she went into the living room and out into the hall to find her purse.

Vito had removed the face of the air conditioner and was extracting bits of sooty viscera from the machine and placing them carefully on the papers spread on the floor. He did not see her as she went by, only heard her tread and caught another extravagant whiff of her scent.

"How are you doing?" she asked, standing just behind him.

"Oh, OK, I think. Mostly it needs cleaning. But I

29

can't tell yet if there's anything really wrong with it. Maybe the commutator in the fan is polarized."

"The commutator? You mean, like a radio commutator? He lives in *there?*"

"No," Vito laughed. He turned around to look at her. "No, there's this thing that goes around and it makes the fan move—"

"Uh-hunh—don't stop talking. I'm just going to get a cigarette."

"Well, sometimes, if the bushing is worn, it touches the housing and naturally that causes it to short out—"

She had come back before him and was fumbling with the snap of her purse, trying to get it opened and at the same time keep her dressing gown from parting. She finally pulled out a small gold lighter but was unable to make it work. "Uh, would you—" She smiled at him.

"Sure." Vito rose to his feet so quickly that he didn't have time to uncross his legs and he tottered backward for an instant. He wiped his hands on his trouser legs and lighted the lighter. His knuckles were white and the flame trembled.

She put her warm hand on his and drew the light close.

"Mmm. Cigarette?"

"Uh, no, not now," he said and sank to his feet again.

"Well—thanks for the light—now, what is this going to mean? I mean, is this something you think you can do, or will I have to get someone from a repair place where they fix these things?"

"Like I said, I'm not sure yet, but if you want to—"

"Oh, no, sweetie, I have all the confidence in the world in you. I was just thinking, you might not want to spend all this time. I mean, maybe you've got a date or want to go somewhere—"

Vito was so shocked at being called "sweetie" that he could barely speak. It was like a caress. No one had ever called him this before. Some of the girls he knew said "honey" and "doll" and "baby" but that was when they were necking. He felt his flesh begin to stir and with it embarrassment.

"No," he said finally, "I'm not going anywhere. I've got all day."

"Oh, you *are* a love. Well, then, you just take your time and later, if you like, I'll fix you a sandwich. And if you want me to hold anything or turn anything on for you, call me. I'm going to finish putting on my face."

She gathered a new hold on her dressing gown so that Vito could see, or imagined he saw, the dark areas of her nipples pressing against the folds of delicate fabric. Then she went back into her room, closing but not quite latching the door. He could hear her singing in a thin but true voice, "I'm gonna love ya, like nobody loves you, aa—ll of the time. Days may be stormy or sunny—"

It was to Vito a beguiling sound. His mother used to sing, he thought. He seemed able to remember her singing.

But it was hard to recall exactly. He didn't remember much. At times he could remember how she smelled. Sometimes when his shirts came back from the laundry he would think about his mother because the smell of clean cloth, soap and starch reminded him of her. And one time—he could remember it very clearly—she had taken him on her lap and she was wearing a blue blouse with a little yellow pin like a butterfly pinned to her breast. He had put his mouth on the butterfly and he could still recall the warm taste of the metal. And then his mother had held his head very tightly against her breast until the scent of soap and starch had made him drowsy.

Sometimes, he didn't do it much any more, in fact, hadn't done it for a long time now, he would lay his cheek on his father's shoulder and there would be a trace of the same scent, of warmth and clean laundry;

but it didn't last very long because the scent of cigars would come through. And his father's shoulder wasn't the same. There was no soft place for his head.

Sometimes too—and this was a funny thing—when he was necking with a girl, like Alice Martullo down the street who had big boobs and would let him feel her if they were alone on the roof, sometimes he wanted to close his eyes and put his face against her boobs. Not bare, but if she was wearing a dress. A cotton dress or a shirt. If she was wearing a sweater it wasn't the same. He was ashamed of that feeling and he never told the other guys about it.

One of these days he was going to get Alice to go all the way. He was working on her. He was already working his hand in and if she hadn't been wearing a girdle the other night, he would have reached her. But his hand had become so constricted with cramp he could hardly move it. Then somebody turned a light on near by and they had to cut it out. But one of these days, if he could only get Alice up there, and if she wasn't wearing a girdle . . . He stopped.

Iris was standing behind him again. He could smell her perfume. Slowly, cautiously, he removed a bolt from the machine and then sank slowly on his hip and elbows so that he was half reclining when he turned to look at her.

Iris was dressed now in her white silk trousers and above it she wore a soft silk foulard blouse knotted at her waist.

"I was going to wait until you got through," she said. "Do me a favor, will you? Open this for me?" She held out a small bottle of nail polish.

"Sure," Vito said, coming to a crouch. Standing, he was as tall as she so that his eyes were level with hers. He didn't want to stand. He reached for the bottle and strained to open it. She watched him thoughtfully. He twisted again, staring at her blankly, his face stiff with exertion. Then the bottle cap moved.

She reached for the bottle. "Thanks," she said. "You're strong for your age. How old are you?"

"Sixteen. I'll be seventeen in February."

"Take my advice. Don't rush it."

"Rush what?"

"February," she said. She smiled at him and went back to her bedroom. This time she left the door opened so that he could see her, facing him but not looking at him. She was concentrating on applying lacquer to her nails.

Behind her head was a wide, white-curtained window. The light gleamed from her blond head and from the polished silk of her blouse. Vito was fascinated. He could not take his eyes from her. He had not seen a woman at her mysterious work before. He picked up a metal plate and rubbed it with his rag—only so that he wouldn't appear to be staring at her if she looked up. But she did not look up. He wished he could stand in her doorway. He wanted to watch her closely. He felt very remote from her.

He cleared his throat. "That smells like airplane glue," he called.

"Oh?" She knew he was there. She didn't look up. He felt foolish and turned back to the machine. One thing, he decided, she sure didn't act married. You could tell she owned the place. It was all hers. And nobody had any claims on her. He could tell that too. He had the feeling that she just didn't give a damn. That she could do anything she wanted, go, come, anything. Didn't give a damn.

No husband, he thought, no—supposing she was a call girl? There were several in the neighborhood, at least everybody thought they were. Good-looking girls, living by themselves. Bimbos. Jesus! supposing she were! He could feel excitement knotting his stomach. He stole another look at her.

In the distance she looked small, bent, strangely girlish and vulnerable. She reminded him of the girls he knew at school. Impossible. Would his father know?

Che coscie, the old man had said, what thighs! He blushed. He hadn't noticed that before. She was so beautiful he hadn't looked at her, not like that. But now he could, now that she wasn't watching him.

Was she—he approached this thought tentatively—could she—did she suspect what he was thinking? If she was a call girl, could he go up to her and kiss her, a soul kiss? Would she open up her shirt so he could see her boobs? His hand was sweaty and he dropped the screwdriver. Would she tell him to take his pants down? Maybe she liked him. Some women liked young guys. What about Mrs. Rosensohn? Why did she go on ignoring him like that? Was she mad at him? He started to whistle. Then he stopped because she had risen and was coming, fingers outstretched, into the living room.

"Do you like this shirt?" Iris said.

"Huh?"

"The shirt I'm wearing? Do you like it with these slacks?"

He turned his head to look at her but she wasn't looking at him. She was scrutinizing her freshly painted nails.

"Sure," he said. "It's nice." He paused. "Say, tell me something—are you a model?"

She raised her eyes to his face. They were steady, unsmiling. "No. What makes you think I was?"

"Oh, I didn't think. I mean—" He was uncomfortable now. He sensed trouble. "I just meant you—the way you look and all—there used to be a model in this building, last year. And you kind of remind me of her."

"Oh?"

"I mean you don't look like the other women around here."

"Go on."

He laughed. "That's all I meant." He shrugged, unable to determine if he had offended her or for what reason. "I just happened to think of it."

"How long do you think you'll be with that?"

"Not much longer. Twenty minutes, half an hour." He blushed. He sensed rebuke. "You want me to take some of these parts downstairs and clean them and then come back? I could do that if you want."

She didn't answer. Holding her hand with the fingers outspread she walked to a window and looked down at the street. The view was empty except for a man who was loading suitcases and bundles of household goods into the back of a station wagon. A moment later the man was joined by a woman with a kerchief around her head leading a small child. Obviously they were going away for the weekend; perhaps, Iris thought, for the whole summer. Maybe—she wondered if she ought to call Juley Franz again. It was only twelve o'clock. He would still be at his office. The hell with that, she thought savagely. She felt a sudden rush of irritation, annoyance. She didn't want to be alone.

"Vito. How would you like some ice cream?"

"Huh?" He was scooping the dust from the air conditioner into a neat pile. His tee shirt had come free of his trousers at the back and she could see the delicate relief of his spine under his olive skin.

"Would you like some?"

"Sure." He smiled.

"Good." She was gay, happy again. "I have a whole quart of it in the refrigerator. Let's finish it, OK?"

"Sure. Unless you want me to—"

"Oh, come on." She held out a hand as if for him to grasp, though she was at the other side of the room. He rose and followed her into the kitchen.

Seated on a tall stool near the sink, Iris watched Vito as he ate his ice cream. His movements were quick, neat, they reminded her of a raccoon she had seen once as a child in the St. Louis Zoo. Her father had taken her on a Sunday afternoon. She had also seen a monkey playing with his genitals. At first she hadn't known what he was doing but it had made her very curious and she grasped one of the iron bars while her father tugged at the other hand. Whatever the monkey was doing, it was bad. She could tell that from her father's face. "Come on," he had said, "that's none o' your business." And he had tugged her so hard that her hand came free of the iron bar. His face was very stiff and angry. Vito, she noticed, had black curls at the back of his neck. He needed a haircut.

Her leg started to tap against her stool. She was getting excited. The tight fabric of her trousers was pressing against her body and the outline was deeply creased and clear. Could Vito recognize this? she wondered. She felt herself getting aroused. She was astonished.

"How do you like that ice cream?" she asked. "Isn't that good? Want some more?"

"Oh, no. That's enough."

"Go on. Have some more." She swung off the stool to fetch him some and when her back was turned, shook her legs a little to remove the cloth of her trousers from the fold of her flesh. Vito watched her covertly. He could see her buttocks flex. His throat constricted violently. He could tell she wasn't wearing anything under her trousers.

She gave him a new plate of ice cream and then, instead of climbing back on her stool, stood behind him. With her forefinger she touched the curls on the back of his head. She was standing very close to him, so close that he could feel the heat of her body on his skin.

"You need a haircut, boy," she said. "Hasn't your mother told you that?"

"I haven't got a mother," Vito said. "She passed away a long time ago when I was a kid."

"Oh, poor baby," Iris said. "Gee, I'm sorry." She stroked Vito's head and put her face close to his. He was in agony. His cheeks burned, even his eyelids were hot. He wanted to touch her, wanted desperately to put his head against her breast. But her perfume confused him, excited him. He started to turn his head and caught a glimpse of her white flesh at the opening of her blouse and he could see the swelling of her breast. He turned his head away quickly.

"I'm sorry," he mumbled.

"Sorry? What for?"

"I—I don't know. I should—I ought to go finish inside. It's going to get hot."

She let her hand slide from his hair to the back of his neck. She could feel the heat of his skin and she wanted to squeeze her hand tightly, to feel the tight muscles beneath the smooth skin but she drew her hand away.

"All right. If you're sure you don't want any more ice cream, you go on in and finish that mess. I'll just clear away these things." She drew aside so that he could move his chair. He didn't look at her when he rose.

"Thanks very much for the ice cream," he said. Awkwardly, with none of his usual lithe movement, he backed away from her and out of the room.

The poor kid, Iris thought, placing the dishes in the sink. Poor, goddam lonely kid. She wanted to do something for him. She wanted, she thought, to hold him, just to hold him and rock him, to hold him on her lap like a baby. She smiled as she thought of it and she could imagine his lean, dark face against her breasts and she could sense the warmth of his breath and the wetness of his lips against her skin and her mind began, incredibly, to fill with desire so that she was completely shaken by it. Oh, boy, oh, boy, oh, boy, she whispered to herself. There was no doubt about it now, she wanted him. Wanted him. Now.

She leaned over the sink and turned the water tap on. She let the cold water play over her hands and her wrists. The feeling subsided. But she felt weak with it. She was suddenly tired. She dried her hands and went to her bedroom to lie down. But she could not keep her eyes closed. Every time she did close her eyes she would be assailed with sex fantasies, so vivid and so immediate and so compellingly sweet that they brought her to the far edge of orgasm.

Impatiently, in disgust, she got up and went to her dressing table. She drew the pins out of her hair and then started to pin it up again, turning her face this way and that, frowning all the while.

"Uh—Miss—Iris. It's finished." She heard Vito's voice in the living room.

She came out of her bedroom quickly, holding her hair up with one hand and holding a box of hairpins in the other. The room was filled with the subdued, rushing sound of the machine. It was like a third presence. Their intimacy was gone.

"Oh, wonderful," she said, her face forlorn. "You did it."

"Uh-hunh," Vito said. He smiled proudly and went to the machine, twisting the dials; it performed perfectly.

"Good boy. What do I owe you?"

"Oh." He gestured. "You gave me ice cream."

"Don't be silly," she commanded. "I want to pay you." She put the hairpins down and reached for her purse. "Here," she said, taking out a five-dollar bill. "OK?"

He had his hands in his pockets and was starting to back away. "No. Forget it. Some other time." He backed toward the door, looking everywhere in the room but at her. He didn't want to leave.

"Oh, come on!" She felt anger at his retreat, his shyness. Moving quickly toward him, she knocked the box of hairpins from the table. "Oh, damn!"

He moved back to her and swiftly bent to pick up the hairpins from the rug. Iris watched him, his lean, swarthy arms emerging from the worn cotton tee shirt, his shoulder blades moving against the cloth. Impulsively, she moved her foot and brought it down lightly on the back of his hand. He looked up uncertainly.

"Now," she said, a little breathlessly, "I've got you trapped. Are you going to take the five dollars?"

He blushed and started to remove his hand but she stepped harder. "Are you?"

"Sure." He smiled. "OK."

"That's better," she said. She lifted her foot from his hand and brought her bare, sandaled toes under his chin. They were cool, scented and her white instep was very close to his lips. Then she drew her foot away and he rose. She put the money in his hand and folded his hand over it so that he could feel her nails scraping his wrist.

"Thanks very much," he said, backing away. "If it gives you any trouble—I don't think it will—but if it does—"

"I'll call you."

"Yeah. Just—"

"I know, just call you."

"Well—"

"Don't get drunk now."

"What?"

"With all that money."

"Oh." He laughed. "Not me. I don't drink."

She opened the door for him, smiling, but there was a trace of anger in her smile. "Well, g'by," he said. She didn't answer. She merely continued to smile and just before she closed the door, she said, "Get a haircut."

He started to laugh but she closed the door. For a moment she stood there, her face against the cool glossy metal of the door. Then she cupped her breasts with her hands. They ached. The apartment seemed dark now, dim. Yet it was only slightly past noon. My God, she said to herself, slowly rubbing her breasts, I think I'm going to cry again. My God. This time she couldn't stop it. The tears came. She walked slowly into the living room, holding her head high to keep the tears from melting her mascara, and turned the air conditioner off.

3

By four o'clock in the afternoon, Vito had walked from East 64th Street, through the Park, over to Eighth Avenue, down Eighth to 42nd Street, over to Times Square. From Times Square he took a subway to the Battery but got off at 14th Street, ate two hot dogs, drank a pint of root beer, had a Fudgsicle, a bag of popcorn, an egg roll and a bottle of Pepsi.

At Third Avenue, with better than three dollars in his pocket, he became absorbed in the display of an Air Force survival kit in the window of an Army-Navy store. Half an hour later he emerged from the store, having examined and having tasted the romance of almost every item in stock. He limited his purchases to a pencil-size flashlight and a can of Sterno. It would be a handy thing to have if he went on a hike.

Then he found a telephone and dialed his father's number.

"Pa? . . . Downtown . . . With some of the guys . . . Oh, you know, horsing around. Having a ball . . . Sure, I ate. I had a hot dog. Listen—" He paused. He did not often lie to his father. "Is it OK if I go to the show? I got money. That woman, that lady I fixed the air conditioner for, 4-B, she gave me a few bucks. . . . What do you mean, ten o'clock? It's Saturday night, for God's sake. . . . All right, before twelve. I know you mean it, that's what I said, didn't I—before twelve? . . . OK, so long—uh—wait a minute—maybe if I don't like the show I'll be home earlier. OK, *ciao*."

Stepping out of the telephone booth he looked at a

clock in a store window. The time was five-thirty. And the question was, Vito said to himself, what am I going to do? What the hell is a guy supposed to do?

What he wanted most to do was to get back uptown, to go back to the apartment, up to the fourth floor, to 4-B. He imagined himself getting on a subway, walking across town, entering the elevator, pacing the corridor. He could even see the dull glint of light on her apartment door. And then his courage failed him.

What could he do? What could he possibly say or do? Suddenly he remembered his screwdriver; he'd left it there. The impulse to run took him so swiftly that he almost dashed in front of a taxicab. He was white-faced when he stepped back to the curb. Then—so what? So I forgot my screwdriver. So what?

Supposing she got angry. Supposing she said, "Go away, kid, you're bothering me. Go away or I'll call your *father!*" He winced.

Supposing there was someone else in the apartment with her. Or she was on the telephone and had to put it down and answer the door. Or supposing she was sleeping or taking a shower. She would be angry.

"I'm sorry to bother you, Miss. . . . Gee, Iris, I hate to trouble you but I forgot my . . . It's just a little matter of a missing screwdriver, ma'am, we'll have it cleared up in no time. . . ."

Shit! He spat, trying to hit a manhole cover and missed. He began walking again, automatically noting the traffic lights, adjusting his course to avoid collision with other walkers, totally unaware of his surroundings.

And supposing—he allowed his fantasy to race unchecked—supposing she answered the doorbell wearing those white pants and supposing she said, "Come on in," and she gave him some more ice cream and came and stood behind him, so close to him that he could feel the delicate scrape of her breasts across the skin of his back, feel it so deeply and so vitally that his heart almost stopped beating. Had she any *idea* what happened when she touched him? Could she *possibly know* what

41

it felt like when she put the weight of her hand on his head, when the warmth of her hand touched his neck? He shuddered and passed his own hand experimentally over his neck and was confounded by the utter absence of feeling.

Well, supposing she did all that—then what?

Well, man, you just go to town, that's all. It was the imagined voice of one of his friends. He smiled. Go to town meant on the roof. Or in the park or the movies. Necking. Trying to push and being pushed back, pushing harder. Impossible. With her he couldn't push.

So, all right, so I'm chicken, he told himself. And maybe you wouldn't be chicken too? he told his imaginary auditor. Huh? Big shot.

"*Che coscie*," the old man had said. What thighs! He felt himself getting hard again, for the hundredth time, the thousandth time that afternoon. He turned to face a store window until he could relax and resume walking.

Let's face it, he told himself, trying, through brutality, to avoid his fears, let's face it, you're nothing but a wop kid, a dago, a mountain guinea. You're just a punk and you haven't even got much of a build. Your nose is crooked, a Jew nose. You haven't got a car.

If only he had a car. If he could borrow a car he could ask her to come for a ride and she would be wearing that thin silk blouse with nothing underneath it and he would drive up the Sawmill River Parkway and they would stop on the grass and begin to neck and he would put his hand inside that shirt and she would open up her mouth and he would feel her tongue—

There was a shocking yelp. He had stepped on an old, half-blind dog. "Why don't you watch where you're going!" a man said. "Damn kids these days, think they own—what's the matter, isn't the sidewalk big enough for you?"

"In your hat, Jack," Vito said.

The man looked at him for an instant, surprised. Then he took a quick forward step. Vito danced away and ran. He sprinted easily for a block and a half and then stopped. The man was lost from sight. He felt better, lighter. He decided to trot all the way East and on up to the U.N. If he paced himself right he might even make it home.

At 38th Street he gave it up. Dripping with sweat, his chest heaving, he walked a block with his hands at his waist, taking great pained gasps of air into his lungs. Then he sat on a standpipe until he cooled off. Iris was still there, still waiting behind the door of his mind.

Oh, man, he sighed tiredly, forget it. Forget it. Darkness hung over the river now. Instinctively, he turned his face toward home. But he didn't want to talk to the old man and he didn't want to talk to any of his friends. He wasn't ready to talk about this yet. If he had a mother, perhaps he could talk to her. Not about all of it, of course, but he could tell her some of the things. He could say—he had difficulty pronouncing the words to himself—I'm in love. He tried it aloud: "I'm in love with her." It sounded less foolish that way. He tried it again. "I'm in love with Iris. Hartford," he added. "Connecticut." He laughed.

At 42nd Street he walked across to Grand Central and had a vanilla milk shake and went into a Trans-Lux. The part about the Japanese fishing birds fascinated him so he stayed to see it twice. It was after nine o'clock by the time he reached his neighborhood.

As he walked along 63rd Street between Second and First Avenues, a girl called his name. He recognized her at once. It was Alice Martullo and she was talking to another girl.

"How come you didn't go to the show?" Alice asked. She was a short, dark-haired girl, wearing a salmon-pink peasant blouse and the back of her head was adorned with a blue kerchief that had been ingeniously folded and pinned to her hair so that it appeared to be clutching her head like an ear muff.

"How come you're so nosy all of a sudden?" Vito said. He walked up the steps past the girls and sat down above them. He lighted a cigarette with exaggeratedly fluid gestures.

"Listen, Vito Pellegrino," she hissed, "if you think I'm going chasing after you, you're out of your little pink mind. If you must know, my father called your father to have a beer with him and he said you went to the show. So shrivel up."

"So calm down. Who's your friend?"

"Mary Callahan, this is Vito Pellegrino, creep, first-class."

"Hi." She giggled.

"Hello."

"How about giving me a drag?" Alice asked.

"What, and have your old man holler bloody murder because I taught you how to smoke?"

"Eyih! Big deal. My father doesn't care if I smoke. He knows I smoke. He just don't want me to do it in front of him."

"That isn't all he doesn't want you to do in front of him."

"Ooh! You listen to me, Vito Pellegrino, I have a good mind to give you a crack in your dirty face."

"Aah, knock it off. It's too hot to get all steamed up."

"Steamed up! Who started it! I'm not going to stay out here and be insulted. Come on, Mary, let's go in and watch TV."

"Maybe Mary likes it out here with me," Vito said.

"She does not. She—"

"Why don't you ask her?"

"Listen, Vito— Mary, I'm going in to watch TV, if you want to waste your time with this creep, it's your funeral."

Mary giggled. She was plump and she had shaved her eyebrows so that her face had a look of gentle surprise. She started to rise, reluctantly, for she was obviously a slow-moving girl. Vito caught her arm. "Wait a minute, Mary. Let her go inside. It's a free country, isn't it?"

"Sure, but Alice is my friend."

"So? I'm not your friend?" Vito smiled at her. He

felt a small stirring of power as he realized that she would submit to him.

"Well, sure, I guess so, but—"

"OK. Then sit down and relax. Let her watch TV."

"Good *night!*" Alice flounced into the house.

"She drinks too much coffee," Vito said. "Coffee nerves." He imitated a person with a facial twitch and Mary laughed.

"Let's go get a Coke," he said.

"I don't think I ought to. After all, if some of the other kids—I mean if I come in with you and Alice hears about it— It's different just sitting here, you know?"

"All right, then," Vito said quickly, "let's go up on the roof."

She blushed. "What's wrong with sitting right here?"

"Come on," Vito said. "I don't like someone sitting over my shoulder." He looked up and there was a distinct movement of curtains at a darkened window.

"Yeah, but I hardly know you."

"What's to know? I'm not asking you to go to Alaska. Just up to the roof."

"Well—I can't stay long."

"Oh, come on," Vito said. He could hardly contain his impatience.

Moving cautiously through a thicket of television antennae, clotheslines and ventilator pipes, Vito led Mary to a sheltered part of the roof. He wished he had remembered to bring a newspaper but it was too late for that now. Mary, he thought, must be inexperienced because she made no objection when he drew her down to him on the soot-covered asphalt of the roof. Maybe she didn't care how dirty she got.

"How old are you?" he asked when they were stretched out together. Against the lampblack darkness of the asphalt their bodies seemed suspended like wraiths over a void.

"Fifteen."

"How come I never see you at school?"

"Because I go to Immaculate Heart. Maybe you know my brother, Donald. I have three brothers."

"Do you know how to soul kiss?"

She didn't answer.

"I'll show you how."

"I think we ought to go back downstairs."

Vito kissed her and she tried to turn her face away. He tightened his grip on her shoulder and tried to kiss her again.

"Wait a minute," she said, and she pushed him away with a strong, square hand. "Let me get rid of my gum." She took it out and looked for a place to put it. "I hate to just throw it anywhere—oh, well." She tossed the gum over her shoulder and then nestled back into Vito's grasp. This time she met his lips with her mouth open. Vito thrust his knee between her thighs and they parted easily beneath her skirt. He fumbled at her blouse.

"You're getting my blouse all dirty."

"Well, then, you open it."

"No, don't open it. Wait a minute. I'll pull it up. There. OK?"

Vito kissed her and kneaded her breast with his hand.

"Not so hard," she said. "Boy, you sure get excited. I can feel your heart beating like a hammer."

He released her suddenly and leaned his head on his elbow. He was afraid he would erupt. He kissed her hand, first the back, then the palm.

"Silly. That tickles." She jerked her hand away.

"You want a cigarette?"

"I'm not allowed to smoke."

"You can take a drag though."

"OK."

She took a deep puff of Vito's cigarette and began to cough. She leaned forward, coughing, and each time she coughed, Vito could feel her body pressing against his knee. He threw the cigarette away and held her until she subsided. He kissed her again.

"For God's sake, wait till I get my breath." She held him away, panting.

He put his tongue in her ear and she squirmed. He kept his knee firmly between her thighs and by this time, her skirt was pulled up high. Tentatively, he put his hand on the warm flesh of her thigh, prepared to keep it there if she fought. But she didn't move.

He moved his hand higher until his fingers found the edge of her underpants. He moved his hand farther, deeper. She was silent, thoughtful. She had not moved. His breathing was very rapid and he could barely speak. But curiously, his excitement began to lower. He was perplexed by her silence, her lack of any response.

"Not too hard," she said once, putting a restraining hand on his arm. "Don't be rough." She laughed to soften the reprimand. Her laughter shocked him. She seemed so much at ease.

"Do you like that?" he whispered.

She didn't answer.

"Huh? Do you?" he insisted.

"It's OK."

He pondered this, his manipulations suddenly becoming mechanical, detached.

"Have you ever—"

"Oh, you and your questions," she said, her voice amiable. Then, to his utter astonishment, she reached deliberately, expertly, and clutched him, obliterating in five or six seconds the accumulated agonies of his day. His breath came out in a sob.

They lay silently for a few moments and then Mary spoke. "I really ought to get going," she said.

"Listen. Wait a minute," he said. He faltered. "I—are you mad at me?"

"No. Why should I be mad? I think you're very nice."

"You do?"

"Yes. But you weren't very nice to Alice."

"Alice?" Vito said blankly.

"Yes, Alice Martullo. Listen, I better go. It's better if I go down alone. OK?"

"Sure. I'll see you."

She waved and disappeared.

Vito leaned his head back against the wall, hunching himself up so that he was in a sitting position. This way he could see the houses across the street. He felt calmer now, rested, but a sense of confusion and wonder replaced the torment that was gone. Idly, out of habit, his eyes found the façade of his building. Then his attention quickened and he sought out the windows of apartment 4-B. The lights were on and the blinds were turned so that he couldn't actually see into the room. Suddenly, he saw movement, a figure, a blur of gold and white light moved past the blind. His moment of serenity vanished. He sat with his chin on his hunched knees, watching, watching, his eyes filling with tears from the strain of watching. Finally, the light went out. He wiped his face and went home.

It was almost twelve o'clock when Iris put down the telephone.

Now I'm sure of it, she thought. I *know* I'm going out of my mind. I'm alone too much. Too much talking to myself. First I get myself all steamed up over a sixteen-year-old kid and now . . .

Why did I ever let him talk me into it? Why didn't I say I'm sick or I have to visit my mother or *some*thing. *Any*thing.

The sound of Harry's pleading voice returned to her mind. The very words he used seemed moist, as if some of the sweat of his hand, some of the humid air of the telephone booth had journeyed with them to her ear.

Poor Harry, she thought. The poor, broken-down, frightened, good-looking, weak-kneed slob. With his child's profile and soft little hands and feet and his heart condition and his shy way of talking with that crazy Tulsa, Oklahoma, accent. Poor Harry. She found herself growing less angry.

Why had she ever married him? An "artist's representative." An agent.

"Who knows," she said aloud. "Who the hell knows?"

They had lived together, if you could call that living together, she reminded herself, for two months.

I must have been drunk or lonely. Or both. Anh— She shrugged. What difference did it make why she had married him.

Because I felt sorry for him, I guess. Stupid. Isn't it?

Then why did I let him talk me into a week's booking in Newark? Why should I bother to help him out? What do I owe him?

Well, of course, it isn't settled yet, she reminded herself. I didn't *prom*ise him I'd make it. I said I'd think it over.

Yet, dimly, she knew that she *had* committed herself. Vague thoughts, images of escape, passed through her mind. She could always go out of town. She could be ill. She could . . .

Why *should* she break her routine? She felt anger rising again. Why should she interrupt this precious three months to do a week's work in a burlesque theater? She pronounced the words in her mind with utter disgust. That was all behind her. She was a star. She hadn't been in a burlesque theater for three years. Nothing but the smartest night clubs, the big hotels.

It was . . . she searched for the word. De*grad*ing, goddamit!

So what if he *was* on the hook? So what if the girl did walk out on him? If he has to make good on his contract that is *his* business. What difference did it make if he *was* finished as an agent? He was a lousy agent.

She stopped suddenly. She found herself pacing the room. Why am I getting so upset?

"Calm down!" she said to herself angrily. "Damn it. Just calm down."

The engagement wouldn't take place for a couple of months. In the meantime, Harry might find someone else to fill the spot. He might find another star to go along with him. Why worry about it now?

He sounded as if he were terrified, she thought. As if he were on his knees. She smiled.

Vito had been on his knees that very afternoon. Picking up her hairpins, on his knees. She had found him irresistible. She smiled again as she recalled stepping on his hand. That must have given him a charge, she thought. He didn't know how close . . .

My God! She stopped herself and went to her mirror. Hot pants, kid.

She turned away, unable to look at herself in the mirror. It was embarrassing. It was like being caught—but she was unable to finish the thought.

So help me, God, hot pants. Burning. I want him now. Right here, on the rug, on the floor. She swallowed. The look on her own face had surprised her. It was a serious face, angry, frowning, and at the same time fearful. She turned the light off and went to the bathroom. She took a sleeping pill and then returned to her bed.

Sitting on the edge of her bed, she began to brush her hair slowly, vigorously. The exertion calmed her.

Why not? She found the words coming to her lips. Why not? Probably he was a virgin. Definitely. Had to be. She could tell.

She would get him to put his head on her lap—and in her mind she could almost feel the warm weight of his head pressing on her body. She would put her hand on his cheek, her fingers would slide down to his throat—

Wait a minute, she told herself. Who needs this? A boy, a kid. Awkward, spastic, hysterical. Who needs—

But as she conjured up a vision of Vito as a callow, overstimulated, frenetic young lover, she was aware that, far from making him seem undesirable, it made her want him more.

This very quality was the thing that attracted her most. It would be rape, she realized. But a different kind of rape. Not brutal, stunning, terrifying. It would be slow, tender, subtle, a rape so skillful and so knowing that it would be a violation not only of his body but of his mind.

Just imagining it, she could almost feel it. She could almost sense the movement of his blood, the aching in his bones, the delirium of wanting to give and not knowing how and the final helpless collapse—the whimpering, mewing fall.

And then she would caress him, she thought, she would wipe the young sweat from the hollows of his dark eyes and she would let him rest with his face against her breast. And then slowly, delicately, cooing to him, clucking to him, she would arouse him again.

She knew just how he would feel. She could almost feel her flesh get hard as his would. She could almost—

She broke off. A new idea presented itself to her.

She could also be a mother to him. He needed a mother. My God, she thought, how that kid needs a mother. Deserves a mother.

The thought filled her with pleasure. She could teach him things—everything. She knew so much. Not only about screwing. She dismissed that thought impatiently. But she could teach him how to dress. How to eat. He would come to her with his questions, with his problems. And she would explain them. No bull. Straight. She would explain everything carefully.

And he would listen, smile, and be grateful. And then she would take him to bed and toy with him, arouse him until he was writhing and straining and then she would release him, free him. And then he would sleep with his young, beautiful lips and those long black eyelashes just touching her breast.

And he would be hers. At any hour of the day or night. Hers.

Now she was very tired. She seated herself at the dressing table and looked at herself in the mirror. "You're a fool," she said deliberately. "A goddam, stupid fool. You're out of your goddam mind."

But that didn't change anything, she thought. She knew what she was going to do. It was going to happen.

She wanted it to happen. Why not? she asked herself again. No answer. She shrugged. She could feel the sedative warming her, claiming her muscles, her nerves. She put her head on the pillow and in another few seconds, slept.

4

At a few minutes after ten o'clock in the morning the telephone rang at Alessandro Pellegrino's elbow. He looked at the instrument woodenly and allowed it to ring three times before he answered it. The noise would rouse his sleeping, malingering son. High time too, Alessandro was bored and lonely. The ringing also signified —what else could it mean on a Sunday morning?—inconvenience, perhaps crisis. He was tempted to ignore the telephone and slip out the door and he would have done so except that Vito would ultimately have had to answer the telephone and deal with whatever calamity had occurred. This, Alessandro thought, would be ignoble. Unjust. Warily, he picked up the telephone.

He listened for a few moments. His voice was very soft when he spoke: "Again? It is broken again?"

"No, not broken, exactly—" It was Iris.

"Ah, not broken, but then?"

"Well, it seems to be making a funny noise and I thought—"

"Ah, a funny noise, eh?"

"That's right. It doesn't seem to be serious and it will probably work all right, but I thought if I called early before Vito—before your son—went out for the day, he might be able to run up, if it isn't too much trouble—"

Alessandro was no longer listening to her words. He was looking at the closed door of Vito's bedroom, imagining his sleeping son, limp, graceful, like fragments of sculpture on his bed. And he was wondering about the urgency in the woman's voice, the note of plea.

Please believe me, it seemed to be saying, please don't ask too many questions. Please do not look too closely, do not press too heavily. When he spoke his voice conveyed a note of exaggerated comfort.

"But, of course, dear lady. Do not even think about it. Do not preoccupy yourself. He'll be happy to come up again. If you like—" He paused and smiled at the closed door—"I'll come up myself and we'll—"

"Oh, no, you'll think I'm being ridiculous. I couldn't *bear* to trouble *both* of you. I'm sure—"

Alessandro smiled. In fact, he covered his mouth briefly with his hand to suppress an incipient laugh.

"All right. In any case, do not worry about anything. Vito will come up, he'll fix your machine and in case it is something he cannot do, I will personally call the repair man so he will be here first thing tomorrow morning. Is that agreeable? . . ."

He opened the door and walked to the bed where Vito lay. The boy was awake. He lay with his head on his folded arm watching his father as he sat on the edge of the bed.

"Ah," Alessandro said. "You're alive."

"I've been awake for an hour."

"Tell me, what movie did you see? Maybe I go myself tonight."

"I didn't go to the movies. I was just—horsing around."

"Mmm. I can see it. You still have lipstick on your mouth."

Vito put his hand quickly to his mouth. His father took his slim wrist and moved his hand away. He held it for a moment.

"Vito, do me only one favor, eh? Just one. Don't make some little girl pregnant, eh? You know what I'm talking about?"

"Sure. I know, Pa."

"And if you go with some girl up on the roof, or I don't care where you go, and if you know, even if you just think, maybe, and if you don't have money to go and buy, you come to me. You hear me? And if maybe you are too shy, you'd don't like to go into Cantor's and ask, maybe Mrs. Cantor is there, you tell me, and I'll go buy for you. You understand what I'm saying?"

"Sure, Pa. Sure, I know."

"Because it's a hell of a thing, you know? You got a girl, you want to get married, oh, that's something else. Then you think about it and you got a job and a place to live. But that's different, you understand me? I'm not bawling you out, eh. I'm not telling you—" He paused and laughed, resuming in Italian. "I'm not telling you not to use your—you know—" He gestured. "But use your head also, eh?"

Vito laughed and slapped his father's hand as it quickly pinched his chest. "Ouch! Cut it out. What was that telephone call?"

"What telephone call?"

"Come on. I heard the phone ring. Who was it?"

"Ah, *figlio mio, figlio mio*—"

"For Christsake! Was it for me or wasn't it? Was it one of the guys?"

"It was your madonna."

"Huh?"

"The blonde, upstairs. 4-B."

Vito sat up quickly in bed. He was frowning. "What did she want? Did I do something wrong?"

His father paused. Many choices came to his mind. He avoided them. "She says the machine, it is making a funny noise still. Maybe if you're not going out, you could go up and look at it again."

"I wasn't going anywhere. Just over to the park, maybe."

"That's what I told her."

"So—"

"So when you get dressed and have a cup of coffee, you go up and see what it is." His voice was very soft, quite neutral.

"All right," Vito said. His tone was similarly hushed. He looked thoughtfully, solemnly at his father's face and was surprised to see that it was taking on an expression of pain. His father continued to look at him, his frown deepening, his mouth narrowing with sadness.

"What's the matter, Pa? Something wrong?"

His father shook his head.

"Your leg?" Vito asked, touching his father's knee.

"There's nothing wrong!" his father said. "Get up. I heat up the coffee."

Vito dressed quickly and breakfasted in silence. His father poured him a large bowl of hot coffee and milk and watched his son as he broke up pieces of soft roll and dipped them in the mixture. When Vito finished eating, he looked at his father who had returned to his chair and was looking vacantly out the window.

"What are you going to do today?" he asked.

His father didn't answer. He drummed his fingers on the arm of his chair and hummed to himself. Finally he spoke. "I think maybe I'll go down to Mulberry Street. Maybe I'll find Don Gennaro. If he's still alive. Who knows? I haven't seen him in a couple of years. Who knows if he's still alive, the old soldier. *Il vecchio generale.* You want to go down to Mulberry Street?" He looked hopefully at his son.

Vito blushed. He shrugged. "I don't know, it depends —you go on. You haven't seen those guys for a long time. Me—I don't know, maybe I'll play ball—or something."

"*Va bene,*" his father said softly. "As you wish. You need a little money?"

"No. It's all right. I still have—"

"*Oofa!*" his father said impatiently. "Here." He took a couple of folded bills from his pocket and tossed them on the table. "Go on. Maybe I come home late. You got to eat something, no?"

"Sure—"

"Well, then?"

"OK. Thanks. I guess I better go upstairs. Papa—" He paused. An idea occurred to him and it was so joyful, so bright with promise that the thought of it illuminated his face. But when he tried to put it into words he became helplessly shy.

"Papa—" he tried again and faltered. "I just thought of something—I mean, I thought of it before. Well, why not, I mean—maybe you could find somebody, like— you could get married again. Huh?"

His father lowered his eyes to the table and moved his fingers aimlessly, gropingly, touching first his books and then moving closer and finally grasping his cane. He lifted his cane from the table and tapped his withered leg.

"Sure," he said quietly, "sure, who knows?"

"Well—"

"I'll see you later."

"All right. You're not mad? It was just something I thought of."

"Go on. She's waiting for you." He motioned with his cane toward the ceiling.

"I'm going."

After the door closed Alessandro sat very quietly, staring out the window, holding an imaginary conversation with himself. In substance, he said finally, talking to himself in Italian, in substance, though it is not my fault and it is not his fault and it is not the fault of God or the government but simply the mindless working of the universe, I have just, from this very moment and for all eternity, lost that which it was foreordained that I should lose—an aspect—may it be no more than that—an aspect of my son.

Iris's mind was very clear as she waited for Vito to arrive. But her limbs, it seemed, were strangely slow. She felt a kind of languor upon her, a heaviness, almost a voluptuousness that caused her fingers to move slowly over the handle of her brush. They seemed reluctant to let it fall. She paused for long moments in front of her wardrobe, idly swinging the door back and forth, listening to the faint insect sound of a squeaking hinge. Her decision was long in coming. In fact, as she plucked at one bit of cloth after another, picking up a skirt and letting it fall, parting her clothes so that the light would fall on this garment or that, she suddenly remembered that she hadn't even yet taken her bath.

Briskly, she swept into the bathroom, turned the taps on full, then paused again and fell to contemplating the rush of gathering water. How green it was! How delicious it looked! How inviting! She slipped into the tub and lay there very quietly, her head back, her eyes focused on the glitter of light reflected from her bath water on the ceiling. Experimentally, she moved her leg and was rewarded with a gush of warmth along the inner crease of her thigh and a corresponding flicker of light above. She waited for the flickering to subside and then did it again. She yawned. Watching the light made her sleepy.

Slowly, as if she were bound by the rules of a game, she reached for her soap and washcloth without taking her eyes from the ceiling. She slid the oval of soap over her breasts, delighting in the coolness of it, then moved it over her stomach and down the triangle of her body, grasping it tightly between her thighs.

She smiled. It was there all right. The feeling of sexual excitement was still with her. Still there. She fell to washing herself as the wave of desire receded. She began to hurry because she didn't want to have to answer the door while dripping on the rug and she didn't want him to go away—

Suddenly she let her towel fall. What about— It's going to have to be in here! In my bed, she thought. Or on the couch, but anyway, in here. She shuddered.

I don't know about that, she told herself. That's not so good. Quite bare, she walked into the bedroom and sat on the edge of her bed. I don't know if I'm gonna like this, she said to herself in a comic voice. This is where I *live*. In another man's apartment, I can walk out and leave him flat.

But—

But this was different. This wasn't a man with hair

and the smell of booze or cigars on him, who made stiff, starchy noises when he unbuttoned his shirt, who dropped his shoes with a sigh. This was a boy. Slim and sweet. God, how sweet! Quiet, supple, like an eel. This was a boy with that smell of freshness on his skin that made you want to rub your nose on him. This was someone, this boy, whom she could take to her bed and hold in her lap. She could fold him up and squeeze him almost like a baby. She could feed him. She could tuck the sheet all around him so that he couldn't move his arms or legs and she could feed him and then put her arm under his curly head and kiss him and stroke him until he slept.

The doorbell rang.

Oh, God, she thought. "Just a minute," she said, putting her head outside her bedroom door and calling. Then, much louder, she called, "Just a minute!"

"OK," she heard. It was Vito's voice.

Dashing to her closet she took out a full peignoir, slipped it on, powdered her face and applied a hasty line to her pale, blond eyebrows. Then she went to open the front door. But she stood behind it as Vito came in.

"Don't look at me," she commanded. She stood behind him, her hand over her face.

"What?"

"Don't look at me because I haven't fixed my face yet." She laughed.

"Oh—all right." Vito stood in the foyer uncertainly.

She put her fingers against his back and pushed. "You go in there and sit down," she said. "I'll be with you in a couple of minutes."

Vito sat in a soft chair and she skipped by him on the tips of her bare toes.

"If you want, I can come back later—" he began.

"No. Stay there. Are you in a hurry?"

"No. It's only—"

"All right then. Stay there. I'll be right out."

"OK," Vito said. He was confused. It was flattering to be asked to wait but her tone seemed, he thought, severe. He sighed. He saw the screwdriver where he had left it next to the air conditioner and went over to look at the machine.

"Hey—uh—Vito. Leave it alone until I come out, will you? I mean, I'll have to show you what it is. All right?"

"All right. Sure. I was just— I left my screwdriver here. I forgot it."

"You didn't think I'd steal it, did you?" she called through the closed door.

"Steal it! A screwdriver? What for?"

"I don't know," she said and her voice startled him. It was much closer and deeper. She had come out of her bedroom and was smiling at him, her face fresh and brilliant.

"You look—" he paused—"you look real nice."

She looked at him quickly and noted his confusion. Then she smiled again. "Why thank you, darling, that's sweet of you." Vito shifted. He was unable to look at her.

"What are you blushing for, you silly boy?" She came up to him and took his hand.

"Oh—" He tried to take his hand away but she held it.

"It's a good thing you don't know how cute you are because if you did, you'd be impossible." She laughed.

Vito succeeded in regaining the freedom of his hand but was at a loss for a way to use it. He rubbed the back of his neck vigorously. He could feel sweat starting to form.

"Look, before you get that thing taken apart all over again, how would you like some breakfast?"

"Oh, thanks. But I ate—with my father. Before I came up."

"All right then, how about a drink?"

"A drink?"

"That's right. Whisky. Scotch, bourbon, brandy, vodka. What would you like?"

"Well—I—I don't—I mean, *you* know, I don't drink much and I—"

"So? Live a little. You're not going to let me drink alone, are you?"

"No—uh—whatever you're having, that's OK."

"Sure? Scotch on the rocks?"

"Sure. I mean, if you want to—"

"There," she said, handing him a glass. "Let's have a ball." She took a deep swallow and Vito took a tentative sip. The taste of strong whisky shocked and almost nauseated him. His face twisted.

"Tastes—OK," he said.

"Oh, Vito. You're a funny boy." She took another deep swallow of her drink. "Now, do it like that. Go on, it won't hurt you. Take a big one. That's how you get used to it."

Vito took a large swallow, started to choke, but held it down. "Pretty good stuff," he said. He faked a stagger. She took him by the hand and led him to the couch.

"Sit back, relax," she said. "What are you afraid of?"

"Me? Nothing."

"Wait a minute. Before you sit back, go over there to that table and get us some cigarettes, will you, sweetie?"

Vito held them out to her.

"Light one for me."

"Huh. Oh." His voice broke. He lighted a cigarette and started to hand it to her.

"Unh-unh." She gestured at her mouth, looking at him with a smile. As he faltered uncertainly, she took his hand and guided the cigarette to her lips.

"Thanks," she said. "All right. Now you can sit down. Don't you want a cigarette?"

"Huh? Oh, yeah."

"Easy! For goodness sakes, boy. You bound so. You almost tipped over my drink."

"Oh, I'm sorry. I guess I'm—I'm kinda nervous."

"What for?" she said. She was sitting with her legs

folded on the couch so that the tips of her knees brushed his trousers and she was smiling at him, at his profile.

"Well, you know. I mean—well, I don't drink much. Oh, this isn't the first time that I've taken a drink but that's like at a party or with the guys, now and then somebody gets hold of a bottle. It isn't like—well—"

"Vito," she said, "put your head back. No. All the way back. Put your head back against the couch and relax."

"OK."

"All the way back. That's it, just relax. Now here," she said, leaning toward him, "hold still. Take a sip. Go on. Don't be afraid. Drink. That's better. OK?"

"OK," he said and laughed. He moved his head so that he could look at her. She smiled and made a little kissing gesture with her lips. His eyes widened with astonishment and then he looked quickly away.

"Have you ever kissed a girl before?" she asked softly, and then added quickly, "Never mind, of course you have. I keep forgetting you aren't as young as you look."

Vito felt a wave of dizziness and he leaned forward instinctively and put his feet flat on the rug.

"Are you all right?"

"Oh, sure." He laughed. "I just—you know." He leaned his head back again and he was breathing hard.

"Poor baby," she said, moving close to him on the couch and sliding her arm beneath his head. "Poor baby." He could feel the warmth of her shoulder and breast beneath the cool scented fabric of her peignoir and he wanted to place his cheek against her. His fingers were stiff with cold.

She took the glass from his hand and placed it on the coffee table, then she leaned back and placed her cheek against his temple.

"Oh," he said softly.

"Poor baby. Close your eyes."

He closed his eyes and she stroked his cheek with her

finger. Then she moved her head and kissed his forehead and his eyes; lightly, softly, she moved her lips over his smooth skin. "Such a baby," she was murmuring, "such a beautiful, beautiful baby. Such long eyelashes." She kissed his eyes again, brushing his eyelashes with her lips. Delightedly, she felt his hand reaching around her waist.

"Ah, there's the baby," she murmured. "There, you hold me." Then she put her mouth on his and kissed him delicately, cupping his cheek in her hand and then she put her tongue in his mouth.

"Oh," he moaned. She slid forward, still kissing him, and gradually pressed him down so that he lay almost full length on the couch. His head was on her arm and she lay close to him, almost on top of him, covering his mouth with hers. His eyes were tightly closed. Reaching down, she slid her hand under his waist band and pulled up his tee shirt, moving her hand over his smooth, hot skin, pressing his nipples and moving down to massage his flat, tense stomach. He began to tremble. "Mmmmuh," he moaned, "muh, muh."

"Ssh, baby," she whispered, "just relax, listen to me, listen to mama, just relax."

"All right," he whispered, his voice catching in his throat.

"Ah, there's a love, there's my doll baby, now just lie still," she warned, "don't move, lie still." She opened his belt and parted his clothing, reaching for his folded and timid flesh which, now remote from the vortex of his mind and belonging less to him than to the cool hand which grasped it, rose, thickened, strained and, as she loomed above him, sensed enveloping warmth, voiding and surging like the flaring of a star, and fell—plunging him dizzyingly, faintingly through blackness, silence, cold.

Cold, Vito thought, cold at his throat, his chest, cold moving over his temples, cold on his eyes. "Mother," he whispered, "mother, mother."

"Hush, baby, hush. I'm here. It's all right. Hush."

"Mother, mo—" He opened his eyes. Iris's face was close to his and she was smiling. "Mother," he said almost without sound.

"My baby," Iris said, "my baby." She kissed him softly on the mouth and he shuddered. He turned his face away and covered his eyes with his hand.

"Please," he said, "please don't look at me." She had taken his clothes off, his trousers, shorts and shoes but had been unable to remove his tee shirt. "Please," he said, and tried to turn away from her. Her gown was open and he could feel the warmth of her body along his leg. He shrank and tried to turn. He began to cry. Turning fetally on his side, drawing his knees up and hunching his head down on his chest, he began to sob, his thin shoulders quaking, his breath making a sharp sucking sound.

"Vito," she murmured, "Vito, darling, doll baby, don't," she said, shaking his shoulders lightly, "don't Vito, it's all right. You're all right. Don't cry, sweetie, don't, please don't." She pressed the cold cloth to the back of his neck and stroked him, curving her body behind his so that she could feel him quivering as if in her own flesh.

"I thought—" he tried to say. "I thought," he sobbed again.

"Ssh. It's all right."

"No." He shook his head. "I thought—for a while—I thought you were my—" He broke down again.

She held him for a long time until he was still.

Finally, when he was still, she asked him, "Are you all right now?"

"Yes," he said, "I'm sorry."

"Don't be sorry. It's all gone. Forgotten." She stroked his head. "How about a Coke?" she asked. "Would you like that?"

"Sure, if you have one."

"All right, I'll go get you one. But while I do, you get up and go put some cold water on your face, all right?"

"OK."

"And then you go and get into my bed. All right?"

"All right," he said, less certainly. Then he added, "But don't look at me. I'm embarrassed."

She suppressed a laugh. "All right, I won't look at you. Go on now."

He hesitated.

"Go on," she repeated, laughing. "Look, I've got my eyes closed."

"All right," he said, laughing. He ran into the bathroom.

Carrying a tray which bore a Coke for Vito as well as a bottle of whisky for herself, Iris paused at the doorway and looked at him as he lay in the bed. His pose was demure. The sheet was pulled up to his chin and only his dark face, slightly rosy and smiling, was revealed. Sensing his modesty, and feeling modest herself—strangely, because she liked to exhibit herself to her lovers and sometimes took a perverse delight in chatting with them for hours all the while that she was wholly or partially naked—she slipped into the bed beside him without removing her peignoir.

"Now, isn't this fun?" she said.

He smiled at her shyly. "I guess I don't hold my liquor so well. I kind of passed out."

"No. Not really, baby. You just—well, the excitement and all. It's natural. Drink your Coke. It'll make you feel better." She held the glass to his lips but he took it from her.

"It's OK," he said gently. "I'm not a baby."

"Of course you aren't. You're *my* baby, but that's different." She paused and looked at him slyly. "This was your first time, wasn't it? I mean really. Inside."

"Yeah."

"Now, are you glad?"

"I—uh—want to say something to you but I don't know—"

"Go ahead."

"I—"

"Go on, say it."

"You're going to think I'm silly because—well, because we hardly even know each other and besides I'm just a kid and you're so—so— What I mean is, I'm—" He turned over on his stomach and buried his face in his folded arms. His voice emerged muffled by the pillow. "I'm in love with you."

Iris felt her eyes fill with tears. She jumped out of bed and got a handful of facial tissues and wiped her eyes carefully in front of her mirror.

Vito was sitting up in bed, his face alarmed. "What did I say? I'm sorry. I didn't mean anything. Please." He was stricken.

She came back to the bed and sat down on it again, wiping her eyes and smiling. She started to get back into the bed, then stood up and stripped off her peignoir. Then she took him in her arms, holding him tightly as she could.

"Oh, Vito," she said, "Vito, darling, darling. You don't have to say that. Don't feel you have to say that."

"But—" He tried to break free but she held him.

"You don't know anything about love yet. You don't know if you love me. You can't."

"But I know how I feel," he said, pulling free of her grasp. "I love you. What's wrong with that?" He looked fierce now, his young face blazing. Then his eyes fell. "You don't have to love me. That's OK. I just love you."

"All right," she said. "All right, we'll see. But I want you to know something—even if you don't mean it, it was a wonderful thing to say. Look, it made me cry."

"But I do—"

"All right, all right." She pulled his head back down to her breast again. She stroked his cheek and his head and ran her hand along his slim back, feeling the wonderfully delicate articulation of his bones and muscles beneath the smooth skin.

"Oh, you're so lovely," she murmured, "so soft and

lovely. You're so beautiful." She paused. "Do you like me?"

"Oh, yes." He kissed her awkwardly, not sure whether he should put his tongue in her mouth. She rose and leaned over and kissed him, expertly, aggressively. She could feel his body coming alive quickly, thrusting against her.

She slid her hand between their bodies and felt his young strength, hot, pulsing, silky. She was overcome with desire to possess him, to consume him, to take this precious, living beauty that was his into her being. She flung the sheet aside and pushed him so that he lay on his back.

"Oh, Vito," she whispered, "darling, you're so beautiful," over and over again she murmured, "so beautiful," pressing her lips to his breast, moving the tip of her tongue along his stomach. He moaned as his flesh, seeking, seeking, felt the warmth of her lips.

"Oh, I love it," she whispered. "I love it, I want it. It's so beautiful, darling, so strong, so beautiful. Mine. I want it."

He went rigid with fear, holding his limbs so stiffly that every muscle sharpened in relief beneath his skin. The horror of what she was doing paralyzed him. He was helpless, alone, unable to speak. He strained frantically, wanting to shrink from the terror that she was bringing to every corner of his mind while at the same time he was conscious of the distant, exquisite purposefulness of his flesh, willful, reckless, carrying with it all his reluctant being.

"Ah!" he cried out. "Aaah, aaah," the sound dying, clattering in his vacant mind. He was lost, alone, dispersed. He could not, at that moment, have answered to his own name.

For a long time Vito lay silent, his eyes squinted shut, his mouth drawn into a wide rectangle of pain. Iris fussed over him, cooing, clucking, tamping the pillow beneath his head, dabbing his temples, his brow. She watched him anxiously, stroking his face, drawing his slim head with its black curls, now damp and matted, close to her breast. Gradually his face softened, the eyelids with their long black hairs trembled, parted and slowly closed. He slept on her arm.

As she watched him, holding herself very still while he fell deeper and deeper into unconsciousness, Iris felt her mind grow cold.

She was terribly awake, painfully, almost sickly alert. Every sound in the room, every clock tick and breath sound, every rustle of the sheet seemed to strike her central nerve. The light was harsh and ugly to her eyes, the glitter from polished surfaces was unbearably bright. In her body she felt a knotted tension. Her hand clenched with the impulse to rend herself, to reach the source of her own agony.

Yet worse than this was her feeling, a thick fog-blanket of isolation, a suffocating feeling of being alone.

With difficulty, she drew her arm from beneath Vito's head. She put her hands to her throat, feeling as if she might gag. Then, desperately, she reached for the whisky bottle and poured the tumbler a quarter full. She drank it urgently, forcing it down, all of it. Then she sat dully, her hands pressed to her aching stomach, feeling the first heat of the whisky enter her blood. Cautiously, she slid down beneath the sheet and pulled it up under her chin. The alcohol grew stronger inside her, more pervasive and finally she could feel it seeping along the perimeter of her brain.

"Ah," she whispered, echoing Vito's cry. "Ah," she repeated, "thank God. Thank God for booze." She threw her leg over Vito's leg and gripped it comfortably between her thighs. Then she went to sleep.

It was after five o'clock when Iris awoke, instantly conscious, fully alert. She turned her head to find Vito watching her. His quick, black animal eyes were steady and his face was grave but when she turned to look at him he broke into a modest smile.

"Darling," she murmured.

"I've been watching you," he whispered.
"For how long?"
"An hour."
"Why didn't you wake me, sweetie?" she drawled lazily and moved close to him, fitting her body luxuriously to his.

He shrugged. She took his hand and placed it on the triangle of her body but it lay there, unmoving.

"I think I ought to go," he whispered, "my father—"

She drew a little away from him and looked at him coldly.

"What's the matter?" he asked.

"Nothing." She shook her head and looked away. She paused for a few moments and rubbed her eyes slowly, meticulously, ignoring him.

"Gee—Iris—don't get sore. I mean, he might be worried. I ought to check in."

"So?" She dropped her hands and stared at the ceiling. "Go."

"I don't want you to be sore at me."

"I'm not sore." She yawned and patted him distractedly, reaching out but not turning her face to him. "Go on home," she said. "Go home and tell your father. And be sure you tell all the kids—all your friends on the block and anyone else you can think of." Her voice was bitter.

He was shocked. His voice strained and almost cracked. "For God's sake! I wouldn't do that. I wouldn't tell anybody. Honest, Iris."

She looked at him steadily. Then she smiled. "All right. I'm sorry. I know you wouldn't. It's just—well, it might not look so hot. Not that there's anything *wrong*"—she emphasized the word with a fierce look—"just that I don't want to get a reputation of being a cradle robber."

Vito blushed. "I didn't think of it that way. I didn't even—I didn't even think of it." He ended lamely.

"It figures."

Vito was silent. His eyes searched her face and then

fell. "Listen," he said at last, "I want to ask you something. I mean—well, we're here, I mean we've—well, *you* know—"

"What?"

"Well, I mean—we're together, aren't we?"

"Yes."

"And that means—or at least, I *think* it means—" he had difficulty getting out the last words, "you're my girl." He paused and whispered. "Aren't you?"

She began to smile and then to laugh. She sat up in bed and laughed and then leaned over him, still laughing, and put her face between his shoulder and his neck.

"Oh, Vito, you funny boy. You funny, funny boy," she said. "I don't have to be your girl. I'm not *any*body's girl."

"But I want you to be—"

"Oh, you don't really know yet what—"

"Yes I do," he said angrily. "You said that before." He sat up, forcing her back on her pillow. He was leaning on both fists buried in the bedclothes, his slim arms were stiff and straight. "I'm not saying we can go steady or anything because—well, I haven't got much dough. But I want you to be my girl. Now if you want to be, all right, but if you don't want to be—"

"Hey! Look who's getting huffy."

He ignored her. "Come on," he said firmly, "what do you say?"

She stared at him for a long time without answering. He appeared absurdly childish, his tousled curls falling on his brow, his delicate, curving lips now tense and his slim arms poking his shoulder blades high on either side of his neck like wings. Yet his eyes did not waver. His face was stern. She was not sure as she answered him whether she was still toying with him or actually giving ground.

"Does that mean, you—I'm not to see anybody else?"

He hesitated. "No. Not exactly. I mean, after all, I can't tell you—it's just, well, how you feel."

"All right, baby." She smiled and reached her arms

up to embrace his head. "All right, I'll be your girl. At least we'll try it. OK?"

"OK," he said, his voice muffled by her shoulder.

"And you'll keep your mouth shut, OK?"

"Of course!" he said fiercely, struggling against her grasp.

"And any time I want it, this is mine, OK?" she said, putting her hand between his legs. She laughed.

He didn't answer.

"Oh, what's the matter," she said, "is the baby mad at me?"

"No," he muttered.

"All right," she said humorously, "after all, if I'm going to be your girl you've got to tell me what to do and what not to do. Right?"

"You're just kidding me. Teasing me."

She laughed. "God, are you serious! I forgot how serious men can be."

"I'm not a man yet." Vito's voice was still muffled by her shoulder but it sounded pleased.

"Honey, if I say you're a man, you are a man. OK? Now, when am I going to see you again, never?"

"Huh?" Vito picked up his head, looking at her with surprise. "I'm just going downstairs to sort of check on my father, you know—"

"Tell you what. Why don't you go down and come back in—say—a couple of hours. Seven o'clock. And I'll cook dinner for you. Would you like that?"

"Sure!" he shouted.

"You mean you're *not* sick and tired of me?"

He made a sound almost like a scream of protest. "Are you crazy!"

"OK, OK. Don't holler. I just thought maybe you wanted to rest or something."

He was unable to speak.

"All right, all right." She laughed. "Now, go get dressed. And be sure to wipe that lipstick off your face before you go down."

For a long time after Vito left, Iris lay idly smoking

and staring at the ceiling. She felt vacant and a little edgy, the after-effects of having been aroused and not released, but she was used to that. Resigned to it. Occasionally, if she knew a man well enough, liked him enough and if she was drunk enough—not *too* drunk, but just enough—she could obtain a kind of frantic, self-willed release which left her physically exhausted and, in fact, feeling hopelessly depressed.

Most of the time she felt it wasn't worth it. No man, she had long since decided, had the strength or the desire or the patience to give her what she really wanted.

Neither could a woman. Dykes, she reflected, yawning, they're worse than men. And so jealous! Jesus, are they jealous! Besides, there was no pleasure in being with another woman. She had tried it and found it joyless, empty. She had felt like an outcast in another woman's bed, more than ever alone.

No matter how unsatisfactory a man was, she reflected, at least she was with a man, not cut off from the rest of the world. The trouble with most men, she reflected, was that they never lasted long enough. Not really. Oh, she thought, there had been a few. Her second husband was slow and even gentle, she thought fondly, but at the end, when she was beginning to feel something, really feel herself going tight inside, he would want to move faster and she would try desperately to slow him down and it never quite became right. And as the months went by, of course, he got worse—faster and faster. Useless.

Too bad, she thought, because she still liked him. But he went out and found another woman. She shrugged.

Maybe, she thought with a sudden flush of pleasure, she could train Vito, actually teach him. In her mind she fashioned careful phrases, "Now, look, sweetie, you give me your hand, like this, and . . ."

He was so sweet, she thought. Such a darling baby. She felt an overwhelming rush of tenderness. Oh, she wished he were there that instant! She would kiss him and hug him, squeeze him and rock him, just rock him back and forth.

She got quickly out of bed. She would cook for him, cook a wonderful meal. She would watch him eat. She would even feed him. She smiled at herself, stretching languidly before the mirror. Then, with her arms high above her head, she stopped.

What would Juley Franz say if he knew? Her hand flew to her mouth. She laughed.

"Oh, brother!" she said aloud. "Oh, buh-roth-*er!*"

Just for the fun of it, she would call Juley in Connecticut. Not to tell him. God! But just to needle him a little bit, just to make him jealous. She giggled.

"Operator," she said in an exaggeratedly highfalutin voice, "Operator, I am calling Connect-icut. I want —in Westport, I want Mr. Fraahnz, Mr. Jewels Fraahnz . . ."

Alone in the superintendent's basement apartment, Vito sat by the window in his father's chair. The room was silent with that special quiet of late Sunday afternoon and he could hear the hum of an electric clock on the shelf. He was glad his father wasn't in the house. He felt an urge to talk and he knew he would have told his father everything that had happened. Yet that, he remembered, was exactly what Iris had asked him not to do. Still—his father was different. Vito decided he wouldn't tell his father *ev*erything. He'd tell him a little, brag a little. His father would laugh at him, poke him in the ribs, pull his hair. He smiled. He wished the old man were at home. Hugging his knees and smiling, he became aware that the small bright-blue rectangle at the top of the window was no longer perfect. A corner was gone.

"Hello, you lousy cat," Vito said, but he stopped. That's what I've been doing, he thought. "Hey, cat," he whispered, "you know what—" But the cat disappeared over the wall. Holy Christ! he thought, I really have. I finally did it! He tried to remember how it felt but he couldn't. He couldn't even remember what Iris looked like. He tried to concentrate, to remember some aspect of Iris, how she smelled, how she felt, but he could not summon up the fantasy. He saw only the room around him, the window, the patch of sky and then suddenly he groaned aloud. His body twisted with the impact of memory. The recollected image of Iris making love to him, kissing his body, consuming him, stunned him with its immediacy.

With a tremendous effort, he thrust it out of his mind. It was a terrible thought, frightening. It devastated him, left him feeling helpless, wasted, felled. Yet, even as his fear subsided, even as his hands loosened on the arms of his chair, he felt the faintest, slightest stirring of pride. And curiosity; this too. Calmer now, he was tempted to re-examine this memory—not fully, not brazenly, but cautiously, secretly, opening that hastily slammed door just a crack.

This, he knew, would be his deepest secret. Whatever else he might dare to recount, he would never discuss this. It was too, too—

Sissy. This was the word in his mind. A ridiculous word, a child's word. He scorned it. Still . . . sissy. And— Never mind, he didn't want to think about it.

But he couldn't stop thinking about it. It kept coming back. Inadvertently, he found himself engulfed again. And again he groaned, grinding his teeth.

He wanted to be—to do—he could barely phrase it in his mind. He wanted to—to—be *nice* to *her!* He wanted to—to give her—

What?

To give her, to do—to make her feel—

"Oh, son of a bitch!" he growled to the empty twilight. "Son of a bitch bastard!" He pounded his fist hard on the arm of the chair.

Suddenly, he wanted to yell. He could feel the tension gathering in his throat and in his lungs. Tentatively, because he was afraid of the sound he would make in the small basement room, he began a low, strangled yell. "Aaarrgh!"

Then louder. "AAAARRRRGGHHH." That felt better. He laughed. Jesus, he was hungry. He would leave a note for the old man. He wished it were seven o'clock already. The clock on the shelf said six. He wished he were upstairs. God, how he wished it. He ached with it. Everything around him was so ugly, so contemptible, such a waste. But she had said seven. He would take a shower and put on his best pants and a clean shirt and a jacket. The thought of getting dressed up was a good one. But first he would write a note to the old man.

"Dear Papa," he started to write and crumpled the paper up. "Dear Whiskers," he wrote again, grinning, using the nickname for his father's mustache, his *baffi*. "Dear Whiskers: I'm up in 4-B having supper with the madonna." He crossed the last word out. "Having supper with that lady with the air conditioner. Pretty fast work. Ha! Don't call *me*. I'll call *you*." He signed it: *Pippo*.

His father would get a laugh out of that. He jumped and grasped the door frame, chinned himself quickly twelve times and stamped, singing, into the shower.

5

In a tributary opening onto the Merritt Parkway, Juley Franz waited tensely, a bulky, tired and rather solemn salmon poised to leap upstream. The dark, sweet, plastic-smelling interior of his silver-gray convertible oppressed him and though he had tossed his weekend bag, shoes and golf clubs into the car before he left, there was still too much room, far too much.

I ought, he thought—and then interrupted his musings long enough to launch himself into a fortuitous opening in the stream of headlights. I ought to get some kind of a dog. His weekend hosts had had a dog, a Kerry blue terrier named Rory who had seemed, on first meeting, utterly inscrutable—couldn't make head or tail out of the goddam thing, Juley reflected, laughing to himself, couldn't even see his face for the hair all over it—and who subsequently revealed a delicate pink tongue, a wet nose and, beneath crisp curls, bright, companionable eyes. These had all been impressed on Juley's awareness with the force of small but poignant revelation.

Nice dog, he thought, already transferring its ownership and affection to himself. But of course who would take care of the thing?

Iris. She could take care of it, feed it, walk it. It would give her something to do. It would also, and this was more important, give them something in common, something animate, that is. They could sit and watch the goddam dog or take it for walks together. It would be fun. It was almost like having a child.

Instinctively he lifted his foot off the accelerator, then resumed speed again. The thought of his children was an unhappy one. Fortunately, his weekend hosts had no children. In fact, if they had he would not have accepted their invitation. The presence of other people's children made him so uncomfortable—guilty, really—that he had learned to evade such encounters.

Not, he reminded himself, that he had anything to be really ashamed of. He loved them, he called them up, took them to shows and the money he spent on them—don't even talk about it, he told himself. Forget it, don't even talk about it.

But the divorce was his doing. He admitted it, why not? In the three years since it had occurred, some of the more painful memories had been dulled but his wife, Minna, *former* wife, he reminded himself, was still, in the eyes of the law and his own eyes, "the injured party." She would have gone on living with him forever, headaches, boredom, rejection notwithstanding, rather than choose massive derangement of her life.

And, of course, the break, when it did come, was far less painful than she had imagined. She had a nice apartment, friends, the children, a summer place, boy friends. Juley laughed. She seemed gayer, prettier, happier than she had for the fourteen years he had known her.

But the children—he shook his head. When you came right down to it, he told himself, they really didn't need him. And that was what hurt the most. What are you gonna do? he thought. What are you gonna do? That's the way kids are. Did I, he went on, in a dialogue with some imaginary judge, did I really give a damn about my *own* father when I was their age? Later, maybe. When I began to grow up and I began to find out what a tough thing it is to make a living. But then?

What are you gonna do? He sighed, changed to the outside lane and accelerated. At my age, he thought, who needs a sports car? The thought was so irrelevant that he smiled.

Immediately, he began forming a fantasy with Iris, a jocular fantasy. I was riding along the Merritt Parkway, he heard himself saying, you know, it was kind of late, and all of a sudden I said to myself, at my age who needs a goddam sports car? How about that? Maybe I'm getting senile, who knows? Iris, of course, would laugh and reply, with that trick she had of making ordinary talk sound a little racy: You? senile! Oh, brother.

Or maybe she wouldn't, he thought grimly. She might just let him have it right in the bread basket.

Bitch, he thought. Sometimes she got him so goddam angry he would like to punch her right in the jaw. But —there was no getting away from it, she had class. You had to hand it to her. Sure she was a strip teaser. And she was good at it. A success. Sure she came up the hard way. She had more goddam class and more goddam guts than any woman he had ever known.

And let's face it, he added, I just happen to be crazy about her. Marriage? I'd marry her tomorrow, he told himself. So, sure I'm nuts. Who isn't a little bit nuts? I can afford to be.

The business, he felt, the vast sums of money that accrued to him were enough to prove him successful, if not sane. This was his most comforting thought, his amulet. And it was the one thing, perhaps the only thing, he reflected, that was proof against all of Iris's gibes.

If only, he thought wistfully, if only she wouldn't needle him so. If only a man knew where he stood with her. But he was always off-balance. She kept him that way. Like that telephone call a few hours ago, he reflected.

"Juju. Darling!" she had squealed into the telephone.

He was surprised, pleased, inordinately pleased that she had called. He hadn't expected it, hadn't even left her a telephone number. All she had was the last name of his hosts in Westport.

"Can I see you," he had said, "can I pick you up?"

"No, baby," she had said, "it'll be much too late and I'm tired. I'll be asleep."

"Asleep! What are you so tired about? I thought you were going to spend a quiet weekend going to the zoo or some damn thing. What did you do, spend the afternoon at a double header?"

"Oh, I've been keeping busy. You know, dashing around." It was the tone of her voice, the swift glaciality of it that bothered him. In the fraction of an instant she had become guarded, aloof, shutting him out.

"Well, look," he had added, knowing that he was on the defensive again, "I ought to be back by ten or eleven, why don't I give you a ring when I hit the city and then if you want—"

"No, don't bother." She sounded dull now, disinterested.

"Honey, doll, I can make it sooner. There won't be much traffic at this hour—"

She hadn't answered.

"Hey, are you listening?" he asked.

"Yeah. Sure."

"I said, if you like, I can—"

"Oh, no. Forget it. I just called to see how you were. I'll talk to you tomorrow."

"It was sweet of you to call. But are you sure—"

"No, Juley. It's too late. Besides, I might go over and see some friends. So, good-by, I'll talk to you tomorrow."

"See— OK. Well—" he faltered.

"Yeah, well." She laughed. " 'By."

Then why had she called him, he asked himself. Because she just wanted to talk to him, just wanted to hear his voice, in the same way that he wanted to hear her voice? Who the hell knows, he told himself. Who knows? Maybe, he thought, he'd call her when he got into the city. Maybe! He knew he would. She might be asleep, she might not even be home. If she wasn't home or if he couldn't get her to come out of the house, he'd have to call somebody. So it would cost him fifty, maybe a hundred. What the hell, for a night's sleep it was worth it. That bitch, he thought, Iris Hartford. Why do I keep knocking myself out?

Seated at Iris's kitchen table, Vito smoked a cigarette and watched Iris as she cleared away the dishes and piled them in the sink.

"The girl," she said, "will do them when she comes tomorrow."

Vito felt deserted, alone. Iris was wearing slim black trousers and a white blouse. She had backless shoes on her small feet, many strands of gold bracelets on her wrist and her hair was smartly arranged. Concentrating on her work, humming as she moved quickly from the table to the refrigerator to the sink, she appeared to Vito as inaccessible as she had on the first moment of their meeting. He could not believe that he had looked so closely into her eyes that he could see the bright pink corners of her lids or the clustered gray and green and brown which had seemed more like jewels than any jewel he had ever seen. He could not remember ever having felt her lips against his mouth. His glance fell on the sharp, tight curve of her buttocks in her tight trousers but he was unable to relate this to anything that he remembered. It made her seem, if anything, more remote, more self-contained. In fact, their having made love, the very real sensations of being in bed together, seeing her flesh, her smile, her frown—all this seemed never to have happened. Timidly, he sought about for some means to rejoin her.

"Uh, that sure was a good dinner," he said. "You're some cook."

"Thank you, doll," Iris said, not turning her head toward him. "You're some little eater."

"If you want me to do the dishes—I do them all the time for my father."

"Forget it. The girl comes tomorrow. I'll have to give her something to do."

Vito was silent. It was hopeless. He felt stiff and uncomfortable in his best suit. It was like sitting in a stalled bus; there was nothing he could do. Then, suddenly, she finished and turned around to face him.

"Baby!" she said. "What's the matter?" She came over to him and pressed his head to her waist. "What are you looking so sad about?"

His sense of relief was total. Her smell, her warmth, the feeling of her hands on the back of his neck. "Nothing," he said. "I'm all right." He rubbed his face eagerly against her warm, silk-covered belly.

"Hey! Watch out for my dinner." She laughed.

"I don't care. I want to squeeze you—like this."

"Oh, baby," she said, leaning backward, arching her back so that her pelvis was pressed tightly against his chest. She began to sway from side to side so that the sharp bone, covered with its small mound of flesh, rubbed against his chest. "Oh, that feels so good. Let's go to bed."

"I was hoping you'd say that."

"Oh, yeah," she said, "wow. Let's go."

Iris was first to take her clothes off and slip into bed. She watched Vito avidly, her eyes bright, as he struggled with his buttons and with his awkward shoes. "Turn around," she commanded, as he started to slide into bed with his back turned.

"No."

"Turn around, I say."

"No. I'm embarrassed. I look funny."

"Oh, you silly," she said, grasping his slim shoulders as he slid under the sheet, "you little silly." She started to rise, to force him down but he held her off. She looked at him, startled.

"I uh—I want to," he said. His dark hand was on her shoulder and he pushed her back. "I want to. OK? You can tell me if—what I should—OK?"

"Sure, doll." An amused smile came over her face.

He was on her with a rush. He held her face between

his hands and kissed her, his eyes closed. She felt his body pressing eagerly against her and as he pressed harder, seeking her, she obediently and good-humoredly opened to him.

"Wait!" she called out sharply. "Not so hard. Easy."

He opened his eyes and looked apprehensively at her face. "I'm sorry," he said. "I didn't mean to hurt you."

"It's all right," she said calmly, "just don't be in too much of a hurry, that's all."

"OK. I won't. Is that—there, is that all right?"

Iris had closed her eyes and she was smiling. "Mmm, that's nice." It was pleasant, she thought, so very, very pleasant. It was so good to be filled, so good to be burdened with this weight, bound, captive. She stretched luxuriously beneath him, feeling his touch everywhere along her body and she twisted her toes so they would engage his feet.

"Oh, darling, this is so nice," she said, opening her eyes to narrow slits and kissing him lightly. She could feel him starting to quicken. "No, don't do that," she said. "Just lie still. Hold me."

Vito tried to obey her but he was unable to restrain his urgency.

And Iris too began to move, feeling his slim hands tightening on her flanks, feeling his quickening thrust, sensing the sweet smell of his curls against her cheek and suddenly something gave way deep inside her, she felt herself falling, falling as if some wall had been swept away, falling, rising, her fingers pressing tightly against the smooth skin of his neck and shoulders, feeling the tightness gather, aching in her loins, moving wildly now, joyfully, seeking, crying, "Oh, yeah, oh, yeah, yeah, yeah," and hearing, dimly, his cry as he burst within her, burst and sighed, strained with one last surge and stopped.

"Oh," she said, finally. "Oh, boy."

Vito raised his head to look at her. There were tears in her eyes.

"What's the matter?" he whispered.

"Nothing, darling."

"But you're crying."

"Forget it. I always cry."

He was silent. "Did I do OK? I tried to do what you told me."

She laughed despite her tears and tightened her arms around his neck. "You don't know how OK you were, sweetie. In fact, that's about the best it's ever been."

"Good?"

"Uh-huh, good." She wiped her eyes and looked at him fondly. She was smiling. "You know something? I almost made it. I damn near did."

"Made it? You mean—"

"Well, you know, finished. Like you did."

Vito paused. "I never even thought of it."

She laughed and pulled his hair. "If you weren't so young, I'd give you a knee right in the you-know-where."

"Well," he said, "I just figured—you know. I mean isn't that what's supposed to happen?"

"I can see you've never read a book about sex. What do kids read these days anyway, comics? Science fiction? That's what you get for watching television, for Christ-sakes. How can you learn anything about sex from watching TV?"

"Oh." He laughed. "I'm not all that green."

"The hell you aren't."

He was silent for a few moments. Then he patted her cheek gently. "It's all right. You'll make it next time."

"Oh, Vito!" She began to laugh. "You kill me. You really do."

He laughed too, proudly. "I'm glad."

"You're glad, are you!" she shouted. "Looka him. He's glad." Then she stopped laughing and kissed him. "I love you," she said.

His eyes opened wide. "You do?"

"Yeah," she said lightly. "But don't let it go to your head."

He lay alongside her, his head on her shoulder. "You're always kidding me," he said. "You make out like I'm just a child."

She turned her face to him and kissed the tip of his nose. "If you want to know the truth, I think you're the sweetest man I've ever known." She kissed him again, putting her tongue between his lips.

Vito felt an exquisite blush of happiness, so swift, so all-pervading that he wanted literally, to lose himself in her being. He pressed against her tightly and discovered, without even having been aware of it, that he had grown erect again.

"Vito!" she said, opening her eyes wide and grasping him, "Vito, what's *with* you?"

"Oh," he said, "oh, oh. Quick, I want to—I want—" He started to rise over her. Then the telephone rang.

"God! Never mind, let it ring. I should have turned it down or put something over it. Go on, baby." But the ringing persisted and Vito, distracted, fearful, felt his strength die.

Iris patted his head and then slid over to the telephone.

"Hello," she said, very softly.

"Honey, I'm asleep . . . Don't argue with me, what do I care if it's only ten o'clock, if I'm asleep, I'm asleep. . . . All right. Did you have fun? . . . Good . . . No, not now, tomorrow. You can tell me all about it then. . . . Yeah, go ahead. . . . A dog! Are you out of your mind! What the . . . all right. I'll talk to you tomorrow. . . . OK, so you're sorry. Not serious. I just want to get back to sleep, that's all. 'By . . ." She hung up the telephone.

Vito lay with his elbows on either side of his pillow, his head on his clasped hands. He was looking at the ceiling and did not turn as he felt her move close to him.

"I want to know something," he said in a tight voice.

She lighted a cigarette and offered it to him but he shook his head.

"I want to know if that's your boy friend."

Iris felt a quick impulse to anger. What right did he have—then she stopped. The sight of his slim, troubled face on the pillow was so young, so touchingly young that her anger vanished. She put her cigarette down and leaned over him so that her breasts touched his delicately boned chest. She pressed her hands against his cheeks so that his lips puffed slightly and she kissed him.

"I have no boy friend," she said. "You're it."

"Honest?"

"I swear to God."

"You mean—"

"Yes, that's what I mean. Now, come here," she said, putting her arm under his head and drawing it close to her shoulder. "Put your hand there," she added, placing his hand on her breast. "That's right. Now lie still and just hold me."

"I—"

"And shut up," she said.

They slept.

6

When Vito awoke in the morning he was in his own bed. He barely remembered having left Iris's apartment, having gone down to the basement and, having discovered that his father was out, having gone quickly to sleep. His clothes were strewn on the end of the bed where he had dropped them. Who needs clothes, he thought, stretching his naked young body under the sheet. He was not used to sleeping naked, even in summer he always wore shorts. But now, it seemed, he was no longer vulnerable. There was nothing to be afraid of. He felt very free.

More than free, liberated. It was as if some tedious, drab and maddeningly petty shell had broken and fallen away. He savored his own nakedness, feeling the worn, cottony surface of the sheets beneath his skin and suddenly, he smiled.

"Oh, God!" he said aloud.

He would never be afraid of a woman again. He would never have to feel constraint, worry, awe. And better still, he would not now have to walk the streets, seeking, seeking with that blind, swollen eye. It knew where to go now, it had its own warm place.

Free, he thought. Oh, Christ, what a feeling. No more plotting, stalking, silent pleas.

He laughed. Oh, how he wanted to kiss her! He wanted to cover her with kisses, thank-you kisses. He could feel a squeal of gratitude forming in his throat. He groaned aloud.

The door opened. It was his father. He looked questioningly at Vito through the dim light of the room and then he broke into a grin.

"So—" He laughed. "Tell me about it."

Vito laughed. He couldn't help it. His laugh was immodest, even a kind of betrayal, but he couldn't help it. He felt a sudden burst of love for his father. Clean, freshly shaved, he was a real good-looking guy.

"Did you have a good time?" Alessandro asked. He didn't want to press too hard.

"Oh, you know, just—yeah. I had a good time. She's some cook. You know? She made supper for me and I ate like a horse."

"Not bad. She can cook too, eh?"

Vito laughed again. There was no point trying to evade that *"too."* "Uh-huh," he said.

"You're a lucky boy, Vito, Vitellone, a lucky boy," Alessandro said, smiling. He put his hand on Vito's arm.

"I know, Pop," Vito answered softly. "Don't think I don't know. Hey—" He paused. "You know what, I think she's just—she's terrific, Pa."

His father nodded gravely. "And beautiful too. Very beautiful. I tell you for a fact, Vito, that is one of the most beautiful women I have ever seen. *La veritá.*"

Vito was silent. His black eyes rested on his father's face in a way that was both trusting and speculative. "Maybe," he said, "I might even marry her. I could quit school and get a job. Hell, I'm sixteen. I'll be seventeen in, let's see, how many months—"

Alessandro sighed. "Listen to me. Don't rush, eh?"

"I'm not rushing, Pa—"

"You wait a little bit, eh? After all, it's still the summertime, you know, take it easy. Maybe you see in a couple of months how you feel."

"What do you mean, 'how I feel'? Look, you don't understand, she said—"

"Yeah, I know, Vito. Better you don't tell me all the things she says, all the things you say. That's your business, OK?"

"Sure. OK."

"All I'm saying is, you got plenty time. You want to get married, OK, you're going to get married. But first you got to be engaged for a little while, no?"

"Yeah, I guess so."

"All right," Alessandro said briskly. "That's all. So you think it over. Now hurry up and finish your coffee because I got to go out." He slapped Vito's flat stomach. "The little cockerel, come and eat. It's almost nine o'clock."

It was shortly after ten o'clock that Alessandro left the basement, walked out of the foyer of the apartment house and into the sunshine. The air was still cool with morning and a flower vendor was laboriously pushing a wooden cart loaded with calendulas and anemones. Alessandro gazed thoughtfully at the flowers. They recalled the anemones of his youth, of the orchards and *prati* around Florence, gray-green with the spring foliage of olive trees, alive with the flutter of young grain and the trembling colors of wind-touched poppies and purple anemones. It had been a long time since he had gathered flowers for a girl, a long time since he had felt those curiously sweet and dreadful convulsions in his stomach and loins that could be summoned by a word, a glance, a touch.

No, he told himself, at last. Not for anything would he intervene. In the first place, it would be futile. Nothing was so unwelcome, so loathsome in fact—like a cold, wet frog in a marriage bed—as the restraining hand of an elder on the arm of a young lover. Restraining, guiding, advising, wise, unwise, it made no difference. It was an abomination in a private place. And who can say truthfully, he asked himself, whether the hand is honest or not? What old longings, shadowy lusts, the ghosts of murdered, broken-backed desires, may not prompt that hand to intervene? What father does not hunger for the youth of his son and for the love of that youth?

No, he repeated. Let him go it alone. He is blessed. He laughed. And how! he thought. What breasts! What thighs. A real madonna. A madonna and child!

What a joke, he thought. What a joke on the priests of the world. He began forming in his mind an elaborate, typically Florentine blasphemy, so ingeniously prurient and so stylishly irreverent that it kept him smiling and preoccupied on the bus all the way downtown.

Vito fretted while Iris slept. Don't call me before eleven, she had said. Impatient with watching the telephone, he picked up the receiver, listened intently to the ensuing hum and replaced it carefully. It appeared to be in good working order. What, he wondered, could he get her, give her, to show his love, to make her love him more. He took the change out of his pocket and found eighty-five cents. There ought to be something he could get with that. A card, a bracelet—no, that would cost at least a dollar, maybe more. Flowers, he thought. Surely he could get a bunch of flowers somewhere and he could write a card to go with them. "To my dear sweetheart . . ." he began composing the card in his mind. He dashed outdoors and caught sight of the flower vendor's cart a couple of blocks away. On your mark, he said to himself, dropping into a crouch. Get set, he whispered, raising his behind in the air like a track man, poising his weight lightly on his toes and knuckles. Go! He hurtled down the sidewalk, caught a green light at the intersection, bounded over a fire hydrant just for the challenge of it and overshot the flower cart by a good ten yards.

Iris awoke to the sound of a ringing telephone. That would be Juley, she decided comfortably, allowing the telephone to ring several times more before she lifted the quilted bedspread off it.
"Hello, baby," she said.
"Doll. Did I wake you up? I'm sorry. . . ."
"It's all right. I was about to get up anyway."
"Have a good sleep?"
"Mmm. Yeah. Like a lonk. Ooh, good. Hey," she

said, her voice becoming quickly alert. "I want to ask you something. OK?"

"Sure, doll, what is it?"

"Look, if I'm so goddam sick, why do you bother with me?"

"That's what I'm trying to figure out."

"OK, and when you find out you'll tell me to drop dead and take off."

"Iris, don't be a jerk."

"But that's what I'm always telling you. I *am* a jerk, a nut. So why don't you leave me alone? Why don't you find some nice, attractive broad who'll be good to you and forget about me?"

Juley paused. "Because you're the broad I want. Don't you like going out with me, having me around?"

"Sure, Juju, but it isn't getting us anywhere."

"Look, will you let me worry about that? You got something better to do, someone you want to see, that's your business. I got no claim on you. But if I want to take you out, that's my business, OK? The worst you can do is say no."

Iris was silent.

"Now," he went on, "the reason I called—I got two tickets for the new show and I thought we might grab some dinner first—"

"Juju. Do you *really* want to take me out?"

"Yes, I do."

"But then afterward you'll want me to come over to your place and sleep with you. And if I don't want to, you'll get sore. And I don't blame you, honestly I don't. Why don't you take out some other broad and get laid?"

"Because—I told you before—I don't want some other broad. I want you."

"Juley, you're crazy."

"I know. Will you be ready at seven?"

"Do I have to get dressed up?"

"Listen, if you came in your overalls—"

"That's the story of my life. I never came in my overalls."

Juley laughed. "You ab-so-lutely kill me. I'll pick you up at seven."

"Seven-thirty."

"So, all right."

"So, good-by. Wait a minute. Are you going to get sore if I don't want to sleep with you?"

"No, I won't get sore."

"Good. Who knows, maybe I'll want to. You have such a lovely stomach. Such a good big stomach. Juju, I hate skinny men."

"Thank God for that." He laughed. "I'll see you."

Iris hung up the telephone, sat up quickly in bed and proceeded to scratch herself, her arms, her back, her belly, as deliberately as an ape.

She could, she thought, as she stopped her scratching and began prying flakes of nail lacquer from her nails, she could marry Juley and leave the theater. She could have a nice house in Westchester or Connecticut. She could have her own convertible and come into town whenever she wanted and shop at Bergdorf's and the antique places.

But, Christ, he was a bore.

Oh, he was nice and he wasn't anybody's fool but—day after day after day of hearing how much money he made—and another thing, she thought sharply, if she did leave the theater and lived on Juley's money she would have to come to him! And if he got bored and started playing around with some broad on the side, what could she do then? She would be trapped. She could feel her hands and feet getting cold. Oh, sure, she could leave him. She had plenty of money put away and she could go back to the theater if worst came to worst. But it wouldn't be so easy to get back once she had been away from it for a while.

One morning he would wake up and look at her and think that she was starting to look like a dog and maybe some little twenty-two-year-old chick in his office, or a hat-check girl or someone like that, would give him the eye and . . . Who needs it? She shrugged.

What the hell. Wasn't there some man, somewhere, who had some guts and some brains and who didn't want *just* to screw all the time, someone she could really be *useful* to? That's what she really wanted, to be useful. Not just in the sack. Because, what the hell, she smiled to herself, she wasn't really so hot in that department. But to be really useful, to cook for a man, organize his socks in his drawers, talk over his business with him, doing something im*por*tant.

Juley, she thought bitterly, needed her like a hole in the head. He'd just as soon eat in a restaurant as eat at home. And the business—hell, it was so well-organized it ran without him. He admitted it.

So what does he need me for? she asked herself.

Who knows?

The telephone rang.

"Hello?" she said cautiously.

"H-hi. Uh, it's eleven o'clock. I—" It was Vito.

"Oh, is it?" She was reluctant to leave her musing. She was tempted to place the telephone back in its cradle but anchored it between her shoulder and head and continued picking at her nails.

"Yeah. I thought—you said not to call you before eleven, so I waited." He paused. "I got you some flowers."

"What's that, honey?" The telephone was slipping away from her ear.

"I said—I said I got you some flowers." His voice was very uncertain.

Suddenly she remembered. She was in the present again. She could hear the child tones, the young maleness in his voice. She could see the thin curving lips and the dark eyes shining behind gloss of black lashes.

"Oh, Vito, you darling," she murmured. She slid back down into the bed and caressed the telephone. "Kiss me," she said, putting her lips to the mouthpiece of the telephone. "Kiss me while I kiss you."

"OK." Vito obeyed. "I want to come up," he said. "OK?"

"Sure, sweetie, only give me a few minutes. Twenty minutes. I'll leave the door open so that if I'm in the bath you can come in. All righty?"

"Twenty minutes?"

"I want to know what your father said."

"Huh?"

"Does your father know that you spent all day and all night in the sack with me?"

"No."

"No? Go on, you're kidding. It was written all over you."

"What! Listen, I never told my—"

"You went out of here last night grinning like a monkey."

"Iris, I swear to God—" Vito's voice was filled with desperation.

"All right. All right. Everybody's yelling at me this morning. I'll see you later," she said shortly. " 'By."

Vito hung up the telephone, weak with confusion. He eased himself gently into his father's chair, aware that he was shaking. When first she had answered him on the telephone it was almost as if she didn't know him, as if he were just some strange kid who was bothering her. At any moment he feared she might put down the telephone and that would have been the end of it. He would have been cut off—he could sense that—forever. There would have been no other way to reach her. So close had he come to this oblivion that he was still trembling.

But then, he thought, flushing with the recollection, she had suddenly said, "Kiss me." He could hear her words again in his mind, warm, wet-sounding and the heat rose quickly to his skin. And even then, when he was open, when he was soft and unguarded, her manner had changed. She had turned harsh, peremptory. He frowned and rubbed his cheek with his hand. Slowly the fear subsided but it left him with a residue of discontent. Maybe, he thought, he'd find a ball game in the afternoon. He hadn't belted out a good long one in about three days.

When Iris heard Vito's knock, she called, "I'm in here." Then she sat up in the bathtub and scooped two handfuls of thick foam from the white blanket that covered the water and placed them carefully on her breasts. When Vito opened the bathroom door she said, "Look. I'm an ice cream sundae."

Vito was startled. He had not seen her naked before except in bed and then he had been aware only of areas of her body, immediately desirable, alien, yet wonderfully compelling. He had not, until now, been able to detach himself sufficiently from his own feeling of urgency to contemplate her as an object, something apart from himself. And in the few moments when he had seen her entirely naked—at a distance, getting into or out of bed—the total view was so overwhelming that he had turned his head or closed his eyes. It had been a superabundance of stimulus, more than his mind could accommodate.

Now he looked, aware of her extraordinary beauty, seeing the small pink nipples beneath their little caps of thinning foam, seeing the water glistening on the white roots of her throat, the curve of her laughing lips and the color of her eyes.

She held out her arms to him and he knelt, feeling her warm wet arms soak the back of his tee shirt. He wanted to sink into the bath with her.

"Mmm, am I glad to see you," he said.

"Ah, the baby. Did you miss me?"

"I thought it would never get to be eleven."

"Ah, ahah," she laughed.

"It seemed like I was just wasting time."

"Oh, my delicious baby. Take your clothes off," she said, unclasping her arms, "and get in the tub with me."

"Good." He took his clothes off eagerly, hopping on one foot as his trousers caught on his sneakers. Then, with his back to her he stepped cautiously into the warm, scented water.

"Turn around!" She said it sharply but there was laughter in her voice.

"All right. I just don't want to step on you."

"Turn around, dammit!"

He turned around and stood over her. The warmth of the water on the lower parts of his legs and the warmth of the bathroom were protecting, reassuring. He suddenly felt brave and confident.

"Look at me," he said, grinning. "See? I'm not embarrassed any more."

She looked at him gravely, her head tipped to one side. "You shouldn't be, Vito. You're gorgeous."

"Oh—" He started to blush.

"I mean it. You're the most beautiful man I've ever seen." She paused. "Do you like me?"

"Oh, yes." He lowered himself into the water and sat awkwardly facing her, his knees hunched up under his chin.

"I mean do you like the way I look? Do you think I'm pretty?"

He tried to speak but faltered. "My God!" he said finally.

Her expression remained serious. "You don't think I'm starting to sag?" She wiped the foam from her breasts and examined them, drawing herself up into a sitting position so that she could see better. "I'm thirty, you know."

"So? So what?"

"Well, I'm no teen-ager exactly."

"I hate young girls. I really do. Christ, they're so stupid, and all the time just—just—I don't know—some of them, they're all right but they're such—cheap chiselers," he finished in confusion.

"Chiselers!" She laughed.

"I mean, hell, they don't know the score."

"And I do, eh?"

"Well—I mean—"

"How would you know?"

"What?"

"The score. How would you know whether I—oh, forget it. Come here." She shifted her body so that he could slide forward and lie alongside her. "Now," she said, kissing him, "close your eyes and just lie still."

"I love you."

"Oh, the baby—"

"I love you so much I want to—I want to—" He began to writhe, straining to reach her. His eyes were open and he was breathing quickly.

"Vito, what are you doing?"

"I want to—" he said, panting and forcing against her.

"Hey! Ouch! That hurts."

"I'm sorry," he said quickly, "but I don't care. I want—"

"Vito! You're getting my hair wet."

"OK," he said, grunting fiercely and sighing as she suddenly parted. Safe now, enclosed, secure, he smiled.

"It'll dry," he said. He looked into her eyes and saw that they were angry but he wasn't afraid of her anger. It couldn't hurt him now. He was where he wanted to be. He was serene. Her eyes changed and they began to smile, reflecting his own smile.

"Oh, Vito, this is nice, so very nice," she said.

"I know," he said, moving slowly. "There. OK?"

"Oh, yeah. But slowly, all right?"

"Don't worry," he said, astonished at his own self-possession and a sudden feeling of guile. He wanted to laugh. Deliberately, even defiantly, he began to move, all the while watching her eyes carefully, seeing them widen with surprise and then grow thoughtful, dreamy. He moved harder, faster, feeling her respond and then he became sly and subdued. But her responses continued and as he watched her eyes, her lips parted and he could see her small white teeth. She was looking at him keenly now, frowning slightly but still smiling, urging him with her eyes. And, without knowing why, he continued to move slowly, knowingly, cynically, at the same time fighting desperately to contain his desire, to ignore the pleadings of his nerves and tissues. His face was stolid, almost cruel with this inner struggle, which, for reasons that he could not possibly know but could only sense, had become vital and which promised some pale victory whose nature was so obscure that he was not aware of what the outcome would reveal nor did he know why he was committed to this test. He knew only that the growing look of urgency in her eyes was something that he proudly had brought into being and this look struck so deeply and happily on his soul that he began to laugh. To Iris, the sound of this short, gay laughter was disconcerting, sweetly confounding. Happily, amazedly, she felt herself sundering, yessing, parting in the deepest recesses of her being with an exquisite ease and willingness, a feeling of want and thankful, oh, so very thankful anticipation of the gift which she was sure, now, and growing surer and delightedly surer of still, she would give to him, to her grave, golden, laughing man child, with his wet black eyes and young red lips, this quick child man who wanted to cleave her sweetly in full innocence and with whom she would, oh, yes, now, she would, yes, yes, with her baby cleave, yes, yes, oh, sweet, oh, sweet. NOW! Oh, yes, yes, for him, yes, was it really—oh, thank God, yes, yes, aye, aye, ahh. She did. Oh, God. Oh, God, she had.

They lay there quietly, trembling against each other, their hair drenched with bath water and the taste of salt and scented water on their mouths.

It was, he could sense, a triumph, and he claimed it surely. "Iris?" he whispered.

She was silent. Then she spoke. "I'm drownded."

"I guess I kind of— I shouldn't have been so rough."

She put her arms around his head and drew his face down and kissed him, sliding deeper into the water so that her whole head was immersed and the water rose up the sides of her face. He started to laugh and tried to lift her up but she continued to hold him, kissing him, pressing the bone of her lower body against him so that they were united with a single sharp point of pain. She finally let him go and he slid to one side, raising her head higher on his arm and gazing into her flushed, dripping face.

"Have you any idea what you just did?" she asked.

"No," he said. He was starting to feel uncertain.

"You just don't know? You have no idea?"

"Well, no," he said. A plaintive note occurred in his voice.

"If that isn't something. If that doesn't beat anything—"

"What do you mean? What are you talking about?"

"Look, stupid, we just made it together, that's all."

"So—"

"So, like that's the first time in Christ, I don't know how long or how many years." She stopped. "Have you any *idea* what this is like?"

"No, I'm sorry, Iris."

"Will you for Christsake stop being sorry!" she shouted at him. "Oh, my God, what am I going to do! What am I going to *do!*" Then, suddenly, her manner changed. She became quietly ironic. "That's all right," she added. "It won't happen again for another five years."

"Huh? Why not? Gee! I don't see—"

"Oh, darling. Oh, baby." She started to laugh. "Oh, I love you so much. I've *never* loved anyone like you. You're too much, too much."

Vito was quiet, confused. He couldn't be sure that she was happy with him or not. Yet he felt she *must* be happy. She was smiling. "I love it when you say you love me," he said.

"Good. And I love it when you say you love me when I say I—ah, the hell with it. Now get me out of this tub so I can put my hair up. That is, if I can still walk."

He stood up and helped her out of the bathtub. She put her arms around his waist and put her head on his shoulder, kissing his wet skin. Her eyes were closed and her voice was sleepy and furred with a gentleness he had never heard before. "Oh, Vito, darling baby, I adore you," she said.

"Gee—"

"Gee!" she mocked him softly. "Now, go on, get out of here and get into bed so I can finish up in here."

"I want to stay and watch you."

"No, Vito, don't be silly. There are some things a woman doesn't want a man to see."

"I want to see everything. I want to know everything about you."

"Oh, Vito, please, go and wait for me." She seemed actually to be pleading with him. There was not a trace of sharpness in her manner.

"OK," he said, putting his arms around her and clasping his hands so that he could squeeze her mightily.

"Ugh," she grunted, throwing her head back. "You're gonna bust mah ribses."

He laughed and shut the door behind him. In her bedroom the curtains were still drawn and the bed lay rumpled as she had left it a little while before. Vito flung himself face down on the bed, arms spread wide, legs hanging over one corner, as if he owned it. On the pillow was a faint remainder of her scent. Oh, boy, he said to himself, burying his face in the pillow, do I feel good!

Iris wrapped herself in a large bath towel and sat down weakly in front of her mirror. She raised a finger and tentatively curved the eyelashes on one eye, looking at her strange, cyclopean expression dully, then let her hand fall back in her lap. That face, she thought dimly, was not someone who interested her very much. It seemed lonely, evacuated, like an empty house on a Sunday afternoon.

Jesus! she thought. She slipped off the towel and got back into the bathtub. The water was mercifully still warm and she closed her eyes. Wow! She could almost feel it again, poignant, convulsing, an echo only, but faithful in miniature. She strained her body and moaned. Almost instantly his name came to her lips and her throat shaped a call, but she stopped. It was futile. He couldn't do it again. Not so soon. Maybe, if she were to—but no. It probably wouldn't work.

And anyway, she wanted to be alone for a little while. There was something—something she had forgotten, something she wanted to remember. She owed her mother a letter. A vision of her mother passed through her mind, small, fragile, encased in layers of clothing far too stiff and crisply protective for—what must have been—the shy, delicate body underneath. Faded, white, crumbling.

That's me, she thought and shuddered. Twenty years. Fifty. Oh, my God. And Vito, twenty years, thirty-six. Hairy, strong, going to fat but still potent, free. Free! He would be sitting in a chair, half turned away from her, his coat off, in a starched white shirt, drinking, smoking, laughing. And he would say, "I'll see you, kid," getting up, tall, careless, a man of substance, putting his coat on and going out the door. While she lay there on her bed in the twilight.

Oh, she wanted to cry.

But no tears came. "Vito," she called. "Vito!"

"Yes?" he answered and came to the bathroom door.

"It's nothing. I just wanted to know if you were all right."

"Sure. You coming out soon?" His voice was thin, absurdly young but so full of color, so astonishingly full of warmth, of his person.

"Yes," she said. She was grateful for his voice. "Say you love me."

He hesitated. "I—"

"No, go on. Say it."

"I love you."

"Oh, brother." She laughed. "What a reading." She felt very happy now, restored to the world, a merry, warm, reckless world.

His voice! She sat up quickly in the bathtub. The

thing she had forgotten, it was coming to her now, getting clearer. I'll be goddamned! she thought to herself.

In the middle of things, when she was feeling him move inside her and enjoying it but still not losing herself, not really, just getting close, but that closeness was still so far—suddenly then, she had heard his voice—heard his laugh, for God's sakes! and all the tenderness welled up in her, all the coolness and the mockery fell away and she had found herself wanting him, wanting him to come to her deeply, wanting to bring him, draw him, go forth to receive him—

But why?

I don't know, she thought to herself. It seemed to elude her. Because he was so young, she guessed. Because he smelled so young and sweet, almost like a baby. Was it? Could it be that? She couldn't be sure.

She got out of the tub and smiled at herself, rubbing her hair vigorously with a towel. "Hey!" she called, bent almost double, rubbing her head, "how you doing?"

"OK," he said.

"I'll be out in a minute." She was anxious now, moving quickly. What did it matter how, why? Who cared? Maybe it could happen again. Oh, she adored him. She wanted to—she laughed aloud—she wanted to eat him up, she thought.

"Hurry, hurry," she said, running out of the bathroom. "Hold me," she said, whimpering an exaggerated stage whimper, "hold me, I'm dying. I'm dying." She curled next to him and he put his arms around her, pressing her wet hair to his chest.

For a long time they lay there dozing. At length Vito roused her.

"Hey, Iris, are you awake?"

"Mmm."

"I'm hungry."

"You insensitive slob," she muttered.

"What?"

"I said you're an insensitive slob. What kind of a way

is that to wake someone up, 'Hey, I'm hungry'? If you're hungry, go and eat. What are you hanging around here for?"

"Are you kidding?"

"Certainly not. You've got the manners of a—a spoiled child."

"What do you mean, spoiled child? What's wrong with being hungry?"

"Nothing. It's a matter of timing, that's all."

"I still don't understand what you mean. Timing? Heck, it's almost twelve o'clock, why—hey, are you *really* sore?"

Iris raised her head and looked at him. Vito was frowning, his expression was one of inquiry but there was no anxiety in his look.

She smiled and took his head in her hands. "I was just teasing you," she said.

"Oh, OK." He paused. "You know something," he said, "I never know whether you're sore at me or not. I mean, sometimes I think everything is great and then the next thing I know, you're mad at me. And I don't know why."

"So what's there to know?"

"Well, like now. You're angry, I mean, anyway, your face looks angry and what did I do?"

"Oh, Vito, that's just the way I am." She turned her face away. "It doesn't have to be your fault. I just get like this from time to time and the best thing to do is leave me alone."

"OK," Vito said. He got off the bed and went into the bathroom, returning with his clothes over his arm.

"What are you doing, leaving me?" she asked.

"Well, sure—"

"What are you so sore about?"

"I'm not sore. Honest. You want to be alone, I'll go—"

"Fine. You come up, have a roll in the hay and take off, so long, kid, I'll see you around."

Vito sat down on the edge of the bed, his trousers

still clutched in his hands. "I don't *want* to go. It's just that I don't know what else to do. Don't you see?"

"You mean you're bored."

Vito laughed and shook his head. "You're always joking with me and half the time I don't know whether you're serious or not. So, what are you going to do? I'm stupid."

Iris moaned. "I'll be a—do you think I'm joking with you, putting you on?"

Vito looked at her uncertainly. "Well—uh—yeah. Aren't you?"

Iris looked at his face for a long time, searching his eyes for some evidence of guile. At length she began to smile and she reached out and grasped his shoulders. "What did I do to deserve this? How did I get myself mixed up with anything like you?"

"I don't know." He laughed, happy that she appeared happy again.

"You don't *know!*" She shouted it.

"No!" he said, falling against her and laughing. "Like I said, can I help it if I'm stupid?"

"You're not stupid," she said softly, running her fingernails over the skin of his back. "You don't know how unstupid you are, thank God."

"Hey, guess what," he whispered.

"Oh, God, you're there again. It's fan*tas*tic!"

"OK?"

"Getting pretty sure of yourself, aren't you, junior?"

"Well—why not?"

"You're right, why not?" she said, and laughed.

". . . According to Putnam County Conservation Chief, Forrest E. Schlosser, the outlook for the coming deer season is somewhat better than in previous years due to heavy spring rainfalls which washed away the snow from upland grazing areas. In general, Schlosser added, the herds seem to be in fine condition but large numbers of does continue to pose a problem. . . ."

"Why," Iris interrupted, "do they have to blame the

poor damn does? Always the woman's fault, every time."

"Well, wait a minute," Vito said, "let me finish reading."

"I don't want to hear any more. It makes me sad. Ugh! Men are such pigs. The does are a problem! Who asks them to go out and kill all those gorgeous deer? Would you kill a deer?" She raised her head from Vito's shoulder and looked at him.

"I don't know. I guess so. If we were living in the woods and we had a cabin and I had to get fresh meat for us—"

"Us? You're not getting *me* in any cabin. Let me out. Let me out. I'm going stir-crazy."

He looked hurt. "You mean you wouldn't want to live in a mountain cabin, all by ourselves, where we could go swimming in a lake and go fishing—and all?"

"You're out of your mind."

"Don't you want me to read to you any more?"

"Not about killing deer, honey. Anyway, I have to think about getting dressed. I have a date."

He put the newspaper down and sat very still. She looked at him expectantly and waited.

"I thought—" he said and stopped.

"You thought what?"

"I thought we—I thought we were going steady." Even as he said it, the words sounded foolish and he blushed.

She saw his blush and was touched by it. The impulse to comfort him rose in her. "Look, darling," she said gently, "I've got my life to live and you've got yours. Anyway, we just met, you know, it's not so easy to turn things off just like that. I've got other friends. Now don't be silly about it, will you? You know I adore you."

"I suppose you're right," he said. "Is this—does this guy—I mean, is he your boy friend?"

"What you really mean is, am I going to sleep with him, right?"

He shuddered. His face went white.

"The answer is no. I'm not. Now do you feel better?"

He nodded.

"So just forget about it, then, will you? This is just an old friend, someone I've known for ages and if he wants to take me out, there's no reason to get angry."

"I'm not angry."

"Well, then, hurt, or whatever. This man is old enough to be my father. Now I've got to start getting dressed." He looked sad. "Tell you what," she added, "if I get home early, I'll call you. OK? And we can have a late date."

"OK," he said. "Can I stay here for a while?"

"But, Vito, I have to get dressed."

"I know. I want to watch you. Can I?"

"Sure, baby," she said. She kissed him and got out of bed.

After she had her bath Vito watched Iris for almost an hour. He was silent most of the time. He spoke only if she asked him a question but as she advanced further and further in her preparations, she became more and more remote until it seemed that she was no longer conscious of his existence. But Vito was too absorbed in watching her to feel estranged. He had never seen a woman at this work before and the intensity of her manner, the suspense that she created—opening tiny vials, tubes, applying a flake of color with cautious, unbreathing movement, drawing very close to the mirror and swiftly leaning back for an intermediate survey—all of this gripped him as if he were watching a drama.

The most astonishing thing of all was the sudden change of expression she assumed when she abstracted herself momentarily from her labors to record her own progress. It was a happy look, Vito decided. She would raise her eyebrows slightly, draw her cheeks together, pout her lips. It was also a strange look, somehow inviting, yet arch, containing a hint of menace, rebuke. It did not animate her face so much as glazed it, fixed it, became a mask.

When she had finished applying her makeup, she

took a cloth from her hair and let it fall to her shoulders. Then she rose and contemplated her naked body before the full-length mirror. She caught Vito's eyes in the mirror, held them for a moment with her own, and then focused again on herself.

"Do you like me?" she asked.

Vito was unable to answer. The sight of her in profile with her stomach pulled sharply back, her tapered hands with their red nails pressing against the white flesh of her hips filled him with such lust that he could not speak.

"Watch," she said. She turned her back to him and began a slow tightening and releasing of the muscles of her buttocks, increasing the rhythm until they blurred in a spasm of movement.

Vito bounded out of bed and put his arms around her, pressing him to her.

"Hey. Let go, you'll ruin my hair."

He put his face against her shoulder. "I want to bite you," he said. "Hard."

"Not where it shows."

"I don't care."

"Well, I care—ouch! You bastard! I'll be black and blue!"

"Good. You're mine. I put my mark on you. Like Zorro."

"Like—like Zorro!" She shouted with laughter.

"You're mine. Go on, say it."

"Well—" She was still laughing.

"Come on. I'll bite you again."

"You do and I'll give you this."

"You're mine. Say it."

"All right, I'm yours. Now, you happy?"

"Do you mean it?"

"I—" She stopped and looked at her shoulder in the mirror where he had bitten her. She rubbed it. "I don't know, honey. Don't rush me, OK?"

"Will you call me when you get home?"

"I don't know, it might be late."

"If it's not late, will you?"

"All right, darling. Now, will you please get going? The guy is supposed to pick me up in about half an hour."

"OK," he said, working his heels into his sneakers, "I'll go. But remember it: you're mine."

The busboy, Iris thought, was really very cute. How odd, it seemed, that she hadn't really noticed men like this before, very young men with this slim, dark, thin-boned grace. She gave him a quick, private smile and was pleased to note the involuntary flicker of his eyes, the stiffening of his young Latin face. Then, as he began to move around the table, he began to preen inwardly, his face taking on a solemn, distracted look. The little jerk, Iris thought disgustedly, and she turned her gaze back to Juley Franz. A small tide of irritation rose in her.

"Italian this, Italian that," he was saying, "in this business, if you haven't got an Italian line, you're dead. Not that we're making shoes any different from the way we ever did but now we have to give them a different name. Crescendo, pasta fazool, something."

"Did you ever ask yourself why you're in the shoe business?" Iris asked. "It just occurred to me—"

"What do you mean? Ever since I was a kid, I got my first job on the road—how old was I?—seventeen, selling."

"Yeah, I know. But why'd you get stuck with shoes, why not hardware or—I don't know—animal crackers? Why shoes?"

"Look, people got to walk, don't they?"

"Yeah, all over you."

"Don't kid yourself, I've had my share."

"So. You went looking for it."

Juley looked thoughtful. The smile faded from his wide face leaving it unguarded, desolated. How many times, he wondered, had he "gone looking for it"? Does anybody *really* do that, he asked himself. You get inklings, sure, warnings, and sometimes you have the sense to pay attention to these warnings but—

"It's like I'm always telling my kids," he went on, "don't look for trouble, it'll find you. You take Jeff, now—"

"How old is he?"

"Fifteen. Just the other day—"

"Got a picture of him? I'd like to see it."

"Sure." Juley was pleased. He pulled out his wallet and handed a photograph to Iris.

She smiled. "Leave it to you," she said. "I was hoping you might not have pictures of your family in your wallet, but I should have known better."

"What's wrong—"

"Nothing's wrong. It's the story of my life, that's all. All the men I know carry pictures of their families around in their wallets."

Does Vito carry a wallet? she thought suddenly. With maybe an old condom tucked away in it? What fun! She must ask him. She would get him a wallet, she decided.

She looked at the picture of Juley's boy but could find nothing in it that moved her. Beneath the boy's expression of amiable bewilderment was a look of complacency, curiously adult, faintly annoying.

"Chip off the old cluck, all right," she said, returning the snapshot.

"Basically, he's a fine boy. Let me show you the latest picture I have of Sandra, my girl."

"Anh! I don't want to look at girls. Just boys."

He laughed. "Hey, how come you're not eating? Something wrong with that? I'll get you something else —wait a minute."

"No, don't bother. I'm not hungry. I think I'll go home to bed."

"Go home to bed! What about—"

"Going to the show?"

"Yes. I've got two tickets for the best—"

"Look, honey, I'm sorry, I know this is rotten, but I'm

just not good company tonight. Finish your dinner and put me in a cab and I'll just go home."

Juley looked puzzled and then his face became angry. He traced a pattern with his manicured fingernail on the tablecloth.

"You're angry at me."

He didn't answer.

She put her hand over his. "I don't blame you for being angry, honey. I told you it was going to be like this. I just don't feel like—you know—just want to go home, that's all."

"All right," he said finally, raising his stricken face, looking at her coldly, then casting about the room for the waiter. "All right, the hell with it."

Iris opened her purse and inspected her face carefully in the mirror. It bothered her to have him really angry. Not that she cared, she thought, not really. And he would get over it, of course, he always did. Still . . .

"So what am I supposed to do," she said, "get down on my knees? Are you going to punish me because I just don't feel up to it?"

"No, I'm not going to punish you. Maybe I can get rid of the tickets."

"Why don't you call up your ex-wife?"

He stared at her, astonished that she had struck so directly at his own thoughts. He was thinking that, despite everything, Minna had always been loyal to him, deferential. He yearned for that comfort now. "Look," he said bluntly, "you live your life and I'll live mine. Don't give me advice."

She shrugged. She could feel her own anger now. It reassured her to be so armed. A glazed, abstracted look came over her face as, in her own mind, she ignored him. What was she doing here? she thought. Why wasn't she somewhere else?

He was speaking to her. Slowly, as if with difficulty, she turned her head back to face him.

"I said I'm sorry," he said. "If you're not feeling so hot, you're not feeling so hot, that's all. I'm just, you know, disappointed. I haven't seen you in about four or five days and I was hoping—"

"God, I wish I had a baby! Look at that broad over there at that table with her stomach all blown out. Doesn't she look gorgeous?"

Juley followed the line of her glance. He laughed. "Baby, any time you want, say the word. There's nothing I'd like better than to make you a baby."

"Really? You mean if I looked like that and got all blotchy in the face and threw up all over the place, it wouldn't make you sick?"

"Are you kidding! I'd love it. I mean that, honest to God, I do."

"Ah, you are sweet." She caressed his hand. The notion of having a baby was so pleasant that his hand seemed suddenly attractive, massive, generous. "I'm really sorry I give you such a hard time, Juju. I really am."

"It's all right, doll, I'm a big boy now."

"Do you realize you're almost old enough to be my father? You *are* old enough. But don't let it bug you. If you were any younger I couldn't stand you."

Juley laughed. "I promise you. I won't get any younger."

"Ugh! God save me from any more young men."

"Me too," Juley said. He laughed at his own joke.

You ass, Iris thought, pulling her fur stole around her shoulders, you poor, thick, unhappy ass. She kissed him fondly when the cab drew up.

"Call me tomorrow?" she said.

He hesitated.

"Never mind. I'll call you." She got into the cab.

7

Vito was stretched out on the rug, reading a newspaper when Iris came over to him. He heard the door open, caught the movement of her legs but, for some perverse and pleasurable reason, kept his eyes on his paper. It was a good feeling knowing that she would come to him, a new feeling, and it gave him a sense of contentment. She walked across the room to him until she stood barefooted on his newspaper. Then she slid her foot forward and gripped his clenched hands with her toes.

He examined her ankle and reached out to hold it steady, feeling the fine bones cool in his hand, seeing the pale ink tracings of veins beneath the skin. "Even your feet are beautiful," he said, bending his head back with difficulty, so he could see her face and then pressing his mouth passionately to her leg.

"You like?"

He nodded his head and grabbed her around the legs, pressing her legs hard against his face and shoulder. She lost her balance and began to fall and he rolled over quickly to catch her. She was breathing hard and he started to sit up anxiously to see if she was hurt but she kissed him, leaning her weight on top of him, breathing sharp gusts of warm air on his face.

"Do you know what I'm going to do?" she said. Her eyes were very hard, narrow. Her face was tight but not with anger. "I'm going to rape you," she said, unfastening his shorts. "Do you mind?"

"No." He began to feel embarrassed but his embarrassment seemed priggish, trifling in the face of her intensity.

"Oh, God," she said, caressing him. "If I could only have this, just once. God, how I'd like to have it, to be a man, just one time."

Vito was perplexed. He no longer felt fear or shame or modesty. He felt aloof. He experienced her ministrations with an esthetic detachment, almost as if he were a spectator, a connoisseur. With a part of his mind he reviewed her exclamations—why? What an astonishing wish! Did he, could he ever want to be like a woman? Had he ever thought of it?—and with another part of his mind he recorded the pleasant but not overwhelming sensations which acted on his nerves. He was quite controlled now, no longer autonomic, and his reactions were experimental, subject to his will and not summoned by her demand.

At length, feeling somewhat rebuffed by his composure, but nevertheless deeply aroused and still intent on subjection, Iris rose and enfolded him. Subjection of whom? Him? Herself? She couldn't be sure.

"Ah!" He was smiling.

"You think so, eh?" Iris's face was gleeful, angry, yet triumphant. Her hair adhered in wisps to her cheeks and she had a wild, tousled look about her.

"You look like a gypsy," he whispered.

"I'll show *you* a gypsy," she said, moving with slow, exaggerated violence. "Now, what have you got to say for yourself, huh?"

"Mmmmm," he said, reaching for her waist.

"Think you're a big man, do you?" She eluded his hands.

"Yeah," he said, "sure." He could feel his control threatened and he knew that in another instant he would submit to her assault and he also knew that he did not want, stubbornly did not want to be conquered, delivered into helplessness by the evacuation of his strength. He heaved quickly, rolling her over, reversing himself. She frowned and started to resist but he placed his mouth on hers, gripping her shoulders tightly until her legs comformed obediently to his hips.

"There!" he said, looking at her hostile eyes. He smiled at her and caressed her face in a protective way, carefully lifting the strands of her hair from the tangle of her eyelashes. She was deeply stirred by this show of love but unable to return his smile, unable to loose the last trace of rancor. Sensing her distress he moved his hands over her body, pressing her, kneading her with delicate elaboration until she responded to the rhythm of his movements. Then, as her eyes closed gratefully and her head turned, smiling, from side to side, he abandoned himself in her gentle abandonment, subsiding quickly and complacently and—as he was even then aware—wanly, as her striving went slow, then slow, then still.

"Oh, Vito," she said at last. It was a small cry.

"I love you," he whispered. It was both truth and, in that moment, a lie. He felt virtuous for having sensed her need and for having requited her. He was conscious of victory—yet, there was also a feeling of detachment, almost estrangement, that he had not known before.

"I love you, darling," she said. Her eyes were wet and she tried to cover them with her hand. "I don't know why this is happening. I shouldn't be crying. I've never felt like this. I'm not used to making it—five times in the last two days. It's never *been* like this before."

"I'm glad. You make me so proud of myself." He felt easier now, comforted. This too was something new, a richer kind of pride than he had known before.

"Oh, Vito," she sighed, wiping her wet eyes and turning her face away from him, "what are we going to do?"

"Do?"

"Yes. We can't just—go on like this. It's impossible."

"Huh? Why? What's impossible?"

"Well, we can't just—my God, we've hardly been out of the apartment for the last three days. We don't see anybody else. It's just ridiculous!"

"You mean because I'm just a kid."

"No, honey." She turned to look at him and touched his face. "It isn't that—"

"All right." His voice was calm. "You want to go and see somebody?"

She paused and looked into his black eyes. There was no sign of hurt on his face. His look was neutral. She felt a wave of sudden contentment. She put her arms around his neck and pulled his head down to her shoulder.

"You know," she said, "the funny thing about it is, I don't give a damn about anybody else."

"Me neither." He kissed her arm.

"The hell with 'em." She paused. "I want to ask you something but you can't get mad. OK?"

"Mm."

"If I give you the money, will you take me out to dinner?"

"Why not?"

"You sure you're not sore?"

"Why should I be sore? If you have money and want to spend it, that's your business. Oh, sure, I could get a couple of bucks from my father, but hell, that's not enough. Besides I'd rather spend your money than his. That makes it like we're together." He paused. "Almost like we were married."

"What gets me about you is that you don't react like most other men. Maybe it's because you're Italian—you have better sense. Things just don't bother you in the same way."

"Well," he said thoughtfully, "I'm not really a man yet. Hell, I'm just a guy. You know, what's the use of beating your brains out? I can't help it if I'm only sixteen."

"I think you've got something there," she said. She looked at the tight black curls on his head, edging the pale olive skin of his neck. "My little wop baby," she said.

"Watch it."

"Oh, you know what I mean."

She felt his face move against her shoulder in a smile.

"My little wop baby," she said again and closed her eyes.

Alessandro laid his newspaper in his lap and slid his glasses down the slope of his nose so that he could watch Vito tying his tie. Barelegged, his voluminous shirt enveloping his slender upper body like a surplice, Vito looked anything but childlike, unformed. He had an air, Alessandro thought, of ease and purpose. He was astonishingly adult and male. How? Alessandro wondered, when? What a mystery that this transformation could have occurred under his nose! And it was not gradual; it was decisive, abrupt. At breakfast Vito had lapped his milk like an animal child. At evening he was the young gallant, deft, smiling, confident, on his way to a rendezvous. Alessandro shook his head.

"You know," he said, "you have a hole in your sock?"

Vito shrugged and grinned at his father, "We need a woman," he said.

"*Per bacco!* We! What insolence! The young cockerel who would give lessons to the old rooster. Are you reminding me of my responsibilities?"

"What are you getting sore about? After all"—Vito laughed—"is it up to me to bring a woman into the house?"

"If it's that one there," Alessandro said, pointing with his thumb to the ceiling, "I would have no objections, not the slightest."

Vito turned quickly and looked at his father. "Uh— What do you mean?"

"Ah," Alessandro said slyly, "now you get angry, eh?"

Vito continued to look at his father's face, reassuring himself at last that he was being teased without malice. He turned back to the mirror. Still, he felt, still . . .

"Listen to me, Papa," he said, and paused. "If you think—I mean, well, she, Iris, isn't that kind of a girl. A woman. She isn't—I don't care what you think."

"Ah! That's what I was afraid of. I believe you. I assure you that I believe you and it is this that gives me fear."

"What do you mean? Why?"

"Ah, Vito, Vito, Vito." Alessandro sighed and relighted the black, poisonous-looking relic of his cigar. "If she was just a—you know—a woman, like *that*—well, then it would be just another, what shall I call it, a trifle, a thing of no importance. But since she is a serious woman, a good person, in short, what can come of it? Harm. I see nothing else."

"Harm! How can I be harmed? What's so terrible I should be afraid of? She's not married, she's free. Nobody's going to shoot me. So what should I be afraid of? What the other kids will say?" He made a gesture of dismissal.

Alessandro was looking out the window, squinting through a cloud of smoke that was as thick and veiny as marble. "The egotism of the young," he murmured, half to himself. "You have nothing to lose, everything to gain. She—" He stopped and shrugged.

"She? Go on."

"Nothing. Forget it. Go put your pants on. Do you need a little money?"

"No. It's all right. Thanks, Pa." He looked at his feet.

Alessandro nodded his head. "*Beh, pazienza.* Go. Enjoy yourself. But one thing, listen to me, eh?—if she's a good woman, you be good to her."

"Pa, I love her. And she loves me."

"Well, then, love her. But be good to her too. Don't be a little turd."

"I wouldn't, Pa." Vito sounded chastened.

We'll see, Alessandro thought. Perhaps not. But we'll see. "Don't forget to take your key. And don't eat beans. They assassinate love."

"If you're not going to eat that baked potato," Vito said, "I'll eat it."

Iris laughed. "My God, what an appetite. Let me fix

it for you. You've eaten all the butter too! Wait till I ask the waiter to bring some more butter."

Vito stayed her with the touch of his hand. "Waiter," he called, "could we have some more butter, please."

"You kill me," Iris said, "you absolutely break me up."

Vito grinned. "All right, so you were seventeen when you married the first guy. Tell me what happened then."

"Do you think it would be all right if I asked for another drink?" Iris said.

"Sure. It's your money. Another vodka on the rocks?"

"You know what I'd like to do to you right now?" Iris said.

"Hey!" he whispered fiercely, grabbing her wrist, "not here. Somebody will see you."

"Don't be silly, darling," she drawled close to his ear. He struggled to remove her hand.

"Aw, come on, Iris, how can I eat?"

"All right, let's see, chapter two. So when I was twenty-two, at least I think it was twenty-two, around then anyway, I got married again. To a guy named Johnny, a musician, who made love to me three times a night every night for six months."

Vito blushed. "You think just because I'm a kid you ought to tease me all the time."

"But darling, I'm *not* teasing you. There's no reason to be jealous."

"Jealous! I'm not jealous. It's just—well, you shouldn't say things like that. Anyway," he finished in confusion, "not while we're eating."

She squealed with laughter. "Oh, Vito, you're too much. I can't stand it. Too much."

Vito was silent, he felt irritation. "All right, so you were married to this—this musician, so what?"

"Look, *I* didn't bring this up. You wanted to know about the guys I married, so I've been telling you. If you don't like what you hear, that's too bad."

"All right. Forget I asked."

117

"All right. Don't shout. God, what a temper. You Latins. Well, let's see," Iris resumed in a light voice, "that marriage lasted about two years. Yes, that's right. Oh, baby," she touched his cheek, "stop pouting. I really was only kidding you. Even if he did make love to me, I didn't really *like* it. It wasn't like it is with you."

He smiled.

"There, that's better, now my baby is smiling." Iris gave him her most skillfully affectionate look. What is there about those black eyes, she thought, that makes me want to kiss them? "You know, if you wore mascara on your eyelashes," she said, "you'd look just like a girl."

"Oh—"

"Hurry up and finish eating, I can't wait to get home."

"Why? What's the trouble?"

"I just thought of something. I want you to brush me all over with your eyelashes."

Vito laughed. "There you go again."

"You mean, always thinking of my stomach?"

He laughed and choked on his food. Iris laughed too, slapping his back, hugging him. When his paroxysm was gone he looked at her and started to laugh again.

"Tell me you love me," she said.

"I must have told you that already a million times."

"Once more."

"I love you. I love you so much I can't tell you."

"Crazy. Let's go home."

"Wait a minute." He put his hand on her wrist and toyed with a gold charm bracelet. "I want to ask you something."

"What, doll?" She smoothed the hair away from his forehead.

"No, I mean it. This is serious. Have you thought about—I mean, I know it's a crazy idea and all, but still—I can't help thinking about it. I mean about getting married."

"Oh, wow!"

"Huh? What's wrong? I mean it's just something I've been thinking about, that's all. You know. There's no hurry. I just—"

"Oh, baby, let's not talk about it now, OK?"

"Sure. I just thought I'd bring it up. You know."

"Yes, I know. I—" She stopped. "Let me put it this way," she said softly, "if I'm going to get married, there's nobody I'd rather do it with, OK? Can we let it go at that for right now, and please get out of here?"

"Sure," Vito said.

"Now, you're not angry, are you?"

"No," he said. He felt a curious sense of anticlimax, as if the sensation he had anticipated had not occurred. Anyway, he thought suddenly, why hurry? School wouldn't start for another two months. "Let's walk uptown a little bit and get some air. Then we can take a cab home."

Back in Iris's apartment, Vito sprawled, in his shorts, on her bed. His hands were clasped comfortably over his full belly and his eyes were directed at a TV set which was animated but silent. From time to time, as Iris removed her clothes, she passed between him and the instrument. His eyes flickered, registering her passage, but he did not look at her face.

"I like it with the sound off," he said, yawning, "then they're not always telling you what to do."

"Hey!" she called sharply, "look at me." She stood before him naked, her hands on her hips.

"I'm looking," he smiled. "You're beautiful."

She looked down the length of her body. "Pretty good for an old broad, huh?"

"You're *not* an old broad."

She was not listening to him. She stood with her legs spread a short distance apart, bending slightly at the knees, her head was tilted forward so that her hair partly obscured her face. Sliding her hands from her hips toward her belly, she began, very slowly, to rotate the lower part of her body, moving her hips in a lateral circular motion and slowly tilting her pelvic cradle up and down so that it took on a helical movement.

Vito watched fascinatedly, noting the movement of the long muscles in her thighs and the creasing and uncreasing of her belly. She lifted her head up and looked at him. Her expression shocked him. Her face was fixed in a faint, abstracted smile. Although her eyes looked into his he was aware that she was not seeing him. She seemed, in fact, to be seeing . . . something, some vision, some memory which had nothing to do with him. She seemed to be listening and as he watched her, startled and immobilized by her air of transport, she began to move faster, shaking her shoulders, breaking her sinuous, figure-eight motion into two separate motions, each increasingly violent. She seemed to be humming to herself. She moved faster and faster, staring at Vito now with an intense, open-mouthed look.

Vito could not meet her look. He was suddenly filled with unbearable embarrassment. There was something fearful and violent about her, something that made him both afraid and hideously conscious of shame. "Hey," he murmured. And then without knowing what he was doing or why, he pulled the sheet over his face to obliterate the sight of her.

As soon as he pulled the sheet up he was aware that she had stopped. He pulled the sheet down again and giggled. Her face was flushed and she smiled uncertainly.

"Hey—" he said and paused. "I—it makes me feel funny when you do that. Don't. I—I mean, you know, it—I just feel—"

"What? Don't be afraid. Say it."

"I don't know. I just—it's sort of—I feel lonely!" he blurted it out and immediately groaned. "No, it isn't that, exactly. I can't really say what I mean."

Her entire expression had changed and she continued to stand before him, still naked, but somehow demure now. He was no longer conscious of the erotic aspects of her body. She was chewing on a corner of her thumbnail and when she raised her eyes from her hands it was to look at him with a gentle neutrality.

"Makes you feel lonely?" she asked.

"Well," he was frowning with difficulty and running his long fingers through his hair, "like, I don't know, like strangers. Does that make sense?"

"Hmf!" she said softly. Then she paused and examined her fingernails carefully. "I was just doing my — That's an exercise. Uh, dancers do it. You know. It's good for your hips and your legs and your stomach muscles. You wouldn't want me to look like an old tub, would you?"

"You! You're—you're *you!* You're—" He stopped. "Hey, don't you be*lieve* me about being beautiful, I mean. I mean, God, I don't know anything but how is it possible to be more beautiful? Don't you see? You're —" He tried to finish but his throat constricted.

"Sure, I believe you," she said with a small laugh.

"Then—"

"Oh, honey, you just don't know women, that's all. Women like to hear they're beautiful. All the time."

"Well, you are."

"Thanks." She gave him a glimpse of a smile and resumed chewing her nail. She seemed to be waiting for something.

He rose from the bed and embraced her. "Come here," he said.

"No, wait, I've got to take my bath."

"All right, all right," Vito insisted, "but come here, anyway." He pulled her to the bed and she sat down. He got up on the bed on his knees and pulled her face against his bare chest. The warmth and smoothness of his skin was so delightful that she rubbed her cheek against him.

"Oh, my," she murmured, "oh, my, oh, my."

"There," he said, "that's what I wanted. Us together.

You're beautiful and I love you. And I want us to be together like this. Not like that. Like this," he said, squeezing her very tightly but carefully against him.

I can't tell him, Iris thought, feeling absolute comfort in his arms. I couldn't. There just isn't any way. A vision of the theater, the smell of hot lights, sweat and cold cream flickered through her mind. She shuddered. "Oh, my darling," she said, "my darling, darling." She kissed the skin of his stomach with such longing that she was almost unable to lift her lips from his flesh.

It was after midnight when she awoke and Vito was deeply asleep. He lay on his stomach with one arm pressed beneath his chest and his legs were crossed tightly, the first two toes of one foot gripping the slim tendon at the heel of his other foot. Iris tried to pull his arm from beneath him but he resisted her in his sleep. Shrugging, faintly irritated, she went into the bathroom and stood blinking in what seemed to be an accumulation of unused light.

She closed the door quietly and then sat on the edge of the tub, dully watching the cold bath water in its ebb. What a disgusting sound, she thought, animate, obscene. Ugh! she grunted. When the tub was drained she turned the taps on again and got up from her perch to escape the spatter of hot water. She looked at herself in the mirror and saw that her breasts were larger than usual. She pressed them with her hands and felt ache. Well, she thought, don't knock it. Besides, while she was having her period, at least, Vito would be easy to control. Fun, too, she thought. She would really drive him wild, give him a long, slow— She stopped. What the hell's the *matter* with me? What am I *doing* with this—this kid?

I love him.

What!

What the hell is this love jazz? This here now love jazz, man?

I don't care, she thought primly, I just do. Look, mother, you have your life, and I have mine. I don't tell you what to do, do I? Besides, it probably won't last, so, for the time being . . .

Why not last? Well, maybe it *could*. It's not impossible. How would they . . . I'll have to tell him. But I can't. I really can't. Besides, I can just see it, waiting in the dressing room and he's helping me on with my coat and I'm introducing him . . . with the big pinky ring . . . come on over to our table I've got some people here want to meet you . . . oh, no. Oh, no, no, no, NO! Goddammit.

You know, some girls they like to make it with the dykes and this one, she's got a kid, I'm telling you, a real kid, like the delivery boy, like my boy in school for Christsakes.

Oh, NO!

"Oh, my God." She said it softly, aloud.

So, what's wrong with telling him?

Oh . . .

Shame.

SHAME! What the hell do you mean, shame? Well, you know . . .

Look, if it makes them feel happy to think they're screwing me, let them. What's wrong with it? You know, big deal. It's an act. And a damn good act. I'm good at it. Here, look at this, three thousand bucks. OK? That something? One week's work? Shame. Balls.

Christ, I'm tired. She yawned.

So, I love him. Sue me.

If he so much as looks at another woman I'll cut—

Oh, come on!

God! what a beautiful body he's got. So beautiful. So silky. He hardly has any hair yet. She laughed.

Why do I make it with him? I can't understand it. Why do I get that feeling that I want to open up and pull him in so deep and I just feel myself coming apart. . . . Oh, my God, what a feeling. And those hands.

I just can't figure it out.

I never hate him.

Even when he starts—you know, like he's a big man. It's so goddam cute.

Cute, hell. He's good. When I think of the stupid, insensitive slobs . . . he's so clean and so, so bright. If I just look at him, he understands. I can see it in his mouth. Oh, I love that pink mouth.

You know you're out of your mind?

Mmm.

So?

So?

So you're out of your mind.

You're getting teed-jus, kiddo. Like knock it off. I think I'll introduce him to Juley. Now, *there's* a gasser. We'll go out together. A threesome.

Fun-ny!

That's just exactly what I'm going to do.

She stood up and reached for her towel.

"Baby," she whispered, kissing his bare shoulder.

"'m asleep."

"It's late, doll. You've got to go home."

"Not going home. Gonna sleep."

She lay down beside him with her mouth against his neck and listened to his breathing. She could barely hear it. He slept even more quietly than a young child.

8

In August all seas are genial seas and the Atlantic is not excepted. Bland, contained and occasionally merry, it claps the shore like a good-tempered grandfather absently patting a baby's rump.

On Long Island the sun rises out of the sea a few points southward of Montauk Light. By ten o'clock, fully dried from its blue sea bath, it hangs white-hot and wafery just above the many miles of silent beach.

Children, freeing themselves from their mothers' clasp, stumble over the sands in distracted little tropisms, to grasp the sun, to bedevil the sea. Sunburned boys with holy medals and piratical cigarettes behind their ears, carry, with exaggerated grunts and considerable attention to the arranging of their favorite muscles, the wood and canvas spores from which spring mushrooms of locus and shade.

By midday, long before it westers in the Atlantic highlands, the sun is sapped, shorn of its long radiance, taken into seeping, oil-daubed flesh. A disk now, thin, quivering, looted, the sun greets late-comers to the shore with a distant, raging look.

Three such idlers, groping, limbs held close like stricken fleas, move across the blinding white rice paper of the beach. A mushroom obligingly blossoms above them and they subside gratefully in its sudden shade. They are safe from the ferocious sun, safe from the fearful journey across the naked sand, safe from all the sharp, hidden objects, the looming, crushing objects, the manifold terrors of wood and metal, bleached shell and glass which threaten to rend their delicate sacs of salt and secret fluids. Safe from all this, saved, secure, they turn their eyes with pleasure to the chortling, mustached sea. Wasn't this—they say it gratefully—wasn't this a wonderful idea?

"Even if I don't get out to this beach club more than half a dozen times a season," Juley Franz said, "I figure it's worth it. So it costs me an arm and a leg, it's still worth it to come out here and relax."

Vito looked at Juley with pleasure. He felt, for this big, broad-bellied man with matted hair on his chest and arms and a smile that never quite seemed to leave his face, a mixture of envy and incomprehension. Earlier in the morning, when he had paused uncertainly next to Juley's glistening automobile, unable to decide whether he should sit next to Iris or get into the back seat, Juley had clutched his shoulder and then rumpled his hair. The feel of that warm generous hand was still vivid, as was the bouquet of essences which surrounded Juley's person. It was so much richer, more pungent and more varied than Vito's own smell. It gave Juley added substance.

"It sure beats Riis Park," Vito said. He looked about him at the uncluttered beach. The air was cool under the umbrella and the sea looked deliciously fresh. It would be unthinkable to pee in that well-kept, expensive ocean. Behind them the gay colors of beach cabins, covered with striped awnings, provided a battery of comforts, of food and oils and soft cushions, all of it clean, quiet and calm. "It's so peaceful," Vito added.

"You like it, eh?" Juley laughed.

Vito looked at Iris who was reclining in a chair, remote behind dark glasses. She seemed to smile at him.

"I sure do. Is it OK if I go for a swim?"

"Be my guest," Juley said. "I want to get a little more sun first. "Iris, honey, how about you?"

"You're mad," Iris said. She yawned and smiled.

Vito walked a few steps and then broke into a run.

He tripped at the water's edge, recovered, lunged forward a few more paces and then fell into the water with a great splash. *Honey,* he thought, as he came up and cleared his eyes of glittering water. But the thought was swept away by a wave of sheer joy which swelled in him as quickly and incomprehensibly as a wave of sea. He began to swim mightily. He could make Paris by mid-afternoon.

"Nice kid," Juley said, looking at Iris. She had slid her sunglasses down the bridge of her nose and was watching Vito as he splashed inexpertly on the first leg of his transoceanic voyage. "Reminds me of my boy."

"So? Why didn't you bring him? They would have been company for each other."

"I told you—the boy is away at camp. Look, honey, this was your idea; you wanted to bring this kid along. Don't blame me—"

"Who's blaming you?"

"Well." Juley paused. "You seem a little edgy."

Iris shrugged. She restored her sunglasses to the bridge of her nose but kept her eyes on Vito.

Juley sighed luxuriously on a striped mat. "Since when," he said with a laugh, "are you becoming lady bountiful? If I didn't know he was the janitor's boy, I might be getting ideas."

"Don't be disgusting."

Juley laughed. "What's disgusting? It happens to a lot of women. Just the other day, a friend of mine, he divorced his wife a couple of years ago and he happened to be down in Mexico City on business and who do you suppose he runs into down there at Cuernavaca —it's his ex-wife, she's fifty if she's a day old and she's got some Mexican kid doesn't look any older than this boy right here. Happens all the time. So? Let her enjoy herself. Am I right?"

Iris shrugged. "Remember what I told you," she said.

"What's that, doll?"

"God, I wish you wouldn't call me doll. Remember

this boy doesn't know I'm in the theater and I don't want him to know. I don't want anybody in the building to know. Last time I had an apartment, over on 51st street, I had to move out of the place. People were bugging me so much."

"I haven't said a thing."

"All right. Don't."

"What's the matter with you? Why don't you just take it easy, relax? Get a little sun, it will make you feel better."

"I wish he wouldn't swim out so far."

Juley raised himself on his arm and turned to look at Vito. He was paddling slowly, about a hundred and fifty yards offshore.

"What are you worried about? It's calm as a millpond out there. Besides, there's a lifeguard. Let the kid have a good time."

"I suppose you're right. It's just, you know—the responsibility."

Juley laughed. "Some mother you'd make. You'd be a nervous wreck."

"I'd bet I'd make a damned good one."

Juley was about to scoff but there was something about her pose, something about the short admonitory glance she gave him before going back to her peering at Vito, that made him alter his tone. "I guess you would at that," he said. He shrugged and lay still, feeling the sun flow into the vessels of his blood.

Vito floated on his back in an attitude of enforced calm. The solitude was beginning to bore him. Reversing himself and starting to dog-paddle toward shore, he could tell from the position of her head that Iris had her eyes on him. He waved and saw her hand flicker in response.

"Come on in," he shouted. There was no answer but he could tell that she smiled. He continued to paddle toward shore until his knees touched the sand and then he fell onto his stomach, allowing the gentle wash to break over his legs. It was a wonderful place, Vito thought, the kind of place he had never seen before, the kind of place that people like Iris and Mr. Franz always went to. And there was only one thing wrong with it, not wrong exactly—but lacking: there was no one really to talk to.

Ever since morning, ever since he met Iris and Mr. Franz in the lobby of the building before getting into his car, Iris had dwindled, growing smaller and smaller, farther and farther away until there was no more connection between them than there was between him and the tiny specks which he knew were people along the edge of the beach.

So far apart had they come that, sitting next to her on the long drive from New York, out on Long Island, Vito was barely conscious of the pressure of Iris's body next to his. The movement of her leg beneath her silk dress, the long cone of her thigh which he knew so well and which he could, at other times, construct in his mind, now had no significance.

Seeing Iris emerge from the bath cabin in her brief bathing suit, catching sight of a few golden hairs on her upper leg and the small pink scar on her knee—even this produced in Vito the very reverse of immediacy. Iris was as distinct from him and as totally contained as an apple hanging from a tree.

Only once during the drive had she turned to him and, by the tone of her voice, a smile and a slight touch on his arm, re-established their unity; but then only for an instant and, before he had had a chance to respond, she had as quickly withdrawn.

It had not seemed, until now, until he found himself lying lonely and a little bored in the shallows, an unpleasant feeling. Up to that time there had been so many diversions, so many new sights and sensations. And, above all, there was the almost constant emanation of Mr. Franz, a persistent, jocular energy which seemed to invade his own being. He had not, until now, felt isolation or yearning.

He looked up and down the beach, conscious that he

was trying to find someone close to his own age—preferably a girl. When he did find her he saw that she was sitting with an older woman and, therefore, inaccessible. But supposing she was alone, supposing she strolled down to the water—then what? The full force of Iris's surveillance beat down upon him as fiercely as the sun.

He wriggled uncomfortably and rose to his feet. As remote and constrained as Iris appeared to be, he knew with an instinctual certainty that she remarked his every movement. He was, in fact, a kind of prisoner in this gay and unfamiliar place. He was there on sufferance, Mr. Franz's and Iris's. The freedom, it might even be said, the sovereignty, that he had known in Iris's apartment, seemed, at least for the time being, arbitrarily suspended. He felt stirrings of resentment and a sullen wish to be home.

Walking slowly up the beach to where they sat, Vito could feel the sun drying the salt water and tightening his skin. His slim muscles were hard and prominent as the result of his exertions and this consciousness of his own physical beauty calmed his discontent. Both Iris and Mr. Franz were watching him and he accepted their glances with secret pleasure.

"Hey, that was great," Vito said, flicking a few drops of salt water on Iris's legs. "Except, I think I saw a shark."

Iris sat up quickly. "My God! You're kidding."

Vito laughed. "Of course I'm kidding. There aren't any sharks around here."

"Clown. Look, darling, why don't you go up and change that wet bathing suit and then we can have lunch."

"Change? What for?"

"Because it isn't good to sit around in a wet suit."

Vito guffawed. "Anyway, I haven't got another bathing suit."

"Then you can wear one of Juley's."

"They'd go around him twice. Three times," Juley

said. He was lying on his back, smiling, shielding his eyes with his hands.

"Well, then, I can fix it with a safety pin," Iris said. "I'll go up with him to the bathhouse and you order lunch."

"But, honest—" Vito began.

"Look, don't argue with me. You shouldn't be sitting around in a wet suit and that's that."

"Never argue with a woman, kid," Juley said. "They always win."

Vito shrugged. He had never seen Iris so tense before. Her suppressed agitation bewildered him. It didn't seem to be anger. He followed her meekly up the steps of the bathing pavilion and padded along beside her over the long fiber mats, his bare feet a silent accompaniment to the blunt taps of her varnished wooden clogs.

At the door of the bathhouse he paused. "Uh, do you want to wait outside a minute while I change?"

"Oh—" She gave him a little impatient shove and closed the door behind them. It was dark in the compartment and astonishingly serene. The robes and towels hanging limply on wooden pegs and the deep shade after the bright sun all combined to produce an air of somnolence. Vito felt drowsy and, after peeling his bathing trunks from his hips, sat down on the wooden bench with a thud. Iris stood with her back to the door, her pale skin glowing in the dim light, her face stiff and grave. She had taken her sunglasses off and Vito could see her eyes glittering. They seemed abnormally large.

"What's the matter," he said, idly rubbing his genitals with a towel, "are you mad at something?"

"No. I'm sorry, darling. Just a little nervy. Forget it. Hurry up and dry yourself and I'll fix those trunks for you."

"He's a real nice guy, isn't he, Mr. Franz?"

"Juley? Oh, sure. As I told you, I've known him practically all my life."

131

"Is he—did he used to be—uh—your boy friend?"

"Oh, he's taken me out a lot—I told you all that."

"I mean—" He paused.

"What?"

"I mean—you know, like us?"

"Honey, what difference does it make *what* I've done? You've got to remember—I'm a woman. I've been married and all that—"

"I mean, does he still—"

"Darling! I spend practically every minute with you. How could—"

"But do you *want* to—I mean, if you went out with him?"

Iris, now that her eyes were accustomed to the dim light, contemplated him. He was standing, his fists clenched at his narrow hips. The slender body with the slightly flaring shoulders that had not yet acquired their full breadth and the narrow torso which was still faintly asexual, not having yet attained its full bulk, seemed fragile yet enormously potent. He looked so slight, so lacking in sheer mass and physical power that the sight of him evoked a feeling of overwhelming compassion.

She was, she realized, her eyes filling with tears, utterly helpless before him. She could respond in no other way. The irritation that had risen in her through the long morning, the outrage that had—just a few seconds ago—been awakened by his questioning, all this was swept away, flushed, inundated by this quick flood.

"Oh," she murmured, moving a step forward to embrace him, "oh, you fool. Oh, how I love you, you sweet, delicious baby fool." She put her mouth to his breast and bit his tiny brown nipple, feeling his arms go around her. And then she slid deliberately from his grasp onto her knees.

"No," he said, pushing her away gently. "It's all right, it's all right, but not now—"

"Leave me alone." Her voice was fierce.

"No," he said again, more firmly, "I don't feel right. I mean—" He gestured at the cabin.

She smiled at him and rose to her feet. "OK, baby, it really isn't fair to be beating his time." She stepped to the mirror and ran a comb through her hair. She tried to tell herself that Vito had not rebuked her. But he had rebuked her, she knew, and she would accept it. She knew that too.

After lunch Iris and Vito lay side by side under the shade of the umbrella. Juley had gone into the club pavilion to make some telephone calls. Lying with his arms at his flanks, Vito could, with one finger tip, touch Iris's leg. He moved the finger slowly over her warm smooth flesh, feeling every now and then a faint muscular tremor which gave him a sense of pride. A person moved past, the movement of limbs causing a flicker of light on his closed eyes, and he modestly withdrew his hand.

"Don't stop," she murmured drowsily, "I like it."

Vito was in a dreamlike state, somewhere between image and reality. As often happened when they lay quietly together, his mind had begun to oscillate until it was pitched between mere feeling and understanding, between simple reaction and conception. Emotions strove to become ideas and sometimes even became words, the symbols for ideas. The process was still tentative and imprecise but as sometimes happened, and was happening now, the feeling was bared and, floating on the surface of this feeling were the thoughts, still formless, still flawed, waiting only for time and the working of consciousness to make them distinct.

He raised his head, bringing his arms up under his chin and looked at her. Her eyes were closed and it was possible to contemplate her face and her body without the interruption of her gaze. Her lips and eyes, freshly made-up, were exquisite. They were perfected objects, like jewels. To think that he had possessed these objects, that he could touch them with his fingers, his lips, his tongue, seemed incredible.

There seemed no connection between what his eyes now inspected and the sensations of love-making which lay in his memory and which, he knew, would recur. But the occurrence, he knew now, without consciously perceiving it, would not match, would never quite match this perfection. It would be marred somehow, clouded. The pleasure would be flawed by fatigue, minor discomfort—the need to move an arm, the faint stinging at the corner of the mouth when it has been wet too long, that most annoying of all banalities, the need to remove a hair from one's tongue—all these, he now knew, were reality. And reality, he had begun to discover, was less than perfect.

The sensations of love were sweet and they would again be sweet. Yet they could not match this— Even, he thought, lowering his head onto his fists, his eyes still lingering on the full fore-slope of her breast, even these would become less than miraculous, less than delicious under his hands, his lips. There would come a time—it had already happened—when those dazzling and prodigal forms, so full of life that they seemed alive, would become simply breasts. And less than breasts, commonplaces.

And still, he was beginning to know this too, there would also come a time for enchantment again. A time when the eyes and breasts which he now saw would again acquire a magical quality, a beckoning, enticing quality and he would be summoned, enchanted and—for a time—drawn out and beyond himself. For a time . . . for a time.

The burden of this meditation was too much for him. He sighed.

In an instant her eyes were open and her face turned toward him with a mildly inquiring frown.

"What is it, baby? You bored?"

Vito wanted to think about that. It was a new idea, boredom. Until recently he had not yet known boredom, not as a concept. But this thought too, seemed difficult and as productive of sadness as the musings he had just entertained. He looked away from her out upon the beach, searching for something to say, something that would relieve the need to express all that which was unutterable in his mind. He turned back to face her.

"Why do you needle this guy?" He saw her eyebrows move upward in surprise. But he, too, was surprised at the words which came to his lips. He had not expected to voice this question.

Iris turned her face back to the sun and moistened her lips carefully before speaking.

"Because he asks for it."

"But—"

"Why does he ask for it?"

"Well, yes—but also—"

"Some guys just like to be pushed around. A lot of people are like that. You wouldn't understand this yet, you're too young."

"Well—" He paused. "You ought to take it easy. I like him. He's a nice guy. He's a big shot but he doesn't act like a big shot, you know?"

Iris turned to look at him again. Her tone expressed curiosity. "Why should that bother you, darling? What do you care what I say to Juley? He's nothing to you. Nor to me."

"I—I don't know. It just doesn't seem right. I can't tell you why. It makes me—uh—feel, I don't know, funny. I mean, he's a big man, with this car and all and all that dough and—well, it'd be different if he was just a big slob or something. But it seems like you have no—no respect."

"You know what?"

"What?"

"You're so right. I haven't."

Vito began to ponder this and then slipped on to another thought. I wonder, he asked himself, what I would do if she talked to me like that, if she called me a slob like that. I wonder if I would hit her in the mouth. He was interrupted by the arrival and sand-shaking collapse of Juley Franz.

"Oh, those poor slaves in New York. I was just checking up on them to make sure they were all hard at work making lots of money for me."

"Don't believe him," Iris said to Vito, "he pays his employees so much they call him Mr. Santa Claus."

"Well, what are you gonna do," Juley said, smiling, "you can't take it with you."

"And nice guys finish last."

"So, who says I'm nice. Hey, kid," he turned to Vito, slapping him on his thin stomach, "how about going for a swim with an old man? How about you, baby, want to come with us?"

"I'm afraid of the water. The mother."

"The mother!" Vito exclaimed.

"It's an old joke," Iris said. "Go. Swim. I ate so much lobster I'm sleepy."

Watching Vito leap with a falsetto whoop into the surf, Juley smiled benignly. Of all the pleasures his money could buy, one of the best was bringing happiness to a kid. While it was true the relationship between himself and his own son was not so simple, not so unguarded as it was with this youngster, still it gave him the kind of satisfaction he wanted: the knowledge that he was doing some good and that he was being appreciated for it. He made up his mind that he would leave New York early on the coming Friday and spend the weekend at his son's summer camp.

"Come on!" Vito yelled. Juley lumbered to meet him, splashing a great heavy-armed fan of water at Vito's laughing face.

"I got a boy. About your age," Juley said when the splashing was done. "Nice boy. He's up at camp. Maybe I can take you up there some time—the three of us. They got mountains, a lake. You ever been to Massachusetts?"

"No," Vito said, smacking the water with the palm of his hand. Then he raised his face and laughed. "I've never been anywhere except Riis Park. And now this."

"You will. You've got time yet." Juley was embarrassed.

Poverty, privation pained him, especially when it affected the young. "Hey, I got an idea. You want to dive from my shoulders? Wait till I get in deeper water. Then take my hands and climb up. OK?"

He caught Vito's slim hands in his and ducked his head under water, feeling Vito clamber up until he was balanced with one foot on each shoulder. He was amazed that Vito was so light. When Vito came to the surface he laughed at him.

"I don't know how you make such a big splash. You sure don't weigh anything. Doesn't your mother feed you?"

Vito looked at him and smiled, sensing and wanting to lighten the embarrassment of the man. "Didn't Iris tell you? I haven't got a mother. She's dead."

Juley's face contorted as if with pain. "Jesus, I'm sorry. I should have—of course she told me. I just forgot and then—well, I said it before I knew—"

"Forget it," Vito said. "How about one more? A triple swan dive this time. OK?"

"OK." Juley reached out a hand and then paused. "Listen, kid, don't say anything to Iris about that, will you?"

"All right. But why not?"

"Well—you know, it's just a slip of the tongue. And she's liable to get mad at me. You know how women are, you never know what's going to make them mad."

Vito tried to look at him but he was unable to meet his eyes. "OK," he said quickly. "Like I said, forget it." He swam away, staying out of range of further conversation. After a while Juley called to him, "We'd better be going back." He answered but he didn't start to come back at once. He waited until Juley turned and plodded back to the beach. Then he swam slowly toward the shore, feeling anger and hurt. Juley Franz, he thought, was still in love with Iris. Didn't she know it —or was she telling him a lie?

When he came out of the water, moving slowly, the long folds of cloth from Juley's bathing trunks hanging like seaweed around his thighs, he was stupefied by the shock of opposing thoughts. Juley, for all his eminence, his magnitude, was also, quite clearly, his rival. The thought of Juley possessing Iris, touching her, being touched, made him tremble with anguish. Yet, Juley, because of his eminence and his magnitude, was also godlike and benevolent. He brought gifts. He was kind and warm as his own father was kind and warm. And, in a way that he could dimly sense, he was pitiable too, as his own father was pitiable. How could he hate his father?

He stopped and carefully fitted the end of his big toe into a fragile snail shell. He raised his leg quickly to send the shell flying, but it remained on the end of his toe. Standing pigeon-toed, he pried the shell off with his other foot. And then, taking a knowing risk, he placed his heel over the lavender shell, and fractured it with a quick thrust. He felt sharp pain and with it, a clearing of his mind. He approached them.

"Vito!" Iris shrieked with laughter. "Vito, Vito, look at you!" She was on her feet, holding the sides of her head, laughing and calling at the height of her voice.

He was surprised but smiled in response to her merriment.

"Oh, Vito, *dar*ling! You look so funny! With those long trunks hanging down and your little belly button all knotted up with cold. You look like Mahatma Gandhi."

Vito started to laugh. He could hear the love in her voice and it flowed into his sea-chilled, fear-chilled body like warm honey. He laughed and shook his head like a dog, sending a spray of cold drops from his curls.

"Oh, Vito," she said, coming to embrace him with a large towel. "Oh, you poor shivering baby. You're blue! You're positively blue." She embraced him, rubbing her hands over the towel and murmuring privately in his ear.

"Take those ridiculous things off," she said. "Take them off before you strangle to death."

"Here?"

"Under the towel, silly. Just undo that safety pin and they'll fall off. I've never seen anything so pathetic in all my life."

Juley stood a few yards away, watching them, smiling, drying himself and combing his thin hair.

Vito unfastened the safety pin and did an exaggerated little dance, waggling his hips as the heavy, voluminous bathing trunks slid to his ankles.

"Let's go home," Vito murmured, brazenly putting his head on Iris's shoulder as she continued to rub him.

"We will, doll, as soon as you get dressed."

"I want to be with you," he said. The intensity of his tone made her draw her head back and look at him. He gazed very steadily into her eyes and repeated it. "I said I want to be with *you*."

"OK, darling, OK," she whispered and patted his cheek. "Soon." And then in a louder voice she added, "Now hurry on with Juley and get dressed. I don't want you standing around wet while you're waiting for me."

In the gloom of the bath cabin Vito and Juley dressed in silence. Pulling on his tiny, knitted underpants, Vito became aware that they were ridiculously small, as trifling as a handkerchief compared to the ballooning opulence of Juley's shorts. Yet he was proud of their economy. He felt girded, trim, in contrast to the clumsy excess of the older man. He felt vigorous, self-contained, superior to Juley's vagueness and indulgence.

"I'm getting old," Juley said, as he bent, wheezing, to tie his shoelaces.

"I hate shoes," Vito said. "They ruin your feet. Did you know the Indians never had trouble with their feet? That's because they always wore moccasins. I wear sneakers. Winter and summer."

"Don't your feet ever get cold?"

"Nanh. I run. Keep moving, that's the way to keep

warm. Gee, I feel great. That water, that's something, eh? I could eat about nine plates of lasagne."

"Where would you put it?" Juley said, laughing.

"Don't worry. My father says I'm not a boy, I'm an appetite with arms and legs. Sometimes I don't eat all day and then, at night, I eat everything in the house."

"Your father's a pretty good cook, eh? Like all Italians, I guess. They all know how to cook."

"I'm going to teach Iris how to make ravioli," Vito said. He was combing his hair before the mirror and he was aware that the flush of sunburn on his cheeks made him incomparably handsome.

"You're getting to be pretty good friends," Juley said.

"Yeah. Pretty good." Vito dropped his eyes from the mirror and gazed at the comb.

Juley remained silent for a few moments, slipping on his trousers and heaving into his shirt.

"Well, that's fine," he said at last. "She's a fine woman."

Vito did not answer.

"And you're a nice boy." He turned to look at Vito who was now leaning at the doorway of the bath cabin. He had opened the door a crack and was peering out into the soft summer light. "You're going to be all right," Juley added, "yes, sir, you're going to be all right."

"My father says in another year I'll start to fill out. It's better if you fill out slowly. If you do it too fast you get soft. If you fill out slowly you stay hard."

"Don't worry about it," Juley said absently, reaching for his tie. "You'll fill out all right. Even if you did look pretty funny wearing my pants."

Vito shrugged. "I just did that to please Iris. You know," he laughed to cover his embarrassment at a fraudulent posture, a lie, "*you* know how women are."

"I sure do, son, I sure do." He turned away from the mirror where he was knotting his tie and looked at Vito. "If you're all finished, why don't you go tell the little lady she can come up and get dressed? It's all clear now."

"OK," Vito said, starting to leave the bath cabin. But he hung back a moment, one hand on the door frame. He caught sight of Juley fumbling with his collar in the subdued light. His face was distracted and grave. "I want to thank you for a real nice time."

"Forget it."

"Thanks," Vito said and he walked down to get Iris, feeling light and springy, as if he could take to the air with every step.

During the long ride back to the city, Vito sat in the front making occasional conversation with an unusually quiet Juley while Iris dozed on the soft leather cushions of the back seat. Juley had, at the outset of the drive, assumed an air of gravity, almost of rectitude. He wanted, he said, to get back early so that he could call his kids in camp. His heavy face was set in somber creases, revealing, Iris thought, another side of him which she rarely saw and which she found highly attractive.

Drowsy with sun and both fatigued and oppressed by the events of the day, she fell into a fitful sleep interspersed with fragments of a terrible dream.

When she awoke it was with a sense of panic and grateful release. The car had entered the Midtown Tunnel and the movement of the white glazed tiles as they slid past under the headlights, made her sick to her stomach. But she was afraid to close her eyes. Still present in her mind, though they were vanishing fast, were relics of the dream, a hideous theater balanced and actually rocking on the edge of a cliff, a dark-haired girl who danced naked in a purple light with a long braid of pubic hair hanging like a breech clout between her legs, a small black poodle who curled comfortably in her lap, licking Iris's fingers until—to her horror—the skin had come away and the blood was draining from her arm and when she tried to remove her hand she discovered she was unable to move. Scream upon scream had risen in her throat until her whole chest ached with unuttered cries.

Jesus! how awful. How godawful! She kept her eyes wide open in the windstream so that the blast of air would cleanse her eyes of the nightmare. The last of the images was swept away but her sense of panic remained.

Oh, wow, she thought, I've got to calm down. And then, suddenly, without knowing why, she thought: I've got to get away. It's like I'm drowning, falling. Why?

Juley caught sight of her head in the mirror, "You finally wake up, honey? Have a good sleep?"

"Mmm," she nodded, noncommittally.

As they came out of the lighted tunnel, Vito turned around in the darkness and put his hand on her arm. But she didn't look at him. She was watching the street numbers, impatient for the journey to end.

After Juley had gone, Iris and Vito rose in the elevator, in silence. Handing him the keys to her apartment, Iris, her head bent, followed Vito quietly into the darkened room. He did not put the light on but simply dropped the bag containing their towels and beach articles and embraced her. Her face was hot against his cheek and a strip of light filtering through the venetian blinds fell across her throat like a scar.

"I'm so tired, darling," she whispered. "I'm so tired."

He unfastened the zipper at the back of her dress and pulled the skirt up over her hips. Dutifully, resignedly, she raised her arms and allowed him to lift the dress over her head. She wore nothing underneath.

"Darling," she murmured, "not now, please. I'm so tired. I don't want to. I really don't want—"

He pushed her, half stumbling, to the couch and laid her down carefully and then, with great intensity, he began to caress her.

Swiftly, ceaselessly, he moved his hands and lips over

the most sensitive areas of her body, feeling her protesting hands on his shoulders, yet moving so quickly, so erratically that she could not organize her objections to his love-making. At last he felt her hands grow slack and she began to moan softly and he felt a stubborn temerity take hold of him as he bent, despite her whimpering protests, to take possession of her in a way that he had never dared, and that had never occurred to him to do before.

"Oh, no! Darling!" she called in soft alarm. But he only gripped her more tightly, determined, rapacious.

"Oh, Vito, Vito," she called, her tone filled with dismay. And as he continued, unrelenting, she began to pull his hair and her voice became hoarse.

"Oh, no, yes," she whispered, "your face. I want to—no—I shouldn't. You shouldn't, oh, your face, your lovely, beautiful face . . ."

For a long time after that they lay huddled and silent on the couch. Iris shuddered and rubbed her face against his neck. He could feel wetness on his skin.

"Why are you crying?" he asked. "What's the matter?"

"I'm cold."

"I'll get something to cover you up. It's the sunburn."

"It's late, you'd better go."

"It's only nine—what is it?—nine-thirty."

"Vito, please go. Please go home." She began to sob heavily. She covered her face with her hands and drew her knees up into her stomach, her whole body shaking with grief.

"Oh," he said, repeating it helplessly in a series of long, lamenting "oh's." "Tell me what it is. Honest I don't know, tell me—please, honey." He tried to remove her hands from her face but her wrists were rigid.

"I'll be all right," she stammered, "just please leave me alone. I won't do anything terrible. Just please leave me alone."

"Anything terrible! What do you—" The notion

stunned him. He was almost afraid to understand what she meant. "Iris, for God's sakes, what *is* it?" he pleaded.

She held her breath in a violent effort to control her weeping. Then, opening her mouth very wide to emit the strangled sound of her words, she said, "I'll be all right. I promise you. It's just too much sun and I have a headache. Please, go down to your father. He'll be worried. I'm going to bed."

"All right," he whispered. He was chastened, awed by her condition. It seemed to relate to him but he couldn't understand how. "Was it because—" He paused. "Didn't you want me to, uh, you know. I mean when I was kissing you, did—"

She began to sob afresh. "Please, please," she said, and this time her voice was so desolate, so full of misery that he felt his heart contract with pity.

"OK, darling," he whispered, "I'll go." He kissed her hair and then went into the bedroom and got her robe and placed it carefully over her.

"Is there anything you want?" he asked.

She shook her head.

"I'll talk to you in the morning. All right?" She didn't move. "All right?" he repeated.

She nodded. He went out and closed the door.

Instead of going directly into the basement apartment, Vito stepped into the back alley and lighted a cigarette. He wanted to sit down but there was no place to sit. Wrapping his towel and bathing trunks into a tight ball, he placed them under his buttocks and hunkered next to the high cement wall.

Suddenly a thought assailed him. Whatever it was, and he couldn't be sure exactly, that had driven Iris to such a paroxysm of despair, he was responsible for it. A faint smile came to his lips as he became aware of his potency, in fact, his supremacy. And just as quickly he rebuked himself for the smile, even wiping his lips with the back of his hand to erase the symbol of the thought.

It couldn't have been, he thought, the way he had made love to her. It couldn't, because she did that to him all the time—or tried to. And—and anyway, he reminded himself, she had liked it, had wanted him, she had said—he recalled her passionate assent. And she had held him tight.

It was something else. Now he no longer smiled. The recollection of her misery was too poignant. It filled him with love and a desire to be tender, to guard her, comfort her. The poor kid, he thought, the poor kid.

But why? He was shaken and perplexed. He felt himself growing stupid and the effect of the long day in the open air made him utterly weary.

Yawning, slouching woodenly, with his hands thrust deep into the pockets of his cotton trousers, and with the damp towel wadded under his arm, he entered the apartment where his father sat reading.

"Hi," he said curtly.

"Ah. At last. Did you enjoy yourself?" Alessandro looked at him keenly.

"I'm pooped."

"You want to eat something?"

"Is there any milk in the house?"

"You want? I'll make you a sandwich."

"No." Vito's voice was irritable. "Sit still. I'll get it." He opened the refrigerator door and poured himself a glass of milk which he drank as he stood, with his back to his father. Then he poured another half glass and turned to face the seated man.

"And tell me," Alessandro said graciously, "how does it go with your beautiful lady?" He made an upward gesture with his thumb and smiled.

"Oh, she's all right," Vito said quickly, looking down into his glass. "She—you know, Pa, she's kind of highstrung. You know what I mean? She's—I don't know." He stopped and laughed shortly. "Are all dames like that?"

"Dames?" Alessandro said. "She is a lady, no?"

Vito blushed at the rebuke. "Well, you know, dames,

women, broads. That's what Iris always calls them, broads."

Alessandro smiled. "I don't know. Something, of course you must expect. You understand with women that every month they have their cycle and this makes them—"

"I'll bet that's what it is," Vito said. "I never thought of that. How do you like that? I'll bet that's just what it is."

His father gave him a long look and then turned his eyes back to his book.

"You going to read for a while?" Vito's voice was much lighter now. He sounded relieved.

"Golden dreams," his father muttered. Vito went to bed.

9

Iris awoke quickly and violently with a feeling of suffocation. She threw the sheet clear and stumbled to the open bedroom window, resisting an urge to claw at her throat.

Slowly she fell to her knees, resting her folded arms on the window-sill and laying her head on her arms. The cool air of morning touched her skin and it had a calming effect. Oh! she thought, thank God, thank God. The choking sensation was over. Exhausted, she continued to crouch at the window, shivering every now and then as the breeze fluttered her gown and fighting the last little waves of nausea that begged the back of her tongue.

It had been a hideous night. Dream upon dream had coursed through her mind, each more frightening than the next. All night long, it seemed, she had been running, never alone, never free of the phantasm who clung gibbering at her heels, a monster with lesioned, purpled flesh, taking on a maiden's form—mockingly obscene, emerging before her in fox mask with slavering tongue, tripping her, clutching her, barring her way and, most terrifying of all, threatening to abandon her to solitary flight.

Awful, she thought. Terrible. Although she felt better now she was still conscious of something having gone violently out of place. Somewhere, deep within her, an enormous change had occurred, a massive internal shifting that was as secret and subterranean as the moving of a geological fault.

Disconnected images fluttered in her mind, segments of the dream, Vito's rejection of her in the bathhouse, the supple, shining folds of his skin, so essentially similar to a child's skin, even an infant's skin, and then—the image that was most disruptive, so productive of fear—the image of Vito's possession of her when they had come home from the beach. Why? she wondered. Why was this so frightening? And at the same time, so lovely, so comforting. He had dominated her utterly, selflessly, seeking nothing, giving only, yet—why had she allowed him to take her like that, why had she allowed him to manipulate her? Why, when she thought of it, was there so much terror that it overpowered delight?

She shook her head to clear all of this from her mind. I've *got* to get away, she told herself. I've *got* to get out of this apartment for a few days. It's like a trap. I can't think. Something is happening. I don't understand it. I've got to think. I've got to get away so I can think. I've got to get away from Vito. Why from Vito? I don't know. But I've got to. I'm losing my mind. I'm—

Juley! Of course. Suddenly, the idea of going away with him for a few days seemed wonderfully attractive. No strain, she thought. Juley was docile, controllable. And she would be good to him. She would be sweet and not tease him and she wouldn't drink too much. Just enough so that she could go to bed with him, but not too much. He'd love it. And he deserved something nice, the poor slob. He was such a good guy.

What about Vito?

I don't want to think about that, she told herself.

But I have to tell him *some*thing.

Why?

Well, you just can't walk out on somebody. . . . He'll get sore. She smiled to herself. She had never seen him angry, not really angry. It was a pleasant thought but it was also a frightening one. She was aware that the smile had grown stiff and cold on her face.

Odd! Really strange. Other men—my God, dozens of them, hundreds—it was kind of fun to needle them, to watch them get angry. She had never felt fear before. Why?

What is there about that little bastard— She stopped. Have you any id*ea* what it's like? she asked her mother. I mean, I can't really explain it to you because, well, because you know, there are some things we just can't talk about. And besides, this is something you've got to *feel*. And you poor thing, you never have. Face it. You just never have.

Have you any id*ea* what it's like, after all this time, with all of those guys, all of it so empty—well, not always, but mostly, anyway, never really caring, not really —and then to find yourself being opened up like a tight flower, being opened up and feeling the sun come in and then, and then! *wanting* to open more, actually wanting, wanting to open up, to spread until there's nothing left, not even you, just opening and warmth, oh, God, such warmth and light—oh, wow. . . .

Well, you just don't know, that's all.

Oh, it isn't like that always. How the hell could it be? You know, sometimes it's an act. But you know something? Sometimes it's an act with him too. I mean, not that he doesn't want to, don't be ridiculous. But sometimes he just puts me on—just—just because he wants to. And that really gets me.

All right, so I'm crazy. But if he wanted me to, I'd tear out my stomach for him. I'd eat his dirt.

And I don't know why. Other guys have tried to be good to me and it doesn't work. He does it and it works. You figure it out. How did this *happen?*

Who the hell knows? Or cares. You know, like I'm hung on him. Is that a gas?

I mean I love him, Mother. It's ridiculous and absurd and I'm sick and I know you think I'm out of my mind. So?

"Honey," she spoke into the telephone. "I'll be back Sunday night. OK?"

She paused and stubbed out her cigarette. "I told

you. I've got some property up in Connecticut. A house I own. And I've got to go up and take care of some legal papers and stuff like that. . . .

"Well, I've got friends up there too. . . . Darling, look, don't be like that, I can't *pos*sibly take you with me. You know, New York is different. I hardly know some of these people. Anyway, you ought to spend some time with your father. I think he's getting mad at me. . . . Take him to a movie. . . .

"And listen, if you go out with anybody, I'll kill you. I don't mean go out, but you know. If you lay any other broad while I'm gone I'll never speak to you again. . . . Well, it could happen.

"Doll. I've got to run. Do you love me? Then say it, for God's sakes! Belt it out. Oh, Christ, like pulling teeth. Like three teeth at one time . . . Good-by, my angel, I've got to run."

Why? Iris thought, as she hung up the telephone. Because I'm getting in too deep, that's why. I'm leaning on him.

What!

The answer was a shock.

Of course I could stay right here. I could even have him run up, if only for an hour. . . .

But, no. She walked into the bathroom and turned the taps on in the tub. No. She felt very virtuous, fully self-possessed. Now all she had to do was call Juley and tell him that he was taking her away for a couple of days.

"God, how I hate New England," Iris said. She stared at the back of a retreating waiter. "They're constipated from the scalp all the way down. They don't talk, they don't think. They even walk like they're afraid to let go of something. Why you should spend your money on these bums is beyond me."

"Well, you know, they're frugal people," Juley said.

"Frugal! Ugh. Except for hate. That they got plenty

of. They make me sick with their pinched noses and their pinched mouths and their righteousness. Weren't you telling me that you moved your plants out of here down South?"

"Sure, but that's a different thing. That's a union problem—"

"Problems, problems. Everybody's got problems. Let's go to bed."

"But you just ordered another drink."

"So? Let 'em bring it upstairs. I want to go to bed with you."

Juley laughed uncertainly.

"What's the matter, don't you want to?"

His laugh was stronger now. "Are you kidding? Come on."

"You're fickle, Juju." She laughed and caressed his cheek. "You have a fickle pickle." She laughed and clung to him voluptuously when he stood up.

"Hey, cut it out," he whispered. "You'll give the place a bad name."

"I'm just *dy*ing to. I dare you to pull my skirt up. I have no pants on. Go on, I *dare* you."

"Iris, for Christsakes."

"Chicken. Ficken chicken," she said, walking very deliberately, with a slow controlled movement of her hips, into the elevator. She was drunk, Juley thought. And he wished he were a lot more drunk himself.

Up in their hotel room Iris stepped out of her shoes and stood in front of the mirror, tugging at her hair with a huge comb. Juley hung his jacket over the back of a chair and then lay down heavily on the bed. He watched her for a moment but found the strain of raising his head tiresome and let his head fall back. He felt bitterly alone. Iris, though she was not really combing her hair, was nevertheless totally abstracted. There was no more bond between them than if they had passed each other on separate trains.

"Are you going to come to bed?" he asked.

She did not answer.

"Hey!"

"Don't rush me," she said. "It's early yet." She turned to face him and brought her arms up to unfasten the back of her dress. Then she slid her dress off her shoulders so that her arms and breast were bare. She peered at her breasts myopically and pressed her fingers to her skin. "I'm coming out in spots," she said at last.

"Oh, for God's sake." Juley started to rise from the bed.

"No. Stay there. Look, you get ready for bed. I want to take a bath."

"But, honey, you just *had* a bath before dinner. . . ."

"I'm going to take a bath," Iris repeated. Her voice was very low; she seemed to be talking to herself. "I smell."

Juley sighed. He undressed, leaving on his shorts, and lay down again upon the bed. He heard Iris run her bath and then he heard her get into it. He waited for half an hour and caught himself several times as he was falling asleep. Then he went into the bathroom and found her. Her head was against the edge of the tub and her hair was caught up in a heavy towel. Her mouth was opened wide and she was sleeping.

Carefully, he awakened her, helped her out of the tub and dried her. She put her arms around his neck and murmured, "Carry me." She was unconscious when he placed her on the bed.

Sunday morning, Juley thought, opening his eyes. Nine o'clock. There was something about the room that was as bleak and disappointing as his own bedroom in New York. Except, he remembered, Iris was there. He turned his head to watch her as she slept. She looked astonishingly young and serene. Even the traces of mascara which she had not totally removed, only emphasized the freshness and delicacy of her beauty. He leaned forward cautiously and kissed her cheek but she did not stir. As he drew back he noticed that her nose twitched slightly and it reminded him of his daughter. It had been a long time since he had watched his child asleep.

Sunday. He would have liked to remain in bed. Perhaps Iris would awaken soon and he could communicate to her some of the warmth and tenderness that he felt. Perhaps she would, as she sometimes did, nestle in his arms in a childlike way, murmuring words in a child's voice and asking him to comfort and caress her. Then, as she became aroused, she would want to make love to him. It was not entirely satisfactory but it was better than nothing. Right now, he felt, he needed it.

But it was Sunday and his children would be expecting him at camp. He rose carefully, trying not to disturb her, and went to the bathroom for his shower.

When he returned he was freed of the traces of night and drink and smoke. His cheeks were tight with shaving lotion and he bent quickly to draw on his socks.

"Why did you leave me?" Iris startled him. He looked at the bed and saw that she was watching him steadily, her eyes just visible above the bed clothes.

"I'm sorry I woke you, baby. I thought I'd let you sleep while I went over to the kids and I'd call you later."

"You're angry at me."

"Oh—" Juley started a denial and then changed his mind. "Well, you know. I didn't expect you to pass out on me."

"Why did you let me drink so much?"

Juley laughed. "Because I was trying to make you."

"Then why didn't you?"

"Because you drank so much."

"So now you're bugged because I passed out and you're going to punish me."

Juley felt a curious, inexplicable anger rising in him and he tried to suppress it. "Look, Iris," he said, "don't start that stuff with me again. Understand? I've had it. If you want to make love, OK. If not, OK. But don't start out first thing in the morning giving me a bawling out. It's a nice day and I feel fine so let's let it go at that."

She was silent and then she turned over in the bed so that she was no longer facing him. He ignored the promptings of irritation and continued to dress. When he had tied his tie she spoke to him again.

"You know perfectly well I can't go with you to see your children, so you're going to leave me here all by myself with a hangover and nobody to talk to."

"I'm sorry about your hangover," Juley said. His face was stern.

"No, you aren't. You don't give a damn about how I feel. You're just sore because I didn't go to bed with you last night. It doesn't matter how I'm feeling—just you're sore because I wouldn't hop into bed with you."

"Iris, look. I told you—it's an old story by now. I don't care. I just don't care any more."

She was silent and he finished dressing. He could feel his anger dissipated now and its absence made him uncertain. His plan to dress quickly, go down to breakfast and drive to the camp, no longer seemed quite so satisfactory as it had. He toyed distractedly with the window curtains, looking out onto the grounds of the hotel.

"You go back to sleep," he said finally, "have a good sleep, and I'll come back and pick you up for lunch. All right?"

She didn't answer.

"Now, what's the matter?" He went to the bed and stood over her. She was crying softly and silently. Instantly, he was moved by pity and a sense of shame. He sat on the bed and stroked her head.

"I'm so lonely," she whispered. "I'm so damned lonely."

"Ah, you poor kid." He patted her. In the place left vacant by the passing of his irritation, he could feel the beginning of poignance and affection. He sighed and shook his head. Loneliness was not something he could ignore, each morning it gathered on his shaving mirror like bathroom steam.

"I'm sorry, baby," he murmured, "don't be lonely. Come on, stop crying. I won't be gone long."

"Hold me," she whispered. He bent over her and cradled her head in his arms.

"I'll get your shirt all wet."

"So, I'll get another shirt."

"Oh, Juju, you're so good to me and I'm such a bitch. Why do you bother?"

"Oh—" He smiled. "Don't worry about it. You're not a bitch. You're just a little mixed up, that's all."

"I feel so much better just having you hold me like this. I know you've got to go, but just stay here a little longer."

"OK," he said, "I'm glad you're feeling better." He could feel desire starting to move in him and he tried to suppress it.

Iris was silent for a few moments; she stroked his hand and kissed it. "Juju," she said softly, "you don't want to make love to me now, do you?"

"No," he said. Then: "Yes! What the hell am I saying, 'no'? Yes, sure I do. What's wrong with that?"

"Oh, Juju, can't you just hold me?"

"Sure. I can do that too. But the fact is, I want to make love to you. Why not? So, if you do, you do and if you don't, you don't. But I don't see why I should be ashamed of it."

"Darling, I'm not saying you should be ashamed. It's just—doesn't it make any difference how *I* feel about it?"

"Look, let's face it. It's always something. Either you're too drunk or not drunk enough. Or you're too busy or too tired or you don't feel well or you're mad at me. Always something."

"Now you're angry at me, aren't you?"

"No," he sighed. "I'm not angry. I just don't know how I get myself tied up like this."

"Get into bed with me."

"But I just got dressed—"

"Oh, please, Juju. Just get into bed and hold me."

"All right." He took his clothes off quickly and slid into bed. She lay curled up with her back to him and when she felt his body next to hers, she squirmed and pressed her behind tightly against him. He slid his hand over her stomach and began to caress her.

"No, not just now. Please. Hold me."

"Iris, for Christsakes!" he shouted at her and she winced, pulling her head down on her chest.

"Hey, don't shout. People will hear you," she whispered.

"I don't care." He grabbed her shoulder roughly and tried to turn her toward him. "What the hell are you trying to do to me?"

She turned her head to look at him, her voice husky with quiet scorn. "You mean you just want to bang me, huh? It doesn't matter how I feel or *what* I feel. You took me up here and you're paying for the hotel so you've got to have your pound of flesh, is that it?"

Juley sat up and stared at her. His throat choked with anger. "What kind of a goddam thing is that to say? What makes you talk like that? Did I ever, for a minute—"

"Anh, you're like all men." She turned away from him in disgust.

Mute with rage, his face showing white at the bone, he grabbed her hair and turned her face to him. "Iris," he said, shaking her head slowly from side to side, "I swear to God, you make me so angry—you make me so goddam angry—I swear I don't know, I don't know what I want to do. You—you—"

"You want to hit me."

"Oh!" He took his hand away and shuddered. His eyes were closed and he shook his head as if he were talking to himself. "I don't want to hit you. I don't want to hit you. You just drive me out of my mind, that's all."

"All right," she said. Her voice was quiet and flat. "I don't blame you. I'll go away." She got out of bed and drew on a robe and walked to the window. "I'll get a cab and take a train back to New York."

Juley was silent. He felt weak and tired. He wanted to lie down on the bed and go to sleep. When he spoke it was as if he heard his own voice from a distance. It seemed unconnected with the workings of his mind.

"Don't be silly," he said quietly. "I planned to leave here at three and we ought to be back in New York around ten."

"Look, if you don't want me around, I'll go. Why knock yourself out? I get on your nerves, so—"

"Iris, you don't get on my nerves—"

"Is that why you wanted to beat me up, because I *don't* get on your nerves?"

"It's just that you keep— Oh, I don't know what it is."

"That's what I mean, honey," she said. She sat down and lighted a cigarette, the robe falling away so that the bottom part of her body was exposed. "I've been telling you that all along. We aren't right for each other. It's not your fault, not mine. I'll just go home and we'll forget it."

"Iris, I don't want you to go."

"Why not?"

"Look—" He faltered. "I—I brought you up here and I'll take you back."

She shrugged. "How do I know you won't get sore at me again and hit me?"

He spread his arms in a gesture of helplessness. "I'm sorry, I didn't mean to— Look, Iris, I know it sounds . . . sounds funny, but I love you. I really do."

"Balls. You don't love me."

"The ridiculous thing is that I *do*."

She frowned and examined her fingernails. "Well," she said flatly, "I don't love you."

He shrugged.

"So I might as well get out of here and stop bugging you," she added.

"Iris—will you please—don't go!"

"Why?"

"I don't know. I just don't want you to go."

"But what difference does it make?"

"Did you hear what I said!" he shouted. "I brought you here and I'm going to take you back. Now that's all!" He was standing before her, bent forward stiffly as if in a formal bow. She pulled her robe together, covering her nakedness.

"You going to hit me again?"

"No," he said hoarsely, "I'm not going to hit you." He sank heavily onto the floor and leaned his forehead on her legs. He could feel the warmth of her flesh under the light silk and smell the perfume of her gown. Even in his despair he sensed how much he needed this scent, this warmth. "Let's just calm down," he said, talking to her knees. "Let's just, for God's sakes stop fighting. I've got to go see the kids, it's getting late. Why don't you go down to the pool and relax and then I'll take you back."

"Are you sure you want to?"

"Yes, I do want to. Don't you? Would you rather go alone?"

"Honey, to me it makes no difference. I've been on trains before. Maybe I could even find a plane out of here."

"I don't want you on a plane or a train. I want you to stay here with me. All right?"

"Hey, did you know you have a wart on your neck?"

Juley started to laugh. He laughed weakly as if he had no strength left in his chest and lungs.

"Isn't that *funny*. That's the first time I ever noticed it," Iris said. "It looks like a salted peanut."

Juley shrugged. His eyes were closed and he was smiling. "So, I'm no Don Juan. Sue me."

"Who knows," Iris said, "maybe if we'd met ten years ago we might have got married."

"Thanks, but no thanks."

"Couldn't take it, huh?" Iris laughed. "Hey, you want a broad? I just happened to think of it. I know a broad who's dying to get laid. My neighbor. She'd be just right for you."

"Please, don't do me any favors."

"I'll bet she'd be crazy in the sack. Of course, she's no chicken, she must be forty, but what the hell."

"Sorry, I like 'em young. Like you."

"Yeah." Iris emitted a short laugh. "That's just my trouble. The story of my life. Let me up, I want to order my breakfast. Ugh! I hate eating breakfast alone."

It was funny, Vito thought, how Prince Valiant, once his favorite comic strip, now seemed so uninteresting. His eyes roamed the page noting the Prince's glossy bobbed hair, his rosy cheeks, a nubile maiden simpering in a doorway. That prince, he thought to himself, smiling as he thought it, is either queer or a big jerk. Impatiently, he turned the page.

"Pa, hurry, we'll be late for the ball game. We've got to get all the way to the Bronx."

"You sure you don't want to go downtown, to Mulberry Street?" His father answered him from the bedroom.

"Oh, for—" Vito groaned. "Pa, you've never *seen* a ball game. Don't you want to at least see one? I'm telling you, you'll like it. Anyway, what's there for me to do downtown? You'll go talk politics to your friends and what am I going to do, watch them play *bocce?* You know they never let the kids play. Only the old men."

"All right, all right," Alessandro said, "I'm coming."

"Anyway," Vito said, laughing, "you can take a book

along. If you don't like the game you can read your book."

"Only the Americans could have invented a game like baseball," Alessandro said. He came out buttoning his shirt. "*Tac!* you move one square. *Tac!* you move to another square. Then you leave the field and let your opposites take their turn. No fighting, no blood. Only self-discipline."

"One square!" Vito hooted. "You're talking about potsie! What kind of squares are you talking about? Pa, be honest. You've never even *seen* a ball game."

"So? I've studied it on the radio." He pinched his nose between his thumb and forefinger. "There's the wine-up," he intoned nasally, "and here's the pitch and it's a long outfield fly to the first base and that's the end of the ball game. *Moh!*" He took his fingers from his nose while Vito shouted with laughter. "Why is it the end of the game? Who knows?"

"Oh, come on," Vito said, taking his father's arm. "Two bits, by the end of the afternoon you'll be a Yankee fan."

The telephone rang.

"Let's leave it," Vito said. "Somebody complaining there's a cockroach in the sink. Come on, let's go."

"No, you better answer," Alessandro said. "Maybe it's for you."

"For me?" Vito picked up the telephone. He was startled by the voice of the operator.

"For who?" he said. "Vito—Vito Pellegrino, sure, that's me. Sure, one moment." He looked at his father. "It's for me, a long-distance— Hello? Hello, Iris? It's me, Vito, hi. Where are—"

"I'll meet you outside," Alessandro said. "Don't forget to lock the door."

Vito nodded. "Sure I miss you. Hey, you know what? This is the first time I ever got a long-distance call. I can't get over it, it sounds like you're upstairs. . . . It's good to hear your voice too, honey. I wish you'd come back. When are you coming back? Ten o'clock? So late? . . . What do you mean you didn't think I cared? What, are you crazy? . . . All right. I'll say it: I love you. I mean it, I really do. . . . Look, don't cry. Think of all the money this is costing—just to cry on the phone. . . . Need you?" Vito paused and frowned. "Sure I need you, honey," he said uncertainly. "I—I never thought about it like that before. . . . Well, of course I'm young, so what? . . . So I've got my father . . . so . . . I told you already, I do—need you—at least, I think I do. I mean, honest, I don't know what you mean. Look," he said, feeling rising confusion, "come on home, will you? Just come on home. . . . What do you mean, what then? What—look, what do you want me to do? . . . I'm not sore, it's just that I don't understand. . . . All right, all right. But come on home, will you? . . . We're going to a ball game. . . . Sure, I like taking you places. . . . OK, I'll be there. . . . Upstairs? Yes, I have the key. . . . OK, I promise I won't go to sleep. I'll put the radio on. Don't worry, I won't feel like sleeping. . . . I want to, too. . . . More than anything else in the whole world. I swear to God. All right? . . . Yes, good-by."

Vito put the telephone down and wiped his palm on his trousers. Jesus! he whispered to himself. What a dame! Broad. What does she mean "need me"? Need —what? I love her, isn't that enough? What—why did she sound so strange? He became suddenly aware that he was trembling. He held out his hand and stared at it.

What the hell is going on? he wondered. Why am I shaking like a goddam leaf? "What then?" he recalled, hearing the sound of Iris's voice clearly in his mind. I never even thought about it, he realized. I never look at it that way. All I ever think about, all I want, is to get into bed and watch her take her clothes off and then—I don't care. I wish she hadn't said that, "What then." It makes me feel so empty, so—I don't know.

Phew! He blew his breath out and wiped the sweat

from his upper lip with his forearm. His father was waiting for him outside.

"So?" Alessandro said.

Vito shrugged. He smiled. "She wanted to tell me she'll be home tonight." He paused. "I never had a long-distance call before. How do you like that? I could hear her like she was upstairs."

Alessandro sat on the steps. His face was drawn and his hands hung limply between his legs. He sighed and shook his head in a gesture of ultimate futility.

"So?" he said.

"What do you mean, Papa?" Vito asked softly.

"What do I mean?" Alessandro gesticulated. "What do I mean? What's going to happen now? That's what I mean. She loves you, no?"

"Yes. I guess so."

"And you love her too, no?"

"Sure, Pa."

"'Sure, Pa.' But it's not the same thing. It's like—" Alessandro paused, trying to find the right words. "It's like holding a candle to the moon. In a small room, the candle is bright and hot. But outside, in the world, the candle is nothing in the moonlight. The wind comes. From nowhere. Pouf! The candle is *spenta*. Out. But the moon shines and shines all through the night."

Vito shifted uneasily. He did not look at his father's face.

"Do you understand me? You're so young yet, Vito." He reached out and clasped the boy's slim forearm. "Even"—he laughed—"you are thin like a candle. And that one, your madonna"—he gestured with his hands—"is round and full like a moon. I don't mean," he added quickly, "only—you know, physically, I mean, also, inside. I—don't know—I don't know what to say.

"For one thing, I'm glad. You have a good woman, a beautiful woman. She loves you, she shows you how to love. This is good. You are lucky. She is not a beast-woman; this, I know. I see how she is with you. So all this is good—the love, the being with a woman, all good. But then?"

"That's what she said."

"Ah! You see? That's the question. After she goes away, what will you do? Will you find pleasure with these little girls in the street, in your school? Will you find another woman like that one? After all, you can't make it a career to go around finding older women to fall in love with you. You don't want to be a gigolo. So you see . . . And what about her? There it is even worse. It is clear she loves you. Really loves you. Ahh—" He spread his hands. It was self-evident. "If she loves you, she wants you. Completely. This is how women are. Ah—" He paused. He tapped his head with his finger.

"I have not been very wise. What could I have done? I don't know. But something better than this."

"Maybe," Vito began and then stopped. "Maybe we could—I could—maybe we could get married." His voice was almost a whisper.

His father looked at him, finding his eyes and holding them. "Ask yourself: do you want to get married? Do you want to be with this woman every day, day after day, morning and night, all the time? Do you want to be with her like that? Do you need her that much? Is there nothing else you might need or want? Nothing else you *could* need or want that, maybe, now you don't know about, but it could happen? Think about that. Never mind about working, about money, about all the rest. Just think about that. Eh?"

"I—I don't know, Pa."

"Of course you don't know. But sooner or later you'll have to think about it. You, Vito. You have to do it by yourself. I couldn't help you. Even if I wanted to help you, I couldn't. You. You have to think about it. You understand?"

Vito nodded.

"Now, you want to go to this ball game?"

Vito smiled. He felt unaccountably embarrassed. "I

don't know. I could give the passes to some of the kids down at the candy store."

"No," Alessandro said, rising to his feet. "Why? It was a good idea before. It's still a good idea, no? You enjoy the ball game, why shouldn't you go? Because you're worried? A little worry won't hurt you. This is just the beginning. There will be more. Besides, she won't be home until ten o'clock. The ball game doesn't last all night, no?"

"No."

"Then, let's go. *Forza!*" He put his arm around Vito's shoulders and squeezed him once.

After they had passed a toll-booth on the Merritt Parkway, Iris turned her head toward Juley to speak. Until then she had been entirely silent, watching the road with her head turned rigidly to the front. Now her face lightened and she drew her knees up on the seat so that she could face Juley.

"Now I know we're going back to New York," she said.

He laughed. "Where did you think we were going, Alaska?"

"You won't believe me, but it scares me to ride in a car. Unless I can recognize the route, I get scared that I'm being taken somewhere, that I'll be taken to the middle of nowhere and get dropped off. And nobody will ever hear from me again. Not that anybody would care."

"I'd care. I'd find you no matter where you were."

"Oh, Juju!" She patted his cheek. "You're sweet. I'm going to miss you—"

"Hunh?"

"Honey, look, we've got to stop this. You know it's no good. How long have we known each other, been going out, I mean, a year? A year and a half? What good has it done us? We just drive each other crazy, that's all."

Juley frowned at the road and finally he glanced at her. "The fact is, you're right. We've been getting worse instead of better."

"You haven't been serious about me for the last four or five months," Iris said. "You've been seeing that other broad—that what's-her-name I met at that party?"

"Vivian?"

"That's the one. Is she good to you?"

"Yes," Juley said judiciously, "yes, she is."

"Well, then, you see? Quit while you're ahead."

"You mean then—you don't think we ought to see each other any more?"

"Juju—don't be ridiculous. Of course I want to see you—you know, now and then. I just mean that we ought to forget about it. There's no future in it for either of us."

"Are you in love with someone else?" Juley asked.

Iris was silent. She turned her head away to look out of the window.

"You didn't answer my question. I said, are you in love with somebody else?"

"What difference would it make—yes, I am in love with somebody else. You know who?"

"I'm afraid to guess."

"Why, afraid?"

"Oh, Iris"—Juley shook his head—"it's—it's just crazy, that's all. I mean, he's a nice kid, a lovely kid. And he's good-looking—" He laughed. "I could go for him myself. But you're not serious. You can't be."

"I know."

"You know what?"

"I know I can't be," Iris said. "You think I should see a head-shrinker?"

"Yes, I do. I really do."

"So what can he tell me? *Why* I'm in love with a young boy? You think I don't know? You think I don't know that this is the only man I've ever been able to make it with in my entire life?" She paused when she saw the expression on his face. "I'm sorry, Juju. This time I'm not needling you. Honest to God, I'm not. I'm telling you the truth. I just can't tell you what it's like to be with him. And I'm not going to try because I know it bugs you. I don't blame you. I'd be sore too if you told me how great it was with you and some other broad. Don't you see, that's why we've got to stop being together—"

"I see, I see," Juley said. "Only what I don't see, and you don't see, is, what's going to happen in the end? What are you going to do about it? You'll be going on tour in the first couple of weeks in September. What are you going to do, take him along in your trunk?"

"I don't know," Iris said. "Maybe by then it will all be over. You know how kids are." She laughed. "He'll get tired of me and take up with the lady gym teacher. That I wouldn't mind so much, better that than the men's gym teacher."

Juley laughed. "Honey, I wish there was something I could do for you."

"Do for me! What's to do? Ah, that's sweet, though." She leaned forward and kissed his cheek. "You really are a doll. Such a wonderful guy. Juley, I can't tell you how sorry I am for giving you a hard time all the time. I hate myself for it, I really do. I don't know why I needle you. You don't deserve it—but sometimes you just bug me, so I can't stop."

"Forget it," Juley said. He patted her knee.

"Can I still call you up at three in the morning if I get frightened or lonely?"

"Sure."

"Can I come get shoes wholesale?"

He laughed. "Not only that, bring the kid too, I'll fix him up."

"You don't have to get snotty about it."

"I was just kidding."

Iris was silent for a long time. She lighted a cigarette,

took a few puffs and then threw it out of the window. Then she crossed her arms and sank more deeply into the seat so that her face was tilted toward the roof of the car. "I guess I really must be going out of my mind," she said at last, "but all I can think about is getting back to him. He's so sweet that half the time I feel like crying—half the time—I don't know." She paused. "Is it *wrong* to be in love with someone half your age? Does it have to be *wrong?* Im*pos*sible? If it were a man, it'd be all right. What are you, forty-seven, forty-eight? All right, there you are."

"But that's—"

"Different. I know. But supposing I was a man and I found this sixteen-year-old chick and I got hung on her? Would it be so bad? In short, if I were a man it would be all right. But because I'm a woman it's not all right. What a lot of crap!"

Juley shrugged. "I don't know what to say, honey. In some ways you're right. Who am I to say what is right and what is wrong? How can anyone say? It depends how you feel, that's all. And how it works out."

"Well, how I feel is that I'm hung on this guy. Like it hasn't happened to me since I was sixteen. And how it works out? Who the hell knows?" She closed her eyes. "Wake me up when we get to the George Washington Bridge, all right? I really dig that bridge. OK?"

"OK." Juley smiled fondly at her.

"Juju," Iris said, opening her lips to smile, and keeping her eyes closed, "I wish to God I could love you."

"Thanks."

"It would make everything so much more simple."

"Never mind." Juley laughed. "Troubles enough I got."

"Who knows," Iris said, "maybe one of these days I will? And you can have the fun of kicking me right in the mouth."

Vito lay in Iris's bed, listening to the sound of the elevator in the darkness. Three times he had heard the elevator rise to the floor level and each time he had known that she was not on it. But this time, he was certain, she had arrived. The room was warm. He had turned off the air conditioner so that he could hear her footsteps in the hall. Although he was naked under the light sheet, his hands and feet were cold.

He heard her key in the lock and he heard her put her bag down with a thud.

"Darling?" Her voice was high, muted and tense. He had planned to answer her with a casual, "Hi," but the sound of her voice was so surprisingly sweet—after the absence of two days—and so exactly tuned to his own anxiety that he bounded from the bed and embraced her with all his strength.

"Oh!" he cried, "oh, oh."

"Oh, Vito, darling, darling." She grunted as he squeezed her and laughed. "Oh, darling, darling, baby." She pressed her body against him, rubbing her cheek against his jaw and neck. "Oh, baby, my delicious, lovely baby, thank God you're here."

Vito pressed his nose to her hair and her skin, breathing in her scent as if it were air itself. He squeezed his arms around her, locking his hand on his wrist so that he could press her until it hurt.

"Thank God *you're* here," he said. "I've been looking for you. I keep seeing women but they're not you. I just wanted to see you."

"Oh, Vito, did you? Darling, I wanted to come back sooner. I really did. Did you miss me?"

"Listen," Vito said. He loosed his arms and took her face between his hands. "I love you. Do you know that? I really love you. For two days it's like—like nothing happened."

"Oh, my God. Help me out of this thing." She tugged at her dress. "Help me, help me." He unfastened her dress and helped her pull it from her head. "Oh, quickly," she said, when she was naked. She pressed against him and they staggered into the bedroom.

"Oh!" she said, as she felt him enter her, "oh, darling."

"I'm home," Vito said softly. He reached down to press her. "This is my home." She smiled and reached for his face, drawing it down to her mouth.

"Now," she said, drawing her legs together tightly, and arching against him, "now you can't get away. Oh, I love you. I love you. I'm not going to let you get away."

Vito stood at the kitchen stove watching the eggs turn white in the pan. He was wearing his shorts and stood with his arms folded, one hand holding a spatula, his chin resting on his bare chest. Iris, wearing a flowered dressing gown, watched him from her perch on a stool. He looked older, she realized suddenly. There was something about his pose, some scant change, so slight that it would not be defined. It had occurred in her absence —or had escaped her notice. But it was there, she could see it, he was no longer a boy, he was becoming a young man.

"So what else happened?" Vito asked, idly probing the pan with his spatula.

"That's all there is to tell, baby," Iris said. "It was a bore."

"Did you see Mr. Franz? Juley?"

Iris frowned. "Yes. So what?"

Vito didn't answer.

"Sure I saw him. He knows the same people I do. We used to hang around with the same crowd. What difference does it make?"

It makes a lot of difference, Vito thought. He could feel his anger rising slowly. It seemed to flow into his limbs and his trunk, heavy, viscous, making his chest tight. He started to speak but closed his mouth. Then he started to speak again and even as he spoke he was surprised at his own vehemence.

"I thought you didn't give a damn about him. Isn't that what you said? So why did you have to see him?"

Iris stared at him. She was startled by his expression. His young mouth looked thin and cruel and his nose looked hawklike under the ceiling light.

"I didn't *have* to see him, darling," she said softly, "I just happened to run into him. Don't make something out of nothing."

"How do I know you didn't go up there to see him?"

"Oh, Vito—"

He paused and stared at her. He turned the flame off under the pan with an angry twist. "So you're away for two or three days and you tell me not to look at a girl, not even to talk to a girl, and I didn't—because, I didn't even want to, and you, you go up there and you're hanging around this guy with all his dough—"

"Oh, Vito, baby—" Iris got off her stool and put her arms around his neck.

"Let me go," he said. He pulled her arms away.

"Honey, you're making a big fuss over absolutely nothing," Iris said. Her voice was crisp. "I told you a dozen times Juley doesn't mean a *thing* to me. So we had a couple of drinks together, so what?"

"So what! It's disgusting, that's what it is. Disgusting!" Vito could feel his anger taking hold of him now. It gave velocity to his words. He was conscious of a kind of exhilaration.

"You're out of your mind," Iris said.

"I may be out of my mind but I'm not a—a traitor!" Vito shouted. He was deeply pleased to see that her face registered fear. She retreated before his violence.

"Look, baby," Iris said, "I'm telling you once more and for the last time: Juley Franz doesn't mean a *thing* to me. And now please let's cut it out."

Vito leaned back against the sink. "All right," he said slowly, "how do I know there isn't somebody else? How do I know you haven't got somebody you haven't told me about?"

"Oh, cut it out, you're giving me a headache."

"I'm giving *you* a headache! What do you think *you're* doing?"

Iris looked at him. There was nothing now, nothing that she saw which evoked her love. He was a stranger. Angry, distant, a source of noise and irritation. Why is this happening? she asked herself. Who is he? She spoke in a dull, tired voice.

"Listen, I don't know what's bugging you," she paused, "and I don't care. I'm tired and my nerves are on edge and I want to get some sleep. Why don't you finish your sandwich—or don't, I don't care—and then get the hell out of here. If you want to call me in the morning, OK. If not—" She shrugged.

Vito opened his eyes wide as if he had been slapped. "Do you mean that?" he said.

Iris didn't answer. She rose from her stool and carefully pushed it back against the wall.

"You mean I can just get out and that's the end of it?" he repeated.

She looked at him quickly. "Who said anything about the end of it? If you're still sore in the morning, don't bother to call me, that's all."

"You—you can—you can just go to hell!" Vito said. He stepped away from the sink and started to walk out of the kitchen. Iris barred his way.

"Damn it—" she began.

"Excuse me," he said, moving past her. "I want to get dressed and go home."

He strode into the bedroom and began pulling on his clothes. Iris went into the living room and lighted a cigarette. She sat stiffly in a corner of the couch and when he came out of the bedroom, still stuffing his shirt into his trousers, she raised her head. His face was pink with anger and he was breathing heavily.

Suddenly she felt her anger fade away. For a moment she was becalmed. It was as if some inner hush had fallen, no gusts buffeted her throat, no clouds scudded across her inner eye. A kind of languor overcame her and she found herself perceiving light and shape and movement in a way that was both voluptuous and detached.

How adult he looked now, she thought, how self-possessed, how direct. Yet, there was something about him that was still boyish, still touchingly awkward. She found herself looking at the prominent knobs on his wrists, white and shell-like under his dark skin. She could feel something stirring inside her, answering, saying, yes, oh, how dear, to this child quality and she was impelled with desire to kiss his wrists. How does this happen, she thought sharply, how does he reach me? He took a jolting step forward.

"Where are you going?" she asked.

"I'm going home, like you said." He pulled his belt with a great yank and forced the folded tongue through his belt loops.

"Don't go away. Honey, don't go away." Her voice was heavy, almost drowsy. It was an effort to make herself alert.

He pondered his belt buckle for a moment. "You told me to get out. So I'm getting out. You want to end it right now, OK. Don't worry, I won't bother you again. You can have your rich friends with their cars and all. So? So I don't care. So long." He reached for the door knob.

"Vito!" she screamed. *Had* she screamed? Still, she wondered. He dropped his hand and faced her. He looked frightened.

"What is it? Why are you hollering?"

"Vito—" Now there was alarm, terror. She knew it. "Don't you *dare* go out of here like that." Her voice shook. "Come back here! Do you hear me? Don't you *dare* leave me. What do you *mean* by—"

"But—" He stood in a slight crouch in front of the door. "But—" He hesitated. She ran to him and jarred him against the closed door. She gripped his shirt in her fists, pulling the thin cloth, dragging him back into the room.

"Oh, Vito, darling, darling, stay. Don't go." She was crying, with her mouth pressed to his shirt. "Don't go." He could feel her hot moist breath on his skin.

"But you told me—"

"Darling, I don't want you to go away. Don't leave me. Stay here, please, please. Hold me."

"Then why did you tell me—"

"Put your arms around me, please." She grasped his hands and put them around her waist.

"All right. All right," he said softly, waiting for her agitation to subside. He began again in a patient voice. "But you told me to get—to get the hell out. Like you didn't care. I thought you were really mad at me."

"Darling, I do care. I love you. Oh, Vito, my baby, I love you so much. You mustn't ever leave me."

"I guess I didn't want to leave—I love you too."

"Do you?" She raised her face and looked at him, her mouth open wide and thickened by her sobs.

"Sure I do." He stroked her head and attempted to press her face against his chest. She pulled away from his hands and kissed him, holding his face and pressing her tongue far into his mouth.

"Do you understand I want to *be* with you?" She shook her head. "You don't, really, do you? Do you understand that I'm giving myself up, that I've been going out of my mind? That I'm so hung on you I can't fight it? I don't even care about anybody any more, just you? Do you realize we might even get married?"

"What?"

"I *know* it's insane. But what else can we do?"

"Gee! I don't know—"

"Never mind." She smiled at him. "I'm not trying to scare you. We won't talk about it now. But let's not fight any more. All right? I don't want to fight with you."

"I don't want to fight either," he said, "only—"

"What? Anything. What is it?" She was unbuttoning his shirt and kissing his chest.

"Will you promise not to see Juley again?"

She looked at him and smiled. "You really mean that, don't you?"

"Sure. What's the matter with that?"

"What's the matter with it? Oh, Vito, people don't just stop—I mean, just because you love somebody doesn't mean—never mind. I'll explain it to you another time."

"What's to explain? Either we're going steady or we're not."

"Steady. Oh, you child." She put her face against his bare chest. "OK, we are."

"You promise."

"Yes, for God's sake, I promise." She rubbed her cheek against his skin. "Scout's honor. You want me to swear on the Bible?"

"No." He laughed.

"Come on," she said, keeping her eyes closed and pushing him toward the bedroom. "Let's get back to bed. So I don't have to keep seeing what a child you are."

"I'll show *you* who's a child," Vito said, "I'm going to bite hell out of you." He gripped her flesh at the base of her neck with his teeth and bit hard enough so that she would have, he knew, a clear violet imprint in the morning.

At eleven Iris awoke with a feeling of laughter on her lips. Cautiously—because she knew this feeling and knew it could vanish unexpectedly only to be succeeded by a feeling of such despair that it was like being buried alive—cautiously, she smiled.

"Mmm," she murmured aloud. She reached down and rubbed her loins. How sore, she thought, how nice and sore. Man, she told herself, that's a feeling. That *really* is a feeling.

Vito had left her bed at about seven. She remembered hearing him rise, feeling his fond kiss and his hand on her breast when he left her. Still heavy with sleep, she had tried to hold him but he murmured something reassuring and she had let go his hand. She had slept serenely since then and her joy was with her still.

She did not, for the time being, need anything else, anyone else. Nor would she, she decided, think about the future. She yawned and stretched. Somehow it would work out. She would have to tell him about the theater, perhaps tonight. If not tonight, then the next day. They would have a long talk and she would explain it all to him. She would wait until they were in bed and she would put his head on her breast and tell him. Before they made love? Or after? After. When they were both drowsy.

It wasn't such a bad thing, after all. He could see that. And there was no reason for him to be jealous. She smiled. It was fun seeing him get jealous, get angry. But the recollection of what had happened halted her smile. He had almost left. She could feel her body growing cold. Stop it, stop it, she told herself. He didn't leave. He wouldn't leave.

She got out of bed quickly. She didn't want to think about that any more. Her good feeling was fading, she could feel it slipping away. Suddenly, unwanted and inexorable, a thought came into her mind.

That was me on my knees last night. That was you, kid. How about that for a switch?

Wow!

She sat weakly on the bed. Her legs felt shaky. Then she laughed to herself aloud.

"I'll be goddamned. He had you on the ropes, kid."

Well, she thought, now you know how the other half lives. I love you, he had said. I want to marry you. Could she believe him?

Hell, yes! He *did* love her. And I love him, she thought. So what's all the panic? He's not going to walk out on you, baby. Stop thinking about it. Try—for the first time in your life you've got something straight and good, oh, God, it's good—try thinking about how to make it work. Not how it can't work. It'll work. Why not? It's got to work.

The telephone rang.

"Harry! I forgot all about you. I thought you were dead. Me and my rotten luck. So, what else is new?"

Half an hour later, Iris pulled up the blinds and stood before the window looking down at the street. The hot sun of midday struck her light robe with such strength that she could feel warmth stinging her flesh. Well, anyway, she thought, laughing to herself, I'm working, one week in Newark—big deal!

It was an oddly comforting feeling. There had been a time, not many years ago, when the certainty of work, the signing of a contract, was as reassuring as the warmth of the sun. But in the last few years, the fears of not working had been almost forgotten in the rush of her success. She no longer courted engagements; she knew the luxury of being wanted, the supreme luxury of refusing work. But still, the prospect of a booking, even so undesirable a booking as this, recalled some of the old fears and some of the old pleasures—the fear of seeking, the pleasure of being sought.

On the street below her a man stood in a truck bed hacking large blocks of ice into chunks the size of skulls. These he forced into an astonishingly noisy machine and each time he did, a white gush of shimmering ice fell into a wooden tub. How nice it would be, she felt, to scoop up handfuls of soft ice, how astringent, how cool.

That sun is sure a mother, she thought, lowering the blind again and restoring the illusion of coolness to the room. She sat heavily in a chair.

Why did I do this? What for? Who needs it?

Tonight.

My God! I've got to get my hair done.

Should I shave or shouldn't I? I told him I wouldn't. Nothing bare. And panties, no g-string.

Now what am I going to tell Vito? I've *got* to tell him. I can't just go away for a whole week and *not* tell him.

St. Louis? Maybe. I'll think of something.

She called her hair dresser for an appointment and then began filling the tub for her bath.

I'm out of condition, she thought, as she slipped into the hot water. Goddamit! *why* did I do this?

How do people get in such *messes?* How can I, a good-looking little broad, five-four, a hundred eighteen pounds, how can I make a big man like Juley, he's almost six feet and must weigh over two-twenty, how can I put him on his knees?

With words!

That's all, just words. Feelings. It would be different if I had a club or a gun or if I belted him until he couldn't—

It's terrible to see someone like this. It was terrible to see Juley like that. Crazy, out of his mind. I kind of liked it—in a way. But—is that why I said yes to Harry?

I'm like that with Vito. On my knees.

The thought almost made her faint. The heat of the bath was suddenly suffocating. She sat up weakly, there was sweat on her face.

I'll give the money to Harry. No, not the whole salary. Half. Then the hell with him. He can go screw himself. No, I don't mean that, not really. He's a sweet guy and even if I did give him a hard time, I shouldn't feel guilty about it. That's the way he wanted it. And it wasn't as if I went out of my way to clobber him. I just couldn't help it.

But that's what I'll do. Charity. Why not? I'll give them a hell of a show and, come Saturday night, I'll turn the check over to Harry and tell him to get lost. For good. Except for a hundred dollars. I want to buy Vito a suit. Something in raw silk. I better make it a hundred and a half. Light gray. From De Pinna's or Whitehouse and Hardy, something like that. I don't want him looking like a Cuban busboy on his day off.

God, what a jerk I am!

But I can't let him down. I just *can't*. He's so sick. So damned sick. Like Juley in a way. Funny. They seem so different. Juley's so big and so loud and so full of money—still . . .

And me . . .

I guess I'm sick, too. I've *got* to be. Why would I keep getting myself involved with people like—

Vito?

There's nothing sick about *that* kid. Oh, brother. You should be so sick.

What'll I tell him? Mother . . . St. Louis . . .

"Harry . . ." She held the telephone in her still-dripping hand. "No, I'm not backing out, though *why* I'm not—I must be out of my skull—listen, I want you to send me a wire. . . . Will you shut up and listen? I want you to make out like it's my mother in St. Louis and here's what I want you to say. . . ."

10

Two blocks east of his apartment house, Vito sat at dusk on a stoop listening to the scream of an ambulance retreating northward along York Avenue. Howling, raging, like a lion with a spear in its side, the ambulance left a broken trail of shock in the quiet of early evening. Yet, long before its cries grew faint, Vito's friends turned their eyes back to themselves, back to their own patch of brick and asphalt browse. Their ruminations were as mindless as breathing; they could not be diverted by alarms.

"What do you bet I had Loretta Mancuso up on the roof? I bet you ten bucks."

"Ten bucks, my . . ."

"Put your money where your mouth is. . . ."

"Big deal! My brother had Loretta Mancuso's cherry. . . ."

"She never . . ."

"Ask your sister. . . ."

"Cool . . ."

"Man . . ."

"Cherry . . ."

"Hey, how about that new science teacher. . . ."

"Oh, Jesus! would I . . ."

"Oh, man . . ."

"Jesus . . ."

"Would I . . ."

Sitting on the top step, his cheek against a warm slab of brownstone, Vito tried to hold the ambulance sound in his ear for as long as he could. The discussion had bored him from its start. Keeping an eye on the animated faces of his friends, he waited for an opening. They moved back and forth, arms figuring the air, shoulders bobbing, in lazy, fluid gesticulations, accompanying their talk of longing with an innocent, tireless dance. There was a lull. Voices and movement subsided in the ending of a strophe. Vito flicked his cigarette stub swiftly, handsomely, into the street.

The effort of being with his friends and remaining apart from them made him yawn. A hundred times in the previous few days he had wanted to talk about Iris and each time his throat had closed above the words. At times he could almost feel these words in his throat and he would have to swallow hard and breathe deeply until the feeling of pressure went away.

If only he could talk about her, he thought, the week might hurry by. A week was made of days and hours and the days could be passed, if there was something real to wait for. But how could it be real if you couldn't put it into words? What a frail reality it was if it existed only in his mind.

But he could not talk. To bring forth the words, to put into the laughing, hungry mouths of his friends the vision of Iris was obscene. His stomach contracted at the thought of it. Recalling the feel of her lips, the widening of her eyes when he made love to her, hearing the sound of her voice rising anxiously as she neared her climax, hearing the sound of her voice as she murmured gratefully in his ear—all of this was the substance and it must remain secret.

Yet, there was something else, something that brought a smile to his lips, that impelled him to talk, an impulse so gay and vigorous that in suppressing it he actually giggled. It was the feeling of ease and confidence and —even though it was not fully conscious, it was nevertheless there—a feeling of supremacy which made him want to laugh and swagger and spit grandly in the street.

His fear of Iris was gone. He could look back on it now and laugh at his timidity. He could, if he wanted, go into her apartment and sprawl on her bed and call her to him. In fact, he decided, he would do just that. He would try it. Take my clothes off, he imagined himself saying, laughing as he said it. And she would do it! She would laugh and do it.

She's my woman, he found himself thinking, the phrase literally forming in his mind. *My woman.* He tested the words silently on the flat of his tongue. It was a rich feeling. Thoughtfully, he rubbed his palms dry of sudden moisture and picked a tar smudge from his trouser knee.

My woman? *Then what?* Iris had asked. He cringed before the thought. I'm only a kid, he found himself thinking nervously. What the hell do I know? He found himself getting angry at the question. He raised his eyes and glowered at the street. It was getting close to suppertime. He hoped his father had cooked something big, a *risotto,* a *minestrone,* something reassuring and warm.

"What the hell you looking so mad about?" one of the boys asked him.

"What the hell do you care?"

"Oh, buddy, right between the eyes. One shot and right . . ."

"Hey, Vito, you want to come to Newark with us tonight to the burlesque show?"

"I'm broke."

"So? Tap the old man for a couple of bucks. Three of us, me, Dom and Fat Herman, are going over."

"Go on, they wouldn't let us in."

"What do you mean? My brother went last night and he's only eighteen and he's smaller than I am. All you got to do is wear a shirt and a tie and have a jacket. What do they care? Ninety-nine cents, you got it, they let you in."

"Anh, I don't know," Vito said.

"Hey, listen, man, they got a great show. My brother

says it's the best he's ever seen. You know who's in it, that broad who lives in your building. Hey, how about that, you been holding out on us."

"Yeah . . ."

"She's living right in his building. . . ."

"What a pair of knockers . . ."

"W-wait a minute. Wait a—" Vito stammered. "What are you talking about?"

"What do you mean, what am I—that blond broad with the big knockers she lives in your apartment, don't she?"

"Yeah," Vito nodded.

"OK. That's the one. The Mystery Girl, from Out of Space. My brother says she made him come in his pants, so help me Chr—"

"You're lying," Vito said. He was conscious of standing up and starting to walk down the steps.

The other boy retreated before him, puzzled by the expression on Vito's face.

"Hey, cool it, man."

"You're lying," Vito repeated.

The other boys, scenting violence, rose to their feet.

"I swear to God," the boy said, "if you don't believe me, ask my brother. He was sitting in the fourth row and he was so close, he said he could see her under her g-string—"

Vito moved so quickly he didn't have time to tighten his fist. He slammed the heel of his hand into the boy's mouth. All he could see was that terrible open mouth and he swung his hand up to stop it.

"Shut up!" he yelled. "You're lying. You're a goddam liar!"

The boy stumbled backward and fell to the ground.

Vito felt their arms around his neck, their hands on his body. He struggled but they held him.

"Cut it out! Cut it out!" somebody was yelling in his ear.

"What do you want to start something for. . . ."

"Why'd you deck Frankie. . . ."

"If you want to fight go in the alley, not on the street. . . ."

"Cool it. . . ."

"Let me go," Vito said. "I got blood on my hand. Let me go! I'm not going to hit him again." He shook them off furiously. He wiped his hand with his handkerchief. "I don't want him lying to me, about who lives in my building," he muttered. He didn't look up at their faces.

The other boy was on his feet and starting to move toward Vito. "Come on," he said softly, "you want to fight, let's go in the back. Come on," his voice was trembling.

"Chickee!"

They froze at the signal. At the street corner, not more than fifty yards away, a white-topped police car pulled slowly to a stop.

In attitudes of elaborate idleness, they scattered away from the spot. Vito began walking west with another boy and crossed the street to gain isolation. Within seconds the stairway was deserted and the last boy could be seen rounding a corner, preparing to run as soon as he was out of sight.

Swaying and staggering as he made his way through the half-empty cars, Vito reached the tail-end of the subway train. There, away from the lights which were the color of bright putrefaction, and the warm, sweet air which smelled as if it had been squeezed from an ancient, sordid mattress, he found a hiding place of shadow and earth-smelling breeze. He combed his hair and settled his tie, using the sooty panes of the subway door as his mirror. Then, carefully adjusting his position so that he would do the least damage to his clothes, he set himself to watching the disappearance of red and green lights as they swept into his vision like asteroids, quivered and then fell back into the void.

Frankie, he decided, was giving him the needle. How much did Frankie know, he wondered. And if he knew anything—if they all knew it—why didn't he come right out with it? Because I would have killed him. He answered his own question.

Then why was he on a subway train, all dressed up, with a pair of his father's old horn-rimmed glasses in his pocket—to make him look older—why was he on his way to Newark? To the burlesque show?

He shrugged. Why not? Maybe she *was* there. You're out of your head, he chided himself instantly. Those crazy jerks couldn't recognize one dame from another. Anyway, he told himself, I've never been to a burlesque show. So? What the hell, for kicks. Why not?

Go on! Get out of here! If she was going to be in a burlesque show, I'd know it, wouldn't I? Wouldn't she tell me?

Besides, it was ridiculous. Iris, a beautiful woman, a lady. Sure she could talk rough and she taught him a lot of—he stopped himself, he was about to say, dirty—a lot of rough words. But there was something about the way she did that—well, she was a lady, that's all. I mean, it's impossible to describe but—

Of course, he thought, I really don't know anything about women. Maybe a woman can be a—a—and at the same time, when you know her and talk to her, she's just like—

Oh, Jesus! He found himself remembering the time Iris had done that funny little dance for him in her apartment. He swallowed hard and tried to concentrate on the lights tumbling by overhead. Was that what they do? Why had he been so embarrassed, so ashamed that he was unable to look at her?

Anyway, so what if she's a burlesque dancer? He began to smile at the thought. But the smile gave way to anguish. Other men would look at her. Other men would watch and feel themselves getting hard and Frankie's brother would—

Oh, he groaned, shaking his head. It was unbearable. He shook his head to clear his mind of the thought and began to yell at the black tunnel of the subway.

"AAAGH! UP UP UP UPYOUR UPYOUR UPYOUR!"

He decided to smoke a cigarette. Keeping the butt hidden and keeping the smoke from being seen would occupy his mind.

Vito wanted terribly to look at photographs of smiling women displayed around the lobby of the theater but he was afraid to loiter under the scrutiny of the ticket-seller. His best chance, he thought, of getting into the theater unchallenged was to walk up quickly, put down his money with a curt "One" and walk in. There was, he noticed, a statement on the marquee, *This Week Only, the Mystery Girl From Outer Space—Right Out of This World*. But he kept his eyes down as he bought his ticket and walked quickly into the hall.

The smell of candy, popcorn and disinfectant surrounded him as instantly and totally as if he had sunk into a pool. It was not an unpleasant odor, yet it seemed to arouse in him a feeling something like anger. He took a seat in the rear of the house and blinked at the blue-white spotlight on the stage.

A very short man in a doctor's white coat was telling a very tall girl to take her clothes off. Everything he said was repeated three times.

"I'm sorry but I'll hafta askya ta take off ya dress."

"Take off my dress?" the girl repeated.

"Yeah. Take off the dress."

The disrobing took a long time. At last when the girl was attired in nothing more than a small brassière and a pair of narrow panties, the man in the doctor's coat applied a stethoscope to her navel.

"Wait a minute," the man said.

"Wait a minute?"

"Yeah, wait a minute. I'm getting some static." He fiddled with the ear pieces of his stethoscope.

And then an amazing thing happened. The stethoscope lost its drooping rubber-hose look. It snapped out straight, rigidly pointing at the girl. She screamed. The man yelled, "Hey, waid a minute, waid a *min*ute, wut's gone on here."

The crowd bellowed with laughter. The lights went off and the curtain went down.

Surprised to find that he could laugh without attracting attention, Vito gazed smilingly around the hall. The theater was half empty and he decided to move down to the tenth row. Just as he took his seat a man in a blue tuxedo with a heavily powdered face, the color of a hothouse tomato, came out and addressed the crowd.

"Now, folks—ya bin a great audience so far—we're gonna get on ta our special show, the feecha attraction, the thing I know ya all bin waitin' for, the onen only, oncena lifetime, the girl with the sonic boom, boom BOOM. I give ya the Mystry Girl Fum Outta Space. Let's really hear it out there!"

The band struck up a slow fanfare, the curtains parted and there stood Iris on the stage.

She was wearing a toy space helmet with a clear plastic visor, a tight tunic of gold cloth, white gauntlets with large, jeweled cuffs, tight trousers of the same gold cloth and she carried an enormous plastic pistol designed to look like a "death-ray gun." Raising her arms slowly to the beat of the music, she took a short cloak from her shoulders and tossed it toward the wings. Then she deliberately raised the visor of her helmet so that her eyes glittered in the light.

Vito rose half out of his chair and then sat back carefully. The shock of recognition had left him all but stunned. He had never realized, he found himself thinking, just how beautiful she was. Framed in the white plastic of her space helmet, her face was as demure and protected as that of a nun.

She half walked, half danced back and forth across the stage with an exaggerated sinuosity.

He leaned forward, resting his arms on a vacant seat in front of him and grinned at Iris as she moved across the stage. She stripped off first one gauntlet and then the next, rolling each one into a cylinder and running the cylinder between a circle made by her thumb and forefinger. She did this distractedly, keeping her eyes high on the spotlights at the back of the hall and then tossing the gloves aside.

Then, turning her back to the audience she moved her buttocks in a slow circle as she unfastened the short tunic and drew it slowly from her arms.

Vito saw her back grow bare except for a gold band of a brassière that passed horizontally just below her shoulder blades. When she turned to face the audience, he could see that her arms and shoulders and midriff were bare and he felt as if something heavy had fallen inside him.

Never taking her eyes from the spotlights, and continuing her slow, circular hip movement, she lifted the plastic helmet from her head and passed it slowly over her body and placed it between her thighs.

Now her expression began to change. She closed her eyes slightly and her mouth opened as if in pain. She swayed, holding the thick helmet between her thighs, passing her palms caressingly over it and then, coming out of her reverie, drew her ray pistol, took aim and carefully shot out the lights. There was an electric buzzing sound as, one by one, the stage and spotlights went off.

Vito closed his eyes in the darkness and rested his cheek on his hands. He could feel moisture on the backs of his hands and knew he was close to nausea.

A spotlight came on again, revealing Iris in front of a curtain. She had moved much closer to the audience now, and had stripped all of her costume except for the brassière and a gold bikini bottom. The music picked up in tempo and her movements now became more violent.

She shook her shoulders and her hips in unison and then stopped abruptly on a musical beat. Her breasts began to quiver, slowly at first, then faster and she moved back and forth across the stage front in profile, jiggling her breasts and touching them now and then with her fingertips, as if to give them added lift. Each time she did this there was a murmur from the crowd. She stopped and took her brassière off and Vito almost choked.

At first he thought that her breasts were bare. Her flesh, beloved flesh. But now he could see there was a thin net brassière still covering her, and under that a shining gold cone covering each nipple. He pressed his fingers against his mouth until his lip hurt.

Now she faced the audience directly, her body bent into a crouch with her legs spread wide, bent at the knees and her weight balanced well behind her legs so that she almost appeared to be sitting down. She drew her hands along the inside of her thighs and began to move back and forth in a flagrantly sexual way. Her head rolled from side to side and she pursed her lips in a continual sucking expression. She curved her hands, as if they were enclosing an imaginary mass and moved them up and down as if they were being lifted by the mass. The music grew louder and louder and there were guttural shouts arising from the floor. She shook her head faster, squinting her eyes, and showing her teeth, rocking up and down on her bent knees. The music became shrill, insistent. The drummer hammered, *thock, thock, thock* on the hoop rim. Iris uttered a high quick cry.

Up, Vito thought. I've got to, and stumbled frantically to his feet. He started to run, then remembered his jacket, grabbed it and began moving up the steep aisle. The music grew louder as he climbed what now seemed to be a cruelly steep hill. Up and up he moved, catching the sight of pink faces straining toward the stage. He flung himself against a heavy metal door, conscious that he was now out of the hall. For an instant he hesitated, desperately seeking direction, and then burst out into the outer lobby. The air was cool. His feet clattered across the terrazzo floor and he found, mercifully, an alley next to the theater.

He ducked into it, put his head against the blessed quiet of a brick wall and vomited explosively between his legs.

"Oh, God," he moaned hoarsely. "Oh, God, oh, God." His voice dropped to a whisper. He rested his forehead against the smooth brick of the wall, waiting for another spasm to overtake him. It came, ripping, erupting, convulsing his stomach muscles and aching in his throat. His knees trembled with the effort to stay erect and only the filth at his feet kept him from sitting down. For long moments he leaned against the wall until the violence died in his gut.

At the end of the alley a single light bulb shone over a rust-colored metal door. He stared at the door, feeling the sweat beginning to cool on his face. He shuddered; his shirt was wet at the sides and back. Behind the door, he thought he could probably find Iris. Putting his coat over his shoulders like a cloak, he took a few shaky steps toward the door. He needed her now. She would take care of him, find a place for him to lie down, she would stroke his head and caress him and then, later, when he felt better, she would kiss him, and get into bed with him and—

He shuddered and broke into a spasm of wracking sobs. Oh, no, he thought, remembering the pink, sweaty faces of the men in the theater. "Oh, no." The sounds squealed from his throat. "Don't let them touch you," he sobbed, "they dassn't—" He broke down helplessly, hunched over so that he was no bigger than a small boy, his hands pressed tightly to his face. "Please," he pleaded now through his tears. "Please, don't let—"

"Hey, you!" Vito heard a shout. He saw a figure on the lighted sidewalk but his eyes were so filled with tears that he could not identify it.

"I said, come here!" He recognized the tones and the uniform of a policeman who had his hand under the skirt of his coat. He wiped his eyes clear and shuffled forward, blinking at the light refracted from his wet lashes.

"What are you doing in there?"

"N-n-noth-nothing."

"What's your name?"

"V-Vito. Pellegrino."

"Where do you live?"

"East Sixty-Fourth Street." His stammering had stopped but his voice was almost a whisper.

"You mean in Manhattan."

"Yes."

"What's the matter? What are you crying about?"

"I'm s-sorry. I—I got sick."

The policeman hesitated. The boy, God knew, *looked* sick. Then he got an idea. "Take off your coat and roll up your shirt sleeves."

"What?"

"You heard me. Take off your coat. I want to see your arms."

Vito bared his forearms, shivering in his damp shirt.

"Now pull up your pants." The policeman peered at his legs. "Did anybody hit you?"

"No."

"You mean you just got sick, hunh. What happened, you eat something lousy? That what it was?"

"Yes," Vito nodded. "I guess so."

"All right. Go on, get out of here. Get in the subway and go back to Manhattan before you get in trouble. You should of stayed there, you understand? If you go looking for trouble you'll find it. How old are you?"

"Sixteen."

"Well," the policeman paused, "you're getting to the age now where trouble can be serious. You get me? It's not kid stuff any more. Now go on, beat it."

Vito nodded and started to move off.

"Hey," the policeman called. Vito turned his head. "You got carfare?"

"Yes."

"All right," the policeman said, making a gesture with his forefinger, "move along."

All I've got to do, Vito thought, is sit here, sit quietly with my head resting against the window and in a little while, I'll be home. Don't do anything, he cautioned himself. Don't think about anything, don't stand up. Don't even move. The subway goes under the river, then I get off at Thirty-Fourth. I wish I didn't have to get off, I wish I could sleep. You can't. Get off, go up to Times Square. Shuttle to Lex. Then sleep. Off at Sixty-Sixth. Then walk home slowly. Slowly. You don't have to wake up. Don't look at anything, smell anything. Stay like this until you get home. Then sleep. Oh, sleep. Sleep. "Please," he murmured, moving his head, "please." It passed. Sleep.

"Vito! Vito! Get up. Come on. It's Saturday. You got to help me clean up the house." Vito heard his father's voice from the other room. He didn't want to get up. He wanted to stay in bed with the shade drawn over the window. But when he turned over in bed and closed his eyes he found himself back in the theater again. He swung his legs out of bed, hesitated for a moment and then got dressed.

When he went into the other room, his father brought him a plate of scrambled eggs. The sight of them made him wince.

"What's the matter with you?" Alessandro said. "How come you sit down at the table you don't wash your face, comb your hair? Just because your madonna goes away you got to look—" Alessandro paused and shrugged.

It was evident that this was no time for banalities. He had himself seen the shape of grief so often—ever since he was a small child, he realized; it was a look that was as familiar as his mother's face, even more so! his mother's face was beyond recall—that he prepared at once for a siege.

Vito's face bore a look that Alessando knew well. The boy's face had gone flat. It was as if the delicate bones, the warm, curving pulp, the glossy black hairs, had been flattened by a great blow. The face appeared smooth and cold, indented, like an ancient marble paving stone.

Alessandro sat down slowly, maneuvering his stiff leg under the table, and folded his hands. He looked at Vito and spoke very softly.

"*Allora,*" he said, "what is it?"

Vito said nothing. His lips moved delicately as if he might have been asleep, but his mouth did not open. His eyelids rose as his eyes focused briefly on his father's face but there was no light of recognition in his eyes.

"What is it?"

No answer. Vito shook his head. He seemed for a moment to be trying to find words but he gave it up.

Alessandro got up and walked around the side of the table. He moved close to Vito and put his hands on the boy's shoulders. Then he picked Vito's head up, cupping him at the crown and at the chin and pressed the boy's head against his belly. Vito twitched, he tried to escape his father's grasp. Alessandro pressed harder, holding the boy's cheek tightly against himself. He moved his hand up from Vito's chin, over the smooth jaw and began to stroke his hair.

"Come on, let's have it," he said. "What's happened? Open your mouth, let the badness out."

He felt Vito's body quiver and then there were tears on his hands. The boy cried quietly, passionately, almost without sound.

"Good," Alessandro murmured, "cry, cry, boy. Cry and you'll feel better." He held Vito's head against his shirt until the crying was done. Then he gave Vito his handkerchief to blow his nose.

"Now," he said, when Vito raised his head. He was able to look at his father's face.

"I saw her last night."

"Oh? With another?"

Vito shook his head violently. "No. You don't understand."

"So, make me understand."

"In the theater. At a—a—burlesque show."

Alessandro looked puzzled.

"She was on the stage!" Vito writhed. "She's a—a dancer—a—strip-tease dancer. She—she was naked. All the men—they looked—she—it was like, like she was showing all the men—they could see—like she wanted them all to—" He was unable to finish. He put his head on his arms.

Alessandro sat quietly for a long time. This, he had to admit, was something he had not thought of. It had occurred to him that she was in the theater, a courtesan perhaps, but this was something else. He shuddered. Something of Vito's shock congealed inside him.

He was, he realized, overwhelmed. He tried desperately to think of something to say, something to *think* that would make it, somehow, not so bad. But over and over again, the phrase occurred in his mind, this is terrible, terrible. This is really terrible.

He rubbed his face. There must be reason somewhere. Sooner or later it would come back. There must be a pattern, a rationale, a way to limit this nightmare.

"She was supposed to be— I mean, she went to St. Louis, no?"

Vito nodded. "That's what I thought."

"So, instead—where did you see her?"

"In Newark. I—I'm sorry. I told you I was going to the show. I went to Newark."

"But how—"

"Frankie. He said his brother saw her a couple of nights ago. I thought he was lying. I hit him in the mouth. But I had to go over and see for myself. You understand, I—"

"Ssh!" Alessandro calmed him with a gesture. "Naturally. I understand."

"And when I got over there and went into the theater, I saw her. She came out on the stage. She didn't know I was there. She wasn't looking at anybody. She—she began to take her clothes off. And she walked around the stage and she was—she—her—you know, her chest—shaking up and down. I—I got sick."

"In the theater?"

"No. Outside. I went outside and threw up. A cop chased me, told me to go home." Vito was exhausted. He laid his face on his arms and appeared to fall asleep.

So that's that, Alessandro sighed to himself. There was nothing to do now. He got up and began clearing away the breakfast dishes. Maybe something would suggest itself later but now there was nothing to do but recover. Just that.

Later in the day he confronted Vito again. The boy was still pale and tense but the organism had reestablished its control. His movements were co-ordinated, the muscles were responding, the appetite was beginning to return. The physical being, the physiology of a sixteen-year-old boy, had begun again to impose its order on the chaos of his mind.

"She's supposed to come back tonight, no?" Alessandro asked. "What time, late, early?"

"Late." Vito's voice acquired sarcasm. "The plane from St. Louis was due in at midnight. She said she'd be here at about one or one-thirty. I shouldn't wait up. I should call her tomorrow."

"So?"

"So?" Vito appeared to be thinking. Then his face grew resolute. "I'm going to call her all right. I'm going to go up there and hit her right in the mouth."

"Why?"

"Because of the *shame! Vergogna!*" Vito hissed.

Alessandro made a gesture. He could understand this.

He could understand the boy's sense of violation, of outrage.

"All right. So you give her a slap. Calm down. What then?"

"What do you mean, what then?"

"You don't love her any more? You don't want to see her any more?"

"I—I'd like to— How could she *do* this to me?"

There it is, Alessandro thought, the cry of the injured gallant. The bravo, the courtier, a female puts her hatpin in his vanity and out comes a sound like this.

"Not just to you." He laughed. "She does it, you know, but not just to you. In fact"—a thought occurred to him—"she tried to protect you. She was not trying to cause you shame."

"By lying?"

"Why not? She wasn't trying to rub it in your face, no?"

Vito pondered this. "Anyway, it's not that," he said finally. "It's—I'm disgusted. It makes me want to vomit. A—a—strip-teaser. A—*whore!* That's what she is. With her fine talk and her fancy clothes and her rich friends. A lousy, goddam whore. I'm sorry," he added hastily.

"You don't have to apologize to me," Alessandro said evenly.

Vito looked at his face and blushed. "I'm sorry—I don't know what to think. I—I get all—I don't know."

Alessandro said nothing. He lighted a black Tuscan cigar and blew thick smoke into the room. "I don't know what to say," he said finally. "I don't like to see you so hurt. Naturally. You're my son, no? But one thing, maybe you can think about. She's a dancer, striptease, all right. You know. Maybe she's a—maybe she's even a whore. But I don't think so. But still, you know, maybe she does love you."

"So?"

"So? I don't know. So, what difference does it make? But—you say you're going to hit her in the mouth. Let

195

her talk first, OK? Then you hit her. *If* you still want to hit her. But first you talk. It's reasonable, no?"

Vito looked at his feet. "OK, Pa. I understand."

"That's all I'm saying," Alessandro said, "nothing more."

He squinted at his son who sat idly turning the pages of a newspaper and scrutinized him as objectively as if he were examining a painting or buying a shoulder of veal. Without doubt the boy was handsome. And equally without doubt women would bestow him with their gifts. So it was not a question of their gifts; those he would have. It was rather a matter of what *kind* of gifts, what kind of women.

"In Italy," Alessandro said to Vito, suddenly breaking the silence, "your madonna would be an important woman. She would be foolish, perhaps. But she would have respect, admiration, love and something more—respect for herself. She would also know how to love. Here—" He paused. "She is, of course, a beautiful woman, a prize for a man. But here she has—only money. Status? No. A fine husband, an industrialist, a senator? No. Not even if she were the biggest *diva* in the cinema. Just to be a beautiful woman would not be enough. She would be required to have more. And she would require it of herself—as no doubt, she does. To be a beautiful woman," he added, "is always to be lonely. But here, it must be much, much worse."

Vito looked at him uncomprehendingly. "I don't understand, Papa, what's so wrong with being a beautiful woman?"

It was better not to attempt an explanation, Alessandro thought, especially since all this seemed beyond his competence. "Nothing is wrong," he said wryly, "except that if you want to slap a woman in the mouth, slap an ugly one, it does much less damage."

11

It was almost midday when Iris awoke. Almost exactly upon gaining consciousness, she reached for the hand mirror on her night table and meticulously examined her face. This is the acid test, she thought, tilting the mirror to catch the light, prodding her skin with her fingers. If I make the grade now, she told herself, I'm in. The inventory was more than satisfactory. She began to smile. The combination of her own bed and a seconal capsule had given her ten hours of dreamless sleep. All the boredom of the past week and the traces of heavy drinking had vanished from her skin.

What a week it had been! Ugh! she groaned. Drunk every night, smashed. Hangover until four o'clock. Dinner with Harry, half-stoned. Oh, my God! Poor Harry, I got a crying jag on every night. Well, that's over. If I never see him again, we're even. Oh, that cruddy theater! She groaned again. Thank God Vito would never have to see her in a place like that.

There's one thing you can say about that goddam grind, she thought, it sure gets you in condition. A night's sleep and you bounce right back. Now all I need is that crazy boy. Oh, wow, another day of this and I'll be playing with myself. She reached for the telephone.

"Darling," she said, grinning into the telephone, "I'm home. How's my angel? How's my sweet, adorable child?

"Speak louder, I can hardly hear you. . . . Louder, baby. What's the matter, is your father listening? Oh, you poor bubbie, you're embarrassed. You silly. Hey, come on up. I haven't even got out of bed yet. I'm not *going* to get out, just come on up. Hurry, hur-ree!

"What? What do you mean, in a little while? So leave the damn dishes, what's that got to do . . .

"All right, all right, make it as soon as you can, OK?

"Did you miss me? *Sure?* What do you mean, sure? Oh, Vito, baby, why do I love you so much? You're getting to be just like a man. . . . I don't care. Hurry. I'll see you in an hour."

Well, how do you like that, Iris thought, as she put down the phone. Talk about a royal welcome. Talk about a royal *what!*

Oh, come on, you're getting just the least bit disgusting. You sound like Juley Franz, for Christsake. So, the boy's a little embarrassed. So what? He's probably got his father down there. You can hardly expect him to be talking a lot of glop into the phone—anyway, you know how boys are.

Take your bath and shut up. Relax.

Still, he *could* have come up now if he wanted. He doesn't *have* to do the damn dishes this very minute. There have been plenty of times when . . .

Oh, cut it out! Goddam it. Stop it! I'm getting angry.

She sighed and smiled at herself in the bathroom mirror, shaking her head and thinking, you nut, you nervous, exaggerating nut. Then she started filling the tub.

Almost an hour later when Iris was seated at her dressing table, she heard the elevator rise to her floor. Her face was freshly made up and she had combed her hair loosely so that it hung to her shoulders. Smiling brilliantly, both in anticipation of Vito and at the pleasure of her own radiant reflection, she pulled her dressing gown close, touched her throat with a last cool wipe of perfume and rose from her chair. As she did so, she heard the front door open softly and she stepped into the living room.

Vito's eyes found her immediately at the far end of the room. He closed the door carefully behind him and took a step forward. Then he stopped. Iris was beautiful, so beautiful that he could hardly comprehend his relationship to her. She seemed just as formidable, as unattainable, as awesome as she had on the first day they had met. He wanted to run to her, to hide his face in the perfumed fabric of her gown, to feel the softness of her body against his flesh, under his hands, to flee the terrifying aspect of her by pressing himself close and allowing the assurance and warmth to come over him in slow waves. He wanted to hide in closeness to her, feeling her hands on his face until it was safe, little by little, to meet her lips, her eyes, her being. He wanted to run toward her. Yet something, he could hardly remember what it was, kept him from moving. Something held him back.

"Look at you," Iris said. She was leaning against the doorway at the other end of the room, a brush still in her hand. Her head was erect, her cheek against the doorframe. "Look at you," she repeated, "standing there, as if you didn't know how beautiful you are. Come here."

Vito walked toward her and stopped when he was a pace away. "Hi," he said, smiling slightly.

"Hi," she said, laughing shortly, nodding her head. Then she moved forward and put her arms around him. She was barefooted and her head came just level with his. She kissed him on the mouth, felt his head grow stiff, saw his eyes blink. Then she took her mouth away and laid her face next to his.

"Oh," she sighed. "Oh, God."

Vito put his face close to her hair and shut his eyes. Her scent poured into him like a sweet oil. He could feel it coating, healing every nerve in his body. She tried to move her head to kiss him again but he held her tightly, grunting into the hair at the base of her neck.

"Come on," she whispered.
"In a minute."
"No, come on."

"I—I want— I'm glad you're back," he said.

"Oh, I'm glad I'm back," she moaned. She pulled his tee shirt free from his trousers and ran her hands over his back, feeling the warm ribs beneath her fingers. Then she pushed him slightly away and brought her palms up to his chest.

"Oh, come on," she said. She was bent back now, pressing the lower part of her body against him. She felt him respond.

"Oh, yes," he said hoarsely, "I want to. Oh, yes." He pulled her dressing gown wide and lifted his tee shirt so that he could feel her breasts against his skin.

Vito lay with his head on Iris's shoulder so that his eyes were just level with her chin. Her head was propped on two pillows so that her neck was bent forward. She held his knee between her thighs. He moved his forefinger along the edge of her lower lip and around her mouth, tracing the outline. Then, in response to the motion of her lips, he laid his finger against her mouth and she kissed it softly.

"I love your mouth," he said. His voice was low and toneless. It was as if he were dreaming awake.

"It's funny," he went on, "how beautiful a mouth can be. I never realized it before. Your mouth is the most beautiful that it is possible to be."

She murmured.

"I was going to hit you in the mouth," he said.

"What?"

He placed the heel of his hand against her lips and pressed slightly. "I was going to hit you right across the mouth. It's funny."

"Vito!" Iris rose up in bed, alarmed. Moving herself up on the bed, she forced him to lift his head.

Now, suddenly, separated from her body, able to see all of her face, the shock and the anger began to return. He moved abruptly away from her and pulled on his shorts.

"Vito. What are you doing? What *is* this?"

He pulled on his shorts and then turned, standing, over the bed. He grabbed one corner of the sheet and flung it over her body and she pulled it higher to cover her breasts. His face was tight.

"Why didn't you tell me?" he said.

"What, for God's sakes?"

"Anyway, it—it doesn't matter." He reached for his trousers and started to put them on. He lost his balance and fell to the floor, holding his trousers around his ankles. "I saw you at the show," he burst out.

"I saw you—naked—doing that, you know, on the stage." His voice was grating, full of the rush of air.

"Unh!" Iris grunted and fell back on the pillows. Her face was white and stricken. She passed her hand over her forehead and smoothed away her hair. "Oh, wow," she said, talking to the ceiling. She drew her fingers down her cheeks and massaged her throat. "It had to happen. Just had to. Well," she added with a short, uncertain laugh, "now you know. You've got the big picture, as we say. OK, OK. So? So what are you going to do now, walk out? Can't stand the thought of it?"

"Do you blame me?" Vito shouted. He was on his feet now, his pants hitched around his waist. "Do you know what I felt like? How would you like it if you saw me—"

"OK," Iris held up a warning hand. "OK, OK! Don't give me the whole routine. I've been through it before. What's a nice girl like you doing in a place like this?"

"What!"

"That's what you were going to ask, wasn't it?" Iris said. She reached over to the night table and lighted a cigarette and then flounced back in the center of the bed. The sheet fell away from her breasts and she held her arms out and twitched her muscles, agitating her breasts furiously. "How about that, eh, how do you like 'ose li'l ol' tits? Like trained seals, eh?" Then she pulled the sheet back and fell upon the pillows again. "OK, go on. You were saying—"

Vito had covered his face with his hands. "That's terrible," he said. "That's just terrible."

"What's terrible?" Iris leaned forward, holding the sheet to cover her. "What's so goddam terrible?" She was raging now.

"Anybody can see you. Anybody in the whole world. Like you don't care—like you don't care about yourself. Like you're dirt. You're not dirt! Do you understand?" Vito screamed. "To me you're *not* dirt. I thought you were the most—most—I can't even say it."

"Oh, Vito!" Iris's voice was hushed. She fell back on the pillows. "I never—oh, wow. I feel dizzy," she said, half to herself and laughed slightly. "It must have been all that booze." Slowly she tried to order her thoughts.

"It isn't that I think I'm dirt," she talked slowly and then stopped. "It's that—*they're* dirt. The audience. Oh, *boy,* are they dirt. But—"

"Then why do you want to show yourself like that? It isn't right. Why do you want them to look at you? Why do you pretend that . . . ? I'd like to kill them. I swear to God"—his voice almost choked—"I'd like to kill every man in that place. When I think what Frankie said about his brother—oh, my God." He leaned against the wall with his chin high and his mouth open, gasping.

Iris felt her anger leaving her. His anguish was soothing, it held promise.

"Look, honey," she began, "I'm sorry. You know? Believe me, it wasn't *my* idea to have you go over there. In fact, I was planning to tell you about this for some time. I just never got around to it, that's all." She shrugged. "You know. Most people get the wrong idea. They think just because you're a dancer, you're some kind of a tramp—"

"A dancer! It isn't—"

"All right, all right. So I give them an act. A damned good one too. You ought to see how lousy most of them are. So what? It's *still* just an act, for God's sake."

"But how can you *act* like that? Like you're actually

—I mean, like us, like we're here and I'm—only it isn't me!" He squealed. "It isn't me. It's all of them. It's every man—"

"Vito, I'm telling you, it's just an act." Her voice began to rise.

"But why?"

"Look, women are different, that's all," she said it tiredly. "Women have to act all the time. Half the women in the country are putting on an act every time they get into the sack with their husbands. Anyway, it's a living. What do you want me to do, sell hosiery? Make like a file clerk? Why the hell should I?"

"I—I don't know," he said. "I don't even know how I could have—just now. I wanted you so much, I forgot about it. But when it's over, I see those men in the theater, and I see how you were on the stage and I feel like I'm going to explode. I want to take my hands and punch them in the faces. I get so angry with you, I swear, I could—"

"Will it make it better if you hit me? Go ahead, hit me. I don't care. I swear I don't. Go ahead."

"Not now. Now I'm ashamed."

"What for?"

"I—I feel foolish. I—I just went to bed with you."

"Is *that* it?" Her voice snapped, whiplike.

"Hunh?"

"You couldn't resist laying me but as soon as you got what you wanted, you start getting squeamish!"

"No." He held up his hand. "Don't say that. That isn't it."

"What isn't it? I'm a good juicy lay for you, aren't I? And you haven't had any all week and you kind of got used to it, didn't you? So you thought you'd just try it once more, just for old times' sake, didn't you? And then maybe in another few days or a week when you get horny—"

"No, *please*. Iris. Stop. Don't talk like that. Don't say things like that." He held both arms out, gesturing with his palms. "You don't understand, please."

"What's to understand?" She had drawn her knees up and was sitting erect now, her eyes wide with anger and her hands clenched into fists, holding the sheet to her throat. "I've taken you up here. I've let you practically live here. Do you understand that? I've never let any man come into this apartment. Never.

"I've let you in here. I've fed you. I've taught you, God knows what I haven't taught you. I've taught you how to behave. I've put up with your stupid fumbling and your stupid innocence—and for what! For *what!*" She shouted at him.

"Iris, I'm asking you—"

"Asking me for what? Do you want to do it again, is that what you want? Here!" She threw the sheet from her body and spread her legs. "Is that what you want?"

"Iris!" he screamed. "Don't talk like a—a *whore!* Don't *be* like that. Iris, for Christsakes, please. Don't," he began to cry. "Don't. You make me want to— You make us dirty—"

"Dirty? *You're* dirty." Her voice was low and hoarse. "You're a dirty little punk kid. You're dirty, filthy, rotten, like all the rest. You're nothing but a snotty wop kid!"

"Oh!" Vito staggered toward her. "Oh!" he said. He slapped her hard across the face. "It's too much," he muttered. She sat with her face against the wall.

"Get out."

He nodded and stumbled through the door. He was breathing heavily and his thighs were heavy. It seemed to take forever just to cross the living room. The metal of the doorknob felt cool under his hand. For a moment he hesitated in front of the elevator, wondering if his legs would hold him up while he waited for the car. But then, he realized, he would never be able to climb down the four flights of stairs. He pressed the elevator button. Then he changed his mind. He thumped down one flight of stairs, then another flight. Then he sat down and rested for a few moments until he felt he could make the trip to the basement.

An hour later, sitting quietly on her bed with a cold cloth held at her face, Iris reached for the telephone. I'm not sure why I'm doing this, she thought. I don't even know what I want to say. Listlessly, she dialed a number. She heard Vito's voice.

"It's me," she said finally. Then she paused. Quite surprisingly her throat began to constrict and she could feel tears. "I want you to come upstairs again. I want to talk to you. I—I've got to."

Vito hesitated. "All right."

"Will you come up now?"

"Yes. OK. In a couple of minutes."

"All right," Iris said. Then she moved the wet cloth to her eyes and began to weep. Why am I doing this? she tried to think against the outpouring of her tears. What's happened to me, why am I drowning? But the questions were scarcely formed, she could hardly even articulate them in her mind, so overwhelming was her urge to cry.

I've got to stop crying, she thought. I've just *got* to. She got up and went to the window and forced herself to breathe deeply and evenly until she had regained control. The thought of losing him just breaks me up. Never mind why, any more. It's a fact. I just can't help it.

Sure, if I were to go away from here and get busy and start running around again, I'd forget it. I'd survive, I know I would. But when it comes right down to the wire, I lose my nerve.

And to think that I started this as a—a kind of game! For kicks! I thought I'd just play with this little kid a few times, this gorgeous baby of a boy and walk away from it as soon as I got bored, as soon as he started to be a drag.

Oh, brother! Is *that* a laugh.

She could feel the tears starting again. Somewhere—once—it seemed, she had had a clue. There was something. She frowned. He needs me, she found herself saying, he's got to need me. After all, he never had a mother. What the hell difference does that make, I never had a father.

"What did you want?" he said. She turned around, startled. She had not heard him come in. Even more startling was the expression on his face. It was not merely angry, it was also stern. He was, she realized with a feeling of dismay, no longer a boy. He was a fully formed man. And not only that. He had in the interval of an hour or so gained some incomparable advantage over her, had attained a position of such safety and angry calm that he was beyond her reach.

"I—I just wanted to talk to you," she said uncertainly.

He shrugged. "So?"

"Look, don't be a pig. I mean, don't be cruel."

"You going to start calling me rotten names again? Because if you do, I'll walk out. But I'm warning you, if you call me—you know—what you did before, I'll flatten you. I mean it." His fists were clenched and his lips were pale.

"Look," she said, making a gesture and sitting down on the bed, "I'm sorry about that. You're right. It was a rotten thing to say and I don't really mean it. You know I don't mean it."

He was silent.

Vito, you've *got* to understand. I don't think those things. You know how I am. I just lost my temper, that's all."

"You called me a—a wop and a kid. A punk." His voice was low. "So—that's what I am. That's the way I was born. Sure, I'm Italian. And I'm only sixteen—I'll be seventeen in another few months. So? What's to be ashamed of? What did I do?"

"Oh, Vito." She shook her head. "Please, please, I know all that. You don't have to say—"

He interrupted sharply. "But what you do you do by yourself. *You're* the one to be ashamed. Not me."

"What makes you think I should be ashamed?"

"What! For running around on the stage with no

clothes on. For doing all those things with your hands and your mouth, doing all that. You mean you're saying you shouldn't be ashamed of that?"

"I told you before—" She paused and sighed. Her voice was a dull monotone. "That's just an act. There's nothing wrong with it. It's been going on since—I don't know when. Men come into the theater to see a girl take her clothes off and they're willing to pay for it. So I do it. I do it better, more artistically, than about ninety-nine per cent of the other broads. So I have this apartment. And these clothes. And I can feed you—"

"I don't want that lousy food."

She went on as if she hadn't heard him. "I've been doing it since I was a young girl. At first I was embarrassed but then I got used to it. I don't even think of the men. You wouldn't understand. When I'm on the stage, I'm just thinking about the act. The men disappear. Sometimes—like last week—I was thinking of you."

"Of me! With everybody watching?"

"Sure. I was thinking of you and how I wanted to buy you a nice suit, a really good-looking suit at De Pinna's. What's so wrong about that?"

"I don't know," Vito said. He was scowling with the effort to find words. "I don't know," he said finally. "It just seems wrong, that's all."

Iris looked at him silently for a long time. She could see the outline of his knuckles pressing against his trouser pockets.

"I was thinking—" She stopped and took a deep breath. She could feel the tears starting again. "I was thinking we might go out to the Coast together. Or maybe I could go out first and then send for you. I might quit stripping and go into pictures. I've had offers. I've got a lot of friends out there."

"I don't want to know your friends." He turned and faced her suddenly, his face thrust forward like a serpent's head. "I hate every one of your friends. I'd just as soon kill them as look at them."

She shrugged. "You're out of your mind."

"I'd like to kill them," he repeated.

"So you're still angry? You're still sorer than hell, aren't you?"

"Damn right."

"OK, all right, OK," she said in a rising note of exasperation. She turned her face to the window.

"OK," he said softly, "I guess that's it."

She nodded, keeping her face away from him, continuing to peer out the window. When she turned her head back to the room he was gone.

12

Iris fell asleep after Vito left, a deep sleep of total exhaustion. When she awoke, it was with a start. Her hand reached for the telephone but when she held it to her ear she was astonished to hear the dial tone. Then she realized that she was listening to a telephone ringing in another apartment. Answer it, she said to herself. Then, suddenly aware of her solitude, she filled the apartment with a burst of sound.

"Will somebody please answer that son of a bitching phone!"

The ringing stopped. Thank God, she thought, yawning spastically. The urge to sleep came over her again. She tossed her rumpled pillow to the floor and slid a cool pillow under her head. Then she sank quickly back into unconsciousness.

At two o'clock in the morning she awoke again. The light was on in the bathroom and she raised herself instantly on one elbow.

"Vito?" she called. "Darling?" She was certain he was there. She got out of bed and went into the bathroom. She even looked behind the shower curtain. Then she shuddered.

He'll call tomorrow, she told herself. Around eleven because he won't want to wake me. Forget it.

But she was unable to get back to sleep. So she got a glass of milk and a book and read until dawn.

At seven o'clock the next evening Iris turned the light on in the kitchen and stood on one leg, rubbing her calf with her foot while she inspected her pantry. Then, slamming the cupboard door with a loud bang, she ran into the bedroom and picked up the telephone. She dialed quickly, pulling the disk back into place with her finger; she was breathing hard.

"Hello—" She paused. "Mr. Pellegrino? Is Vito there?"

"No. He's not here."

"He's not there!" She stopped. For a moment she was unable to go on. "But—he's got—Mr. Pellegrino?"

"Yes."

"I'm sorry." She laughed. "For a moment I thought I had the wrong number. This is Miss Hartford, Iris Hartford up in Four—"

"Yes, I know."

"I—uh—guess you know me. Oh, boy, is *that* a line."

"Pardon?"

"Uh. Did, uh, Vito tell you—uh, where is he?"

"He went out."

"Out?" She felt herself getting desperate. How could he— "I, uh, don't suppose you'd like to come up and join me for a drink—"

"Pardon?"

"I—I'd like to talk to you. I was wondering if you could come up for a little while."

"Now?"

"Well, yes, if you're not too busy."

"That's very nice of you. Very nice."

"Well, will you come?"

"I will come," Alessandro said. "In about five minutes. Thank you."

"This is a pretty funny scene, when you come right down to it," Iris said. "Oh, damn!" In offering Alessandro a glass of beer she spilled some on the rug.

Alessandro shrugged.

"I mean, you're old enough to be my father—not that you *look* old, but you know what I mean. And I'm trying to get hold of your son—it's like I was the man and I'm going to you to ask if I can marry your daughter."

210

Alessandro laughed. "In that case," he said, "I'm glad this isn't the old country, because I would have to tell you how much is her dowry. Maybe if I had had a daughter I would have had to work harder and save some money."

"Quit while you're ahead," Iris said. "Take my word for it, you're lucky."

"Ah, that's good. Cold beer on a warm night. You'll be sorry if I get drunk and talk too much. Vito tells me that when I get drunk I am like an old woman." He stopped and looked at Iris. "Let me tell you something." His manner changed, his tone became grave. "This is the first time I get a close look at you and I want to tell you that you are a very beautiful woman. I didn't know until this moment just how beautiful you are. No, wait—" He held up his hand to forestall her interjection. "One moment more." He smiled. "Let me be honest, I don't understand you at all. Vito loves you, this I can understand. But you love him? This is hard to believe. If you were—please excuse me, but I am not saying something so terrible, after all—if you were just amusing yourself, I would understand that. Much more easily. So, forgive me, I really must ask you, I need to know—what do you feel about the boy? Please be honest. You can say anything."

"I wish it was that easy," Iris said. She laughed. "I'll try to be honest with you, I mean really. No double talk. It's just that—I'm not sure I'm being honest with myself."

Alessandro nodded.

"I—dammit, I haven't felt anything like this about a guy—a boy—for years. I'm—I'm hung on him. Why? Who knows? It's ridiculous. I *know* it's ridiculous. I've told myself that a thousand times. But there's something about him, something that happens to me when I see him . . . I don't know—" She gestured helplessly—"Maybe it's an infatuation. Maybe it isn't love at all."

"Who knows what love is or what it isn't?" Alessandro said. "But what I wanted to know was whether—

forgive me—you were being cynical or not. Mind you, not that this is a crime. I just want to know."

"The funny part about it is," Iris said, "that every time I start talking about it, I feel like I'm going to cry. Cynical. Oh, boy, am I cynical."

Alessandro shook his head and sighed. "That's what I was afraid of," he said.

"I'm sorry, I don't—"

"Look, Miss—Miss—I'm sorry, but I must talk to you, I must—I have a duty to my son, no? I am a father. And I love my son, eh? So, I must say things, maybe not so kind, you understand?"

"Sure." Iris frowned.

"You know, perhaps—excuse me—together with you, he is a man. You know? We Italians, we mature very young, I mean physically. But he is still a boy. You see? And"—he interrupted himself with a laugh—"you see, I was a boy, a long time ago, but still, I know—what he saw, this, this dance, this hurt him very, very much." He paused.

"I'm not trying to make you feel bad. But I want you to understand. This is a boy, you see. And when he saw you, the woman he loved, it was—well, for a man it might be different. But it never really was clear to him that you could have been with another man—"

"But—"

"I know, perhaps you told him. But a boy is like—like Adam. He is sure he is the first. Sure. And the only one. He is sure of that, too. He doesn't know about tomorrow. Or yesterday. Only about now. This minute. So—when he saw you, and when he saw the other men watching you, it—it was a terrible thing. You cannot know what a terrible thing it was. I'm sorry." He spread out his hands.

Iris was silent for a long time. "I didn't want him to see me," she said. "I guess somehow I knew all along it might be like this. I guess that's why I never told him."

Alessandro shrugged. "Even telling him—I don't think it would have mattered. You see, there is one thing more. He—Vito—has not had a mother. This is my fault. And now I see it very well. I have been too selfish. Maybe I wanted him too much to myself to marry another woman after my wife died. Maybe I was afraid to marry another woman—I feel—I feel I am a burden, a cripple, you know. Perhaps there would be other children, I might not be able to support them. Who knows? But it was a bad thing for the boy to grow up without a mother. And I think"—he paused and carefully placed his beer glass in the center of an ash tray so that it would not mar the table top—"I think that he felt for you something of what he would feel for a mother. I do not say that he is a baby, not at all. But I think perhaps he began to feel a little of this and then, you see—"

"He sees his mother taking her clothes off and shaking her ass in a burlesque theater— Oh, my God!" Iris covered her face with her hands.

Alessandro watched her patiently. "I'm really very sorry," he said gently. "For you and for Vito. Maybe it is my fault. I should have tried to stop it. I see now that I could have come to you. Only, how did I know — I'm sorry, I beg you to forgive me, but I thought it was a good thing for the boy. I didn't think you would really feel about him the way you do."

"Oh, I've been such a fool," Iris said, "*such* a fool."

Alessandro smiled. "Don't blame yourself too much. He *is* a fine boy. A beautiful boy. And after all, it has to end sometime, no?"

"End? Why? Why does it have to?"

Alessandro made a gesture of helplessness. Then he leaned forward. "Surely, you're not serious? You don't think you can just go on like this?"

"I suppose not," Iris said quietly, "but you know something? I wish it could. You said let's talk frankly and all right, I will. I may be out of my mind. I may be committing a criminal offense, corruption of a minor or whatever it is, but the one thing I want, the thing I want most in the whole world, is to have Vito back. Right now, this minute. There's the God's honest truth."

"Now, I really don't know what to say," Alessandro said, rising with difficulty to his feet.

"Will you try to stop it?"

"Pardon?"

"Will you try to keep him away from me?"

He thought for a long time before answering. "No," he said finally. "Why should I do that? What harm there is has been done, no? He has fallen in love, he has—if you'll forgive me—fallen out of bed and bumped his head. What more could happen to him? He could become brutal, perhaps, but I don't think so. He is not that kind of a boy. As for you—dear lady—what can I tell you? You're a grown woman." He spread his hands wide.

"Thanks. That's very decent of you."

"Decent? That's a word like nice. Something one ought to do. Believe me, I'm doing the only thing I can do. Nothing. By the way, to change the subject, your lease is up in a few weeks, no?"

"Three more weeks. Then I'm due on the west coast."

"Ah, then, you see? It would have ended anyway."

"I wish I'd known you a long time ago," Iris said.

"What! an old man, a cripple?" Alessandro laughed. "No, seriously, you're a good woman. I'm grateful for my son." He limped quickly through the door.

Vito was perched on the side of a fire hydrant, bouncing the end of a broomstick on the asphalt. The stick trilled briskly, making a wooden bell sound in the street. The days were getting cooler, he thought. Summer was almost over. The asphalt was quite hard. It would get softer in the afternoon but right now it was perfect for stick ball, soft enough so that it provided sure traction but not so soft that it was spongy. He gazed about him pleasurably. It was good to be playing ball with his friends. He hadn't done it for a while— a long while, it seemed.

There was nothing difficult here, nothing hidden. The urge to violence would appear instantly, summoned instantly by the speeding blur of a ball. Then, pow!—he took a mighty swing with his broomstick—the urge was gone.

"Hey, Vito-oo. The Duke. Hey, Duke, you're up next," a boy called. "I'm gonna murdelize you."

"You're dreaming," he answered easily, smiling. It was pleasant to understand with such clarity, to respond so naturally. "I'm gonna put it in the river. Lay back, now."

"Who's he kidding?"

"All right, I'm warning you—" Just as he prepared to swing at the ball, he caught sight of his father walking up the street. He smiled in anticipation and hit the ball so that it fell not far from where his father walked.

"Homer!" he yelled exultantly. "How about that?" He loped easily down the street to his father.

"Hey," he said, pointing to the paper bag, "is that heavy, you want me to carry it?"

"No. I can do it," Alessandro said. "Nice day, eh? Now the cool weather begins. Soon school starts, no? When?"

"Next week," Vito said. "Next Monday."

"You got to get some new pants," Alessandro said. "Oh, there was a telephone call for you. I'm supposed to give you the message."

"Oh?" Vito's face grew tight.

"She—Iris—she wants you to have dinner tonight with her. Upstairs." He gestured.

Vito frowned and thrust his hands in his pockets. "She called, hunh?" He was thinking it over. "What did you tell her?"

Alessandro shrugged impatiently. "What did I tell her? I told her I'd tell you. *E basta.*" He paused. "Are you going to go?"

"I—I don't know," Vito said. He looked at his father and blushed. He could feel himself getting eager, he could feel his sexual appetite stirring. For three days it had lain quiet and it startled him to discover that he was so vulnerable. "Maybe I will," he added. "What do you think, should I go?"

Alessandro sighed. "What *I* think—it's what *you* think. You want to go, you go. I just want to know, so if you're not going to have supper I won't cook for you. Anyway, you better call her."

"All right. I'll call down at the store."

"Oh, and I forgot to get a can of peas. Get a can before you come home."

Still carrying his broomstick, Vito began a long, exaggerated trot to the corner. Halfway down he stopped and hid the stick carefully under a stairway. It seemed suddenly foolish to be carrying it in his hand.

There was no doubt in his mind now. He *was* going to have dinner with Iris. He wasn't sure what he would say to her on the telephone. Nor was he really sure what he felt. Fear, there was that. Awkwardness, too. But over-riding these feelings was an erotic hunger that gave him a quick erection as he walked.

For Christsakes, he scowled at himself, looking down at the cloth of his trousers. Then, suddenly, the erotic impulse faded. The daylight and the street shapes flooded back into his mind, replacing the sounds of Iris's voice, the sight of her body.

It wasn't the same any more. Loving her, making love to her would never again be the total absorption it had been. It was no longer the end of all his thoughts, all his longings.

Now there was quite distinctly another terminus. It was what came *after* love. And it was bleak, oppressive. Now he was aware and worried by the moment when the spasm of love had passed. That moment was gray, clouded with dismay and confusion and some anger still.

"Hi," he said into the telephone.

"Hi. Are you still sore at me?"

Vito shifted in the telephone booth. "No." He laughed. "I'm not sore. I just got hot and then I cooled down. You know."

"Sure, I know. Will you come upstairs later? For dinner?"

"Uh, sure. What time?"

"Any time." She paused. "Are you sure you want to?"

"Uh—sure. Sure."

"I want you very much. Darling?"

"Yes."

"Are you listening to me?"

"Sure." The telephone booth was getting hot. He opened the door.

"I said I want you very much, Vito. It's hard for me to say this, I mean—let's not fight again."

"OK." He laughed.

"Do you love me?"

"I—sure."

"Say it. Tell me you love me." Vito was looking through the open door into the store. A pretty girl walked in. She had pointed breasts like lemons.

"I—uh—look, I'm in a phone booth, you know?"

"All right. You brat. You inarticulate brat. I'll see you later."

Stepping out of the telephone booth, Vito was grateful for the cool air. He wiped his damp face. Phew! He realized that his stomach muscles were constricted. The dark wood floor of the store and the stacks of groceries were reassuring, peaceful. It occurred to him that it might be nice to work in the store, to stay behind the counter where it was cool and to stack the cans in geometrical constructions.

The girl glanced up from her shopping list and appeared to smile. She was really quite pretty. He felt the impact of her glance in his flesh. Her upper lip was full and deeply beveled inward so that a tiny portion of her teeth showed when she turned her face toward him. Her mouth was sweet and warm, it reminded him of a persimmon.

"All I want is a can of peas," he told the clerk. He looked at the girl quite closely now. She was about his age, perhaps a bit younger. Her hair was pulled back but a small tendril of brown hair quivered at her temple. It was agitated by the slow movement of the overhead fan. Now and then Vito caught a scent of her perfume but it got lost among scents of vinegar and cheese.

Her hand, when she held it up to receive her change, looked astonishingly naked. Vito knew, he realized now, just how soft and warm that hand could be. He knew what the small pointed nails would feel like on his skin.

"You're new in the neighborhood," he found himself saying.

"We moved in this summer. In June," she said, smiling at him. Her eyes were very dark and she looked at him with surprising ease. "I'm Carol Kenney," she said.

"I'm—"

"Vito. Vito Pellegrino. I know all about you."

"You do? What do you mean? How'd—"

"Oh, I get around."

"No, I mean, wait. No kidding." He began to walk out of the store with her, the can of peas heavy, grenadelike in his hand. Her sweater was very tight and he could see the faint impression below her shoulders, where her brassière compressed her skin. Releasing that brassière, Vito thought, would yield him an astonishing softness. And her nipples would become hard. He knew how to make them hard now. "How come you know about me?"

"I'm a secret agent for the FBI. No." She laughed and touched his forearm, her fingertips lingering a trifle longer than her smile. "Actually, I'm good friends with some of the girls around, Alice Martullo, Mary Callahan. You know, gossip and all that jazz."

"Oh." Vito laughed. "Sure, those kids—"

"You've got quite a rep. The big lover boy." She tossed her head and began to walk uptown. Vito accompanied her.

"What—I mean—uh, what's this lover-boy jazz?"

"Oh, we'll have to have a long talk sometime. I know all about you and your actress—"

Vito recoiled. Then he smiled. "Well, you know. I can't help it." He tossed the can of peas high in the air and caught it with a smack. "Some women just can't stay away from me. You know? What are you going to do?"

"I guess you really know your way around, don't you?" Her voice was full of exaggerated irony.

"Can't deny it." He looked at her boldly, allowing his eyes to fall on her breasts. "You know, like I say, why fight it?"

She blushed. "Well—I—this is my corner. See you around."

"Sure," Vito said. He was smiling. She was no longer so self-possessed. "Kenney, hunh. You in the book?"

"Try me." She gave him an impudent look and walked off.

At six o'clock Vito was drying his face with a towel when the telephone rang.

"Hello, is this—is this Vito?"

"Yes," he said. "Who's this?"

"Can't you recognize the voice?"

"Uh, sure—no. Do I know who—"

"It's Carol Kenney. Boy, are you fast on the uptake."

"Oh—sure. This morning—"

"What a memory! I was just wondering—well, have you got a date tonight?"

"Uh, no. Well, yes. I don't know. It depends on what time."

"Oh, look, don't bother. If you think I want to be a late date for someone, you're—"

"No, listen," Vito said quickly, "it isn't that. I've just got to go to dinner." He was determined now.

"Oh, well—" Her voice sounded caressing in the telephone. "My parents are going out about eight-thirty, and

I was wondering if maybe you want to come over and watch TV."

"Sure. Great. What's the number?"

"Two-thirty-four East Sixty-Fifth, apartment three-C. And you don't have to go shouting all over the block that I called you. All right?"

"Now why would I do a thing like that? Who do you think you're talking to, a jerky kid?"

"Well, I'm no kid either," she said, speaking very gently again. "If I was, I wouldn't be calling you up. You dig?"

"Crazy," Vito said. "I'll see you."

He finished dressing quickly and then stepped outside into the cool air. How about that! he thought, grinning. He smacked his palms together several times. The world seemed bright and glittering again. Man! he thought, remembering Carol's hard little apricot behind in her flannel slacks. Then his joy collapsed. There was still the meeting with Iris. He gnawed his fingernail. It was a little like going up to see the principal at school. Why had he thought of that? He shrugged. Better get it over with, he thought. Maybe he could just sort of eat dinner quickly and then get out. I've got to see the boys, he found himself saying, we're getting up a team. . . .

Iris opened the door at his knock. She was wearing an apron and her hair was pulled back and tied with a ribbon. Her face was only lightly made up so that she seemed duller, less aggressively beautiful than Vito had ever seen her—except, he reminded himself, in the early morning. He frowned, trying to suppress this thought.

"God, I'm glad to see you," she said. She put her arms around him but he remained stiff.

"Hi."

"Are you still so angry with me? Come on, you're not serious. You *can't* be."

"No, honest." He felt his flesh getting hot. "I'm not angry. You know—it's just—"

"It's just—what? You just don't give a damn about me any more? Is that it?" Iris folded her arms and smiled at him.

"No!" His voice broke. "Look, you know—I get embarrassed." He embraced her clumsily but dropped his hands to his sides.

"All right. Look, I asked for this. Now, how about a drink?"

"No, no thanks," Vito said quickly.

"Afraid it'll start all over again, is that it? That's how I made you the first time. Afraid I'm going to try it again?"

"Look, Iris—" He faltered. "Don't say things like that. Honest—"

"Why not? Why the hell not? Why not say what you mean? If you're bugged, say so. Don't keep shifting around—"

"I'm not shifting, it's just—"

"OK, OK. I know a dead horse when I see one. Well." She sat down and took a long drink from her glass. "That's that, I suppose."

"Hunh?"

"Look"—her voice became hard—"before you go barreling out of here in a panic, I just want to say one thing for the record, OK?"

"Sure." He was frightened.

"I just want to say, no matter how ridiculous it sounds, that I love you. Do you realize that, you—you brat?"

"Sure." His voice was a whisper. "I—I love you too."

"No, you don't." She moved over to him and took the point of his chin in her hand. "Look at me. Look at me!" Her voice was imperious, yet pleading. "Now look at me and tell me you love me."

"I—"

She sighed and rose to her feet. She went to the window and pulled the curtain aside so that she could look out the street.

"Do you want some dinner?"

"I—I'm not very hungry."

She paused. "You want to split? Cut? You want to go?"

"Well—"

"It's all right." She turned to face him. Her throat was working and her voice came out haltingly, but very gentle. "It's all right. Go on."

He stood up and moved a step in her direction.

"No, forget it." She motioned to him. "It isn't fair to you. I know this feeling. Believe me, I know this feeling. Go on."

"Iris—I'm—"

"Just go," she whispered, "go." She turned her face away and gripped the curtain.

The corridor was stunningly silent. Vito stood in front of the elevator and looked at Iris's door. He could hear no sound, no movement. Instinctively he held his breath. For a moment he thought he ought to go back. If he heard a sound, if he heard her voice, he would go back. He listened and there was no sound. Then, walking carefully, he began to go downstairs.

For a long time Iris stood at the window, staring down at the street. In the doorway of an apartment a few houses down, a pair of young girls sat like ornaments on opposite sides of the stoop. They're like cats, Iris thought vacantly. The girls were moving their arms slowly, raising their hands to their hair, smoothing their clothes and slowly but ceaselessly turning their heads to survey the street, as rhythmically and effortlessly as a watchful cat moving its tail. Suddenly they stood up, dropped lightly from the stoop and landed on their toes.

Men! Iris thought, her lips curving in a smile. Boys. She peered up the sidewalk but it was difficult to see far in the darkness. I'll bet anything, she told herself, I'll bet a hundred bucks. She waited, the smile stiffening on her cheeks.

Then she uttered a sharp laugh. "Sure enough!" she said it aloud. Two boys had come into view. I owe myself a hundred bucks, she thought, turning away from the window to look into the room. I owe myself a bill.

For a moment the lights seemed painfully bright. She blinked until her eyes narrowed. Then she stood uncertainly in the center of the room.

She walked over to the dining table and switched off the overhead light. Then, on impulse, she grabbed the end of the tablecloth and pulled it hard. The water glasses toppled, spilling wetness on the cloth. For long seconds she watched the dark water stain spreading on the blue linen, then she blew out the candles and, moistening her fingertips with spilled water, snuffed out the smouldering wicks.

Holding her hands to the sides of her head she walked into her bedroom and sat down at her dressing table. She took off her earrings and laid them in a box. Very deliberately, she looked at herself in the mirror and spoke aloud. "I'm not going to cry. I'm not. The only thing it does is make you look lousy."

She raised her fingers and stroked the lines at her throat. Lifting her chin high made the faint horizontal rings almost disappear. Then she dropped her head and closed her eyes and let her hands fall slack in her lap.

Printed in Great Britain
by Amazon